The
INVENTION *of*
SARAH CUMMINGS

Books by Olivia Newport

The Pursuit of Lucy Banning
The Dilemma of Charlotte Farrow
The Invention of Sarah Cummings

The
INVENTION of
SARAH CUMMINGS

A NOVEL

OLIVIA
NEWPORT

Revell

a division of Baker Publishing Group
Grand Rapids, Michigan

© 2013 by Olivia Newport

Published by Revell
a division of Baker Publishing Group
P.O. Box 6287, Grand Rapids, MI 49516-6287
www.revellbooks.com

Printed in the United States of America

Library of Congress Cataloging-in-Publication Data
Newport, Olivia.
    The invention of Sarah Cummings : a novel / Olivia Newport.
        pages cm. — (Avenue of Dreams ; Book 3)
    ISBN 978-0-8007-2040-7 (paper : alk. paper)
    1. Anonyms and pseudonyms—Fiction. 2. Wealth—Fiction. I. Title.
PS3614.E686I58 2013
813'.6—dc23   2013015723

This book is a work of fiction. Names, characters, places, and incidents are the products of the author's imagination or are used fictitiously. Any resemblance to actual events, locales, or persons, living or dead, is coincidental.

13 14 15 16 17 18 19   7 6 5 4 3 2 1

For Mark,
at my side all these years

1

The hat crooked its finger at Sarah Cummings.

The gesture was sophisticated. Seductive. Irresistible.

Sarah pushed open the shop's door for a better look from the inside of the display window. Under a flood of sunlight, the gold bead trim adorning a narrow crimson brim doubled as a prism, sending hues to chase and dance around the milliner's shop.

She did love that hat.

The classic oval shape of the crown and simplicity of design would make it versatile—worth every penny of the price. The coins in Sarah's purse were a long way from sufficient, though. She had not yet attempted to make a hat herself, but having mastered gowns and suits, she contemplated her next frontier unafraid. A hat would require such a small swatch of fabric. The attraction was all in the design and the trims, and she had a small trunk full of ribbons, beads, and buttons harvested from gowns over the last three years.

Considering the afternoon she had just experienced, Sarah felt she deserved an indulgence.

"Don't you just adore that hat?"

Sarah turned toward the voice. The eyes fastened on her were speckled—she was unsure what color to call them. Not quite blue. Not quite hazel. Certainly not green. But bright. And not tired at all. She had seen those eyes before. The not-quite-any color was uncommon enough to be memorable. But they did not belong to anyone on Prairie Avenue that Sarah could remember.

"I've been marveling at that hat through the window for two weeks," the young woman confided. "Even my mother agrees it's exquisite, and we rarely agree about any matter of fashion. You should have seen us choosing gowns for a wedding we attended."

And then Sarah knew. Florence Pullman's wedding at the end of April. The immense parlor of the George Pullman home had been decked in green and gold, with vast wreaths of orchids and lilies of the valley cascading down the pillars. Florence had taken her vows in the bay window, wearing an opulent ivory satin gown. Sarah remembered the train cut on the bias. Mrs. Pullman had asked Flora Banning for the loan of her maids, including Sarah, to serve at the reception that lasted until midnight. More than two hundred people had been there for the gala and eaten from the five-tiered cake with the angel on top.

Including the owner of this pair of indescribable eyes. The voice rang familiar to Sarah now as well. She had heard this young woman's laugh as she offered her the tray of finger foods and Johnny Hand's orchestra played behind the screen of palms. Sarah smiled weakly and glanced back at the hat. Across the shop, a clerk perked up at the prospect of business. Sarah estimated the steps that would take her back to the sidewalk, out of range before the young woman with the laugh and eyes began to remember as well.

"Oh my goodness," the woman exclaimed, placing a hand on Sarah's forearm. "Were you planning to buy that hat? All this time I've spent gawking at it, I didn't consider someone else might buy it before I made up my mind. I suppose I could ask the owner to make another just like it, but my mother would never abide that. It would be too much like buying clothes off the rack from Marshall Field."

Sarah bristled. Her father had worked at Marshall Field— proudly. And Sarah had spent the better part of her afternoon trying to convince the manager of the ladies' dress department that she could sew a garment that matched anything on the rack. Certainly she was qualified to sell them. For the third time in a year, Sarah was denied a position for which she believed she had eminent qualifications. Her every application met with the response that the economic depression meant that the store had few open positions.

Withdrawing from the woman's unsolicited touch, Sarah smoothed her copper crepe skirt with one hand, confident no one could tell it had once been part of Flora Banning's Christmas ball gown. "It's true I have been admiring it," Sarah said, "but I'm not sure it's right for my wardrobe."

"Then I'd better snatch it up while I can." The young woman extended a hand. "I'm Lillie Wagner."

Sarah took the hand reflexively and met Lillie's eyes, innocent and devoid of any recognition. In their formal black-and-white service garb, the servants of Prairie Avenue were faceless. Why should Lillie Wagner remember Sarah Cummings?

"I'm Serena Cuthbert." The name sprang to Sarah in that moment, startling in its familiarity. "It's nice to meet you."

"Do you live nearby?" Lillie asked.

"Not too far," Sarah answered. That was true. Prairie Avenue was only a few blocks away from the Michigan Avenue shop, though she could hardly explain that she was a parlor maid for the Banning family across the street from the Pullmans. Lillie Wagner never would have spoken to Sarah if she suspected her employment status. Lillie probably would not even have spoken to her if Sarah had managed to wrangle a position at Marshall Field's store. Only her clothing suggested she would be a match for Lillie's social status.

"I must try on that hat." Lillie gazed at it. "And you must give me your honest opinion of whether it flatters me."

The shop's clerk approached, and Lillie swished her skirts as she pivoted with a nod toward the hat in the window. A moment later, with the creation on her head, she moved to a mirror and motioned that Sarah should stand beside her. "What do you think?"

Sarah studied the image in the mirror. Lillie's round face featured strong cheekbones and high eyebrows under auburn hair. Sarah was sure the hair would hang to Lillie's waist if let loose. Her own common brown eyes were set wider than Sarah would have liked and her hair, while a satisfying ebony shade, was thinner than she wished.

Lillie adjusted the tilt of the hat. "You haven't said anything, Miss Cuthbert."

"It's lovely," Sarah answered honestly. "It suits you quite well."

Lillie lifted the hat from her head. "You should try it on too."

Sarah shook her head. "I've already decided against the purchase."

"Just try it on." Before Sarah could protest further, Lillie had perched the hat atop her careful coiffure.

"Serena Cuthbert, you look spectacular!" Lillie's eyes met Sarah's in the mirror. "The men must gobble you up at the balls."

Sarah stared at her own reflection. The hat did suit her. Eager eyes soaked up the details of design, memorizing rapidly where the seams were in the crown, the angle of the peak, the proportions of the brim. She removed the hat from her head and turned it in her hands a few times.

"You should have it," Lillie urged. "You were looking at it before I was."

"I wouldn't think of it." Sarah handed the hat back to Lillie. "It's not right for me. The color does not go with any of my suits."

Lillie laughed. "My mother would have a suit made to match the hat." She glanced at Sarah's skirt and blouse. "You must have a wonderful dressmaker."

"She is quite skilled." It had taken years of practice for Sarah to topstitch a collar with the precision of a sewing machine. If someone offered her a free machine, she was not sure she would take it.

"I would love to have your dressmaker's name," Lillie said. "We only moved to Chicago a few weeks ago, and while my mother has interviewed several dressmakers, she hasn't taken a fancy to one yet."

Sarah knew just when the Wagners had arrived in Chicago, right before the Pullman wedding at the end of April and right before Sarah had renewed her resolve to find employment outside the Banning household. How newcomers had squeaked onto the guest list she did not know. Sarah fanned herself with her fingers. "My goodness, it's warm today."

"It *is* the first of July," Lillie observed.

"If it's this warm now, what will August bring?" Sarah wondered. "I should be going. They're about to close the shop anyway. It's nearly six o'clock."

"Then I'd better complete my purchase. I cannot take the chance of someone else drooling over my hat."

"It was lovely to meet you." Sarah moved toward the door.

"Oh, Miss Cuthbert, must you run off?" Lillie asked. "I was about to invite you to dinner. I'd like to get to know you better."

"Dinner?"

"I suggest one of the hotels nearby," Lillie said. "My parents will be going to a dinner party given by one of my father's business associates, and I've already told Cook I would eat out. I'd love to have your company—unless your own family is expecting you."

"No, my family is not expecting me," Sarah said softly as the image of her parents' simple twin grave markers wafted through her mind. Identical in size and shape, they also shared a final date. She had not been to see them for over a year.

"Are they attending a dinner party as well?" Lillie asked.

"They're in Europe." The words slipped out as if they had always been there in the truth column, waiting their turn to rise to the top and be spoken. "They just left last week, and I do not expect them back before New Year's." How easy it was to say that.

Lillie's eyes widened. "Are you on your own, Serena?"

Sarah pulled a pair of short white gloves out of her bag. "My aunt checks in on me every now and then, but I insisted I didn't want to be trouble for anyone. We closed up the house and I've taken a small suite with just one servant." Her room *was* small, and Mrs. Fletcher was the only other servant down the hall at the moment.

Lillie's head bobbed with enthusiasm. "That sounds so practical. I'm twenty-one, but my parents treat me as if I were fourteen. They would never leave me on my own for half a year, but they do let me go out to dinner when they're not going to be home. My father set up accounts at all the best places as soon as we moved here. Please say you'll join me."

Sarah pressed her lips together and mulled the offer. It was Wednesday, her day off, so whatever work awaited her at the Banning house would be there tomorrow. Besides, the Bannings had left to spend several weeks at their summer house in Lake Forest. The next few weeks in the heat of a Chicago summer were sure to be sluggish and the pace of work more forgiving than usual. Mrs. Fletcher, however, had been adamant she would bolt the doors of the house at eight-thirty and go upstairs to the servants' quarters. She was not going to sit up half the night waiting for the parlor maid. Planning only to wander the shops and get something to eat if she got hungry, Sarah had promised to be home by eight-thirty.

"Please?" Lillie pleaded. "I know it's only six o'clock and that's like eating in the middle of the afternoon, but I didn't have lunch. I wasn't hungry then."

Sarah fingered the cuff of her cream shirtwaist. The servants at the Banning house always ate dinner at six o'clock. Then Sarah would put on her whitest apron and help the butler serve the evening meal to the family promptly at eight. Lillie looked at her with such hopeful eyes, and Sarah admitted to herself that she was hungry.

"I'll be delighted to have dinner with you." What good were all the dresses she had made over the last three years if Sarah buckled now? This was her moment.

"I'm so pleased. May I call you Serena? I love your name. You'll have to tell me how your parents ever came up with something so unusual."

It had just popped into her head. "It was my grandmother's sister's name. I don't know where it came from before that."

"I suppose I sound pathetic," Lillie said. "I've met many people since we moved from Cincinnati, but they're all connected to my father's business somehow. My mother kept saying she was going to give a party so I could meet some young people, but she never did and here we are in July. Now she says we may as well wait until September."

"Many people do leave the city to escape the heat," Sarah acknowledged.

"How about you? Do you go away?"

"I was at the lake house the last two summers," Sarah said in all truthfulness. This year she had been selected to stay behind with Mrs. Fletcher, the cook, and look after the Banning mansion while the family was in Lake Forest.

"With your parents away, it's probably easier just to stay in the city," Lillie observed. "I don't blame you."

Sarah nodded. That was as good an explanation as any.

They moved to a small counter near the door and Lillie gave the clerk her mother's account information. A few minutes later, the hat was tied neatly in a box hanging from Lillie's slender fingers.

"My carriage is just outside," Lillie said. "Do you need to dismiss your driver?" They walked a few slow steps outside the shop.

Sarah shook her head. "I walked to the shops today. I was in need of some fresh air."

"That makes it easy. We can go in my carriage and I'll drop you at home later."

"I'm sure I can find a cab," Sarah said. "I don't want to take you out of your way."

"It's no problem. I live on lower Prairie Avenue, a few blocks from here. My parents had hoped to find a house farther north, but nothing suitable was on the market and Father did not want to build something new." Lillie leaned in close to Sarah. "The

George Pullmans live up near Eighteenth Street and they have quite a swanky house. Have you ever seen it?"

"A number of times," Sarah answered.

"Oh, here's my carriage." Lillie laid her gloved hand in the driver's palm and accepted his assistance.

When he turned and offered his hand to Sarah, she sucked in a slow breath and entered the carriage. Lillie murmured instructions to the driver and the carriage began moving north, toward downtown.

A few minutes later, they stepped out of the carriage in front of a hotel Sarah had only ever passed on foot, not daring to enter. Inside, the dining room was enclosed in glazed gray-marble walls. Waiters in stiff formal wear glided around offering every attention to detail with barely noticeable gestures. Lillie ordered a favorite meal for both of them. They ate their way through the soup, the fish, the meats, the vegetables, the salad, and dessert. Smiling and nodding and chatting, Sarah was more proud of herself by the moment, even as every detail of serving the same series of courses each evening at the Banning house jabbed at her thoughts. Three years ago, Charlotte, the kitchen and serving maid, had married and left her position, and Lina, the parlor maid, was lured away to work in another of the mansions of Prairie Avenue. Sarah's duties expanded, and washing and peeling vegetables fell to Mary Catherine, the new scullery maid fresh from Dublin. Mrs. Fletcher had made a proficient cook of Sarah during her years in the kitchen. Sarah could glance at the food set before her and instantly reconstruct how it had been prepared. Years of laying tables three times a day readied her for the menagerie of silver and crystal before her.

Three years! Sarah had never meant to stay a day past her eighteenth birthday. That would have given her eighteen months in the employ of the Bannings—long enough to take a letter of reference with her. Now for a year and a half she had been applying for other positions, and no one seemed to think she could do anything but be in service.

By the time the seasoned roast beef was served, Serena Cuthbert had emerged fully formed with a past life far more scintillating than the orphan girl who had been put into domestic service at the age of sixteen and discovered her own talent with a needle and a cast-off ball gown. Lillie seemed to have no doubt that every word Sarah spoke was true.

Sarah felt as if she had stepped into her own skin for the first time, and she was not going back. This was too easy.

But where was Serena Cuthbert going to stash Sarah Cummings?

2

*S*arah slipped through the female servants' entrance and bolted the door behind her.

In the kitchen a moment later, Mrs. Fletcher glimpsed the clock.

"Three minutes to spare," Sarah announced, breathless. After the meal she had lost valuable time graciously declining Lillie's insistent offer to deliver her home in an open carriage. Lillie's suggestion was reasonable, of course, but the whole evening would have been undone if Lillie had come to the corner of Eighteenth Street and Prairie Avenue and seen which entrance Sarah used to the Banning mansion. Fortunately, Sarah had found a streetcar easily and boarded it out of Lillie's view.

"I'm going on up." Mrs. Fletcher pulled herself out of the stuffed chair that always sat below the window. "It's about time I had a summer break instead of dragging up to the lake year after year. I don't know what made Mrs. Banning decide to hire a summer cook, but I'm grateful."

"It's my turn to make breakfast for Leo, isn't it?" Sarah asked.

Mrs. Fletcher nodded.

"At least he always eats." Sarah laid her handbag on a counter. "I used to find it annoying to go to all the trouble to serve breakfast and hear Oliver say, 'I'm not hungry' or 'Just coffee, please.'"

"Well, Oliver's gone and married now. Lucy too. Richard will be gone to school soon enough."

Sarah was glad to be rid of the whole bunch.

"There's bacon in the icebox, and plenty of eggs," Mrs. Fletcher said. "Leo will be down at seven-thirty as usual."

"It must be the engineer in him that makes him so precise." Most of the household staff had journeyed up to Lake Forest to look after Flora and Samuel Banning and Richard for seven weeks. With Leo home and Samuel dropping in periodically to tend to his law practice, Mrs. Fletcher and Sarah had been left behind to keep them comfortable and the house running smoothly. Karl, an under-coachman, was around for odd jobs and Leo's minimal demands for transport.

Looking weary on her feet, Mrs. Fletcher gestured toward the kitchen table. "Another note came for you from Simon Tewell."

Sarah straightened her skirt.

"This is the third note he's sent," Mrs. Fletcher said. "What does he want?"

"So far he just says he wants to discuss something with me and asks would I come to St. Andrew's at my convenience."

Mrs. Fletcher scoffed as she pressed her gray hair back on her head. "He knows you're in service. There is no convenience."

"I'm certainly not going to spend my day off ferreting out his mysteries," Sarah said.

"With the family away now, you should have time to find out what he wants. Just let me know when you're going to be gone." Mrs. Fletcher shuffled toward the stairs leading up from the kitchen to the servants' quarters. "I'm going to bed. Make sure you put the lights out when you come up."

"Good night." Sarah listened as the older woman scaled the stairs with weary steps. Three years ago the two of them had regarded each other warily. Sarah was not any more content now with the thought of a life in service, but she no longer regarded Mrs. Fletcher as her captor. Finding a way out was just taking longer than she had hoped.

Tonight's dinner had been easier than Sarah ever imagined. Lillie Wagner needed a friend, and Serena Cuthbert was up to the challenge.

Sarah moved to the table and picked up the envelope, certain its contents would be the same as the previous two.

Simon Tewell had been the assistant director at St. Andrew's Orphanage during Sarah's later years there. She had liked him well enough—as much as she liked anyone at that place. In fact, he once had listened to her tearful rant about the injustice of having both her parents killed in an accident and being left alone, and never once had he told her it was the way of the world and she would just have to adjust. It had been three years since she'd left the orphanage and joined the domestic staff of the Bannings'. Lucy Banning Edwards held a more or less permanent volunteer position at the orphanage. When she came to family dinners, Lucy occasionally reported that Simon had asked after Sarah. Lucy had arranged Sarah's placement at the Bannings' in the first place. In Sarah's mind, though, that did not entitle Lucy to be making reports to the orphanage director. If Lucy wanted to do something to help her now, she should use her influence to find Sarah a new position with some dignity.

Sarah had not been back to the orphanage even one time. Why should she go there? She wanted a future, not reminders of her past. Wasn't the point to get children out of the orphanage and on their own? Wasn't that why she had gone into service in the first place? Going back to St. Andrew's was movement in the wrong direction.

"This was not supposed to be my life," Sarah murmured to the empty room. "My father was a department manager for Marshall Field. We had a home. He wanted more for me than this."

Her parents had been killed instantly in a traffic accident. Sarah had been at school in the middle of an arithmetic lesson. The question that had haunted Sarah every day since her parents' death was why her father had not made sure she was provided for. He'd filled her full of dreams that shattered with his death, his only legacy an empty bank account and an untraceable family tree.

Serena Cuthbert, that's what Sarah wanted—and not just for a random, serendipitous evening. Serena Cuthbert did not come from an orphanage dormitory or sleep in a servant's narrow attic room. She did not cook and serve meals and sweep floors. If she liked a hat, she bought it. If she wanted a gown, she had it made from fresh, unspoiled textiles direct from New York. Sarah's own father would have been proud of Serena Cuthbert.

Sarah picked up Simon Tewell's envelope with its tidy handwriting but did not break the seal. She would take it upstairs and put it with the others, unpersuaded she had any reason to go back to that place.

Lillie flopped onto her bed, tummy first, feet up in the air. The quilt was new, the appliqued rose and leaf pattern commissioned by her mother to match the freshly installed wallpaper. In a few minutes Lillie would send for her ladies' maid to help her undress, but for now she wanted only to savor the evening. How fortunate that she had been in the milliner's shop at the same time as Serena Cuthbert. She and her mother had taken tea a few times with the wives of her father's business associates, but Serena was the first young woman Lillie had met in Chicago who she felt might be a true friend.

With the thought of Serena at her side, Lillie dreaded the upcoming Fourth of July celebration a little less. Serena had accepted the invitation to celebrate with the Wagners readily enough. With the Cuthberts in Europe, Serena would not have her family's traditional party on the pier at the lake house. Serena's description of the Cuthbert gala did make it sound fun, though. Next year Serena would invite Lillie to celebrate with her family, perhaps even in Lake Forest. For the time being, Serena was free to make whatever plans she wished for the holiday. She had said she would be delighted to go meet the Wagners at Jackson Park.

Paul Gunnison would be there, of course. Until she moved to Chicago in April, Lillie had not seen Paul in ten years. She had been a child, and he a teenager with no particular interest in the wide-eyed, round-faced little girl whose eyes trailed his movements when their families socialized. And when his family moved to Chicago to launch the Midwest branch of the candy-making business, he faded from Lillie's mind. Lillie and Paul had barely recognized each other the first time they met again in Chicago, but the spark was instant. Paul had called on Lillie four times already. Of course, he stayed only fifteen minutes each time, because to stay any longer would be rude, but Lillie felt the way he looked at her now and the attentiveness he offered even in those brief interludes. She was sure Paul planned to speak to her father and ask permission to escort Lillie formally.

She was going to need some new gowns if she were going to be seen on the arm of Paul Gunnison. Lillie slapped her own face in chastisement for neglecting to get the name of Serena's dressmaker. Though Serena had worn only a simple skirt and shirtwaist, Lillie could appreciate the attention to detail in every tuck and topstitch. The garments draped Serena's frame perfectly.

Lillie sat up straight on the bed. Bradley Townsend was also going to be at the Fourth of July party. She would have to make sure he was formally introduced to Serena. Though she hardly knew him and he seemed nice enough, Lillie had no interest in Brad herself. He was sure to appreciate the pleasant bearing and conversation of someone like Serena. After all, they both had spent considerable time in France, and Serena's parents were there now. They were sure to find common ground.

Lillie had offered to have her coachman see Serena home tonight, but her new friend had refused. Lillie supposed it was part of Serena's determination not to be a bother to people and to learn some independence. It did seem rather exciting to think of navigating around Chicago alone. Serena could get into a cab and go anywhere she wanted. No one told her where she ought not to go or decided on a destination without even consulting her. Lillie lolled on her back, pleasantly imagining such delicious independence.

She heard Moira's familiar soft knock on her bedroom door and bid her enter.

"Shall I turn down your bed now, miss?"

3

The thread color was two shades too light, but it would have to do. With careful stitching, Sarah could hide the thread under the trim.

Independence Day morning found Sarah rummaging through her supply of assorted trims and scraps of fabrics. What was she supposed to wear to a Fourth of July party? The conundrum had rattled around Sarah's mind for two days. The party would be outdoors, where the crowd would await fireworks over Lake Michigan culminating the evening, so she drifted away from selections that seemed too formal for the setting. Finally she settled on a blue fan skirt, knowing that the fullness in the back of the skirt would make the front seem narrow and her waist slender. The lightweight crinkled cotton garment had once belonged to Violet Newcomb, Mrs. Banning's sister. Sarah had taken in the waist nearly a year ago and paired the skirt with a cambric blouse loose enough to be comfortable in warm weather. In honor of the patriotic holiday, she decided to tack on bands of red ribbon around the collar and cuffs of the blouse and roll some ribbon into a flower to attach to the skirt at the hip on one side.

The ribbon she had in mind had come off a hat Flora Banning had wearied of two years ago. Both Flora Banning and Violet Newcomb were generous with clothing that went out of style from season to season. Occasionally Lucy Banning Edwards parted with something, but her clothing choices tended to the sturdy rather than the fashionable, and her own day maid, Charlotte Shepard, was often on the receiving end of discards. Sarah had long ago gotten over any hesitation about wearing hand-me-downs from the wealthy women for whom she poured tea. By the time Sarah dismantled the garments and reassembled the pieces to suit her own figure and tastes, even the donors could not recognize their own clothes. Flora, Violet, and Lucy had all begun to ask Sarah to do alterations from time to time. Her talent with a needle was indisputable.

However, a parlor maid had little use for dinner gowns and fashionable day suits. Sarah's room in the third-floor servants' quarters was the same miniscule size as everyone else's. It was meant to be a place to sleep and little else—certainly not a wardrobe collection. The narrow closet had become insufficient before Sarah had been there a year. She had pounded hooks into all the walls and appropriated three unused dilapidated trunks she found in a spare room. On a daily basis, Sarah still wore dark, solemn dresses covered with white work aprons. Only on Wednesdays and every other Sunday afternoon, when she was off duty, did Sarah have the opportunity to don her handiwork and venture out into public—usually alone. Sometimes she took a train to Marshall Field's store downtown, where she could lose herself for an entire day drifting from floor to floor. She always made sure to walk through the men's department her father had once managed. If she could afford it, she might treat herself to tea and a sandwich in one of the store's restaurants. Occasionally Sarah felt a man's eyes on her, but without a proper introduction, a glance was all she could hope for.

This party could change that. This party could change everything. Lillie had assured her—Serena—that the guest list included a number of eligible bachelors.

Men of means.

Men she could never meet any other way.

Men who did not know Sarah Cummings.

All she had to do was be Serena Cuthbert. Really be her, flawless in demeanor, unhesitating in conversation.

"I *am* Serena Cuthbert," she said aloud as she licked her bottom lip and put the first stitch through the ribbon and onto the left cuff. If she played her cards right, even a position at Marshall Field's would be beneath her.

⌒⌒

Paul Gunnison offered his arm and Lillie took it gladly.

"I hope Serena arrives soon." Lillie surveyed the expansive green behind the Field Columbian Museum, where a crowd amassed slowly but steadily in Jackson Park. "I made her promise to be at the East Lagoon by seven."

"Didn't your mother say the picnic would be laid by seven-thirty?"

Lillie nodded. "Yes, that's right. We're told the fireworks won't be until at least nine-thirty, so we have plenty of time to enjoy our meal."

"What does your friend Serena look like?"

"Dark hair and brown eyes, a little taller than I am." Lillie laughed nervously. "I suppose that describes a third of the women here."

"At least a quarter." Paul gestured ahead of them. "If we stroll toward the North Bridge, you might spot her."

Lillie smiled at the excuse to walk along the lagoon with Paul Gunnison and let him pull her hand through the crook in his elbow. She was tempted to lean into him slightly, but restrained herself from being so forward.

"Oh, there she is now." Lillie pointed in exclamation a moment later. She broke loose from Paul and with a hastened pace closed the distance keeping her from her new friend. "You made it!"

"I wouldn't miss it for the world." Serena Cuthbert toyed with the broad brim of her hat.

"Miss Serena Cuthbert, may I present Mr. Paul Gunnison? Lillie gestured from Serena to Paul. "Paul, Serena is the friend I mentioned to you."

Paul bowed slightly and offered his hand to Serena. "I'm delighted to meet you, Miss Cuthbert."

Lillie's pulse beat in her throat. In the waning early evening light, Paul's eyes glimmered, and she could not believe her good fortune at being on his arm tonight. He bore his unusual height with gentlemanly grace and flicked his eyes in her direction frequently, even in a crowd.

"Lillie speaks very highly of you, Mr. Gunnison," Serena said.

Lillie touched the ribbon on Serena's stripes. "You look quite fetching. Remind me later to ask you again about your dressmaker. If you tell me now I'm sure to forget."

"Why don't we join the others?" Paul nudged Lillie's elbow. "Your mother will be looking for you before she opens the buffet."

Lillie nodded. Together they ambled toward the blue-and-yellow-striped canopy the Wagners had erected at the south end of the lagoon to stake out space for their private party. Under the tent, a full complement of domestic staff took up their stations behind the buffet laden with mounds of food. Tables and chairs hauled in earlier in the day now spilled out from the tent, arrayed toward the lakeshore.

"It seems to be quite a large party." Serena removed her hat and used it to fan herself delicately.

"Most of the guests are Father's business connections," Lillie explained. "I don't know many of them well, but I'm eager to introduce you to a few."

"I'm looking forward to it."

As they approached the tent, Lillie felt a prod on her elbow and turned toward it. "Mr. Townsend! This is perfect. I was hoping to run into you soon. I'd like you to meet my friend, Miss Serena Cuthbert."

Lillie smiled as Bradley Townsend's face shimmered in greeting. She watched him examine Serena as quickly as he blinked his blue eyes under jet-black hair. She flushed at the mutual pleasure she saw in them both. Chicago would be so much less dreary and lonely if Brad and Serena and she and Paul could be a foursome.

Lillie introduced Brad to Paul. The men shook hands, but Lillie could see that Brad's eyes barely left Serena's face. Serena's full lips formed a warm smile, and Lillie wanted to giggle.

"Let's get something to eat," Lillie said, leading the way to the buffet table. "Then we can all get to know each other."

They sat together at a table for four looking out on the lake, the glittering alabaster museum in the background and their plates heaped with cucumber salad, baked ham, lobster tail, berries and melons, brie, assorted breads, and double chocolate cake.

Brad took in his surroundings as he accepted a glass of lemonade from one of the circulating Wagner footmen. "I haven't been to this part of the city for some time," he said. "I wasn't sure what it would look like with the fair gone. It's a bit odd to be having a picnic with the evidence of such an extravaganza obliterated."

"The evidence is not obliterated." Paul nodded toward the Field Columbian Museum. "That was the Palace of Fine Arts at the fair."

"So it was. That building will be there for a hundred years or more," Brad speculated. "The walls have a brick core under the plaster—not likely to burn."

"I assume the Field Columbian Museum is named in honor of Marshall Field." Lillie put a delicate bit of ham on a fork and moved it toward her mouth.

Brad nodded. "He is the major benefactor—and he donated the land for the world's fair."

"The land where we're sitting on right now?"

"That's right."

"I have so much to learn about Chicago," Lillie said. "Did you attend the world's fair, Mr. Townsend?"

"Certainly," he answered. "Several times. How about you?"

"We never made it from Ohio. We meant to, of course, but somehow it did not happen. One thing after another interfered with our travel plans. What about you, Serena?"

"Mr. Townsend, I wonder if we were both at the fair on 'Chicago Day.'" Serena leaned toward Brad.

He chuckled. "Quite likely. It was a popular day. If only I'd had the pleasure of knowing you then."

Lillie stifled an unladylike giggle. Brad and Serena liked each other. She could see it in their eyes.

"It's unfortunate the fires destroyed so many of the buildings after the exposition closed." Paul's cutlery clinked against his plate as he prepared his next bite.

"The city council should have taken immediate firm action about the tramps squatting in the buildings." Brad leaned back in his chair and stretched his legs.

"Some people are down on their luck," Lillie offered cautiously.

"No matter." Brad slapped one knee. "From what I see, the Olmsted firm is doing an admirable job with their new design for the area. Don't you think so, Miss Cuthbert?"

"It's truly lovely." Serena met Brad's eyes and one corner of her mouth turned up.

"What about the Ferris wheel?" Lillie glanced from Brad to Serena and allowed herself a smile at their glances. "Did you ride? That was the attraction I was most disappointed to miss."

"It ran for several months after the fair closed," Brad said. "Then they took it apart, moved it north, and put it back up. You can still ride it."

"I would be honored to take you." Paul offered Lillie the bread basket on their table, though she could reach it easily unaided.

"I'd go in a heartbeat." Lillie would go wherever Paul Gunnison offered to take her.

"The wheel made money for the fair," Brad said, "but now it's losing money hand over fist. I don't expect it will last long."

"Then we'll go soon," Paul said.

Lillie flushed. Surely Paul would speak to her father before long.

"Have you met the Bannings yet?" Brad asked, looking at Lillie. "I realize they're situated a few blocks north of you on Prairie Avenue, but I wonder if you've had occasion."

"Do you know the Bannings?" Serena casually took a bite of cucumber salad.

Brad gave a playful grin. "I've seen them at the odd party, but no, I don't know them. They are well regarded, however. I'm sure I would enjoy meeting them. How about you?"

"I've seen them at the odd party as well," Serena answered.

"I haven't met them yet," Lillie said, "but I look forward to the opportunity."

"The Glessners live very close to them," Brad said, "as well as the Pullmans and the Fields."

"I was introduced to the Pullmans at their daughter's wedding," Lillie said. "Mother would love to know them well."

"There are some eccentric characters at that corner," Brad said.

"It's finally getting dark." Serena waved a hand toward the water. "Do we want to move closer to the lake before the fireworks begin?"

⚘

Sarah breathed controlled relief. The conversation had at last turned away from the residents of the corner of Eighteenth and Prairie.

She felt the rip as she stood up from the table. The red ribbon flower at her hip snagged on the corner of the table and now dangled precariously. Sarah's hand caught it just in time, or the damage to her skirt might have been drastic. No one else seemed to notice, but she could not leave it hanging like that, not with Bradley Townsend at her side for the evening. He did not appear inclined to drift off with any other guests. It seemed the foursome would have their own party within a party this evening. The moment was too important to lose to a hanging ribbon.

"I think I'll find another glass of lemonade to take down to the lake," Sarah said brightly. "I see one of the footmen right over there. I'll just be a minute."

"We'll wait for you," Lillie said.

"Nonsense. You all go on and find us a good spot to watch from before the light fails completely. I'll be right there."

Lillie laughed. "I haven't known Serena long," she said, "but I do know she's independent. A modern woman!"

As the others left, Sarah moved away from the Wagners' guests to examine the damage more discreetly. She had to remove the flower without snagging the skirt's fabric and without the benefit of scissors.

———

Simon Tewell straightened the shoulder of the reluctant boy. "Try to look confident, Alonzo. People are not going to buy Cracker Jacks from someone who doesn't look as if he wants to sell them."

"I've already sold six boxes." The boy's face flushed in protest.

"And we have twelve cartons to sell." Simon gripped the left point of the boy's collar between thumb and forefinger and pulled it into line. "Remember, if we sell enough concessions, the whole class can take the train to Springfield in the spring." He turned the boy around and nudged him toward the drifting crowd, then followed his movements for a few minutes. Business was picking up.

Simon turned to track the progress of several other boys from St. Andrew's Orphanage hawking various concessions to the crowd congregated for the fireworks. The assembly seemed as mixed as the population of Chicago—glamorous catered gatherings of the wealthy as well as blankets and sandwiches of the working class. The boys selling snacks had a wide market to take advantage of. As Simon sauntered across the lawn, a vaguely familiar form came into focus, bent over slightly. Intuitively he moved toward it until recognition dawned.

"Sarah Cummings? Is that you?" Simon quickened his steps, stumbling slightly over a depression in the grass.

Her head lifted and she looked at him.

"Mr. Tewell!"

"'Simon,' please. You left the orphanage long ago. There's no need to stand on formality." Sarah Cummings, Simon was pleased to see, had come a long way from the scrawny, arrogant girl who had so vehemently protested residing at St. Andrew's. In fact, if Simon had met her for the first time in this setting, he might never have supposed her to be a servant.

Sarah pulled something from her skirt and balled it in her hand as she glanced toward the lake. "It should be a good show tonight."

"I'm sure it will be." Simon swallowed. "You're looking very pretty tonight. I hope I'm not too forward in saying so."

"No. I mean, thank you. It's kind of you to notice." Her dark head bobbed briefly.

"Lucy has commented often that you are doing well at the Bannings'. And your skill with fashion has not gone unnoticed, according to her reports. I assume you are wearing one of your creations tonight."

"I'm afraid I've gotten separated from my group." Sarah looked toward the lake again. "I don't mean to be impolite, but—"

"Of course." Simon took a step back. "You'll lose them in the shadows. I won't keep you long, but I have been hoping to speak to you."

"I'm sorry I haven't answered your notes."

"I suppose it was hectic getting the Bannings ready for their summer at the lake. I understand you're busy, but I wonder if I might prevail on you for just a few minutes."

"I promise to come see you at St. Andrew's," Sarah said.

"Soon?"

"Yes, soon."

"It was lovely to run into you."

"Likewise, Mr. Tewell. Simon."

Clearly her mind was elsewhere, but at least she had promised to come see him. It would be better to discuss the matter in his office anyway. Sarah turned to leave, and Simon made no effort to delay her as he admired the graceful swing of her hips and skirt.

4

*T*he hydrangea bushes in the front were bigger than Sarah remembered. The main door was painted a deeper shade of red. Otherwise the place looked the same. The wide alley on one side hosted boys oblivious to their unkempt state as they played a make-shift game of base ball. Sarah had not discovered the appeal of the game, but the orphanage never lacked for boys who wanted to play.

The brick of St. Andrew's Orphanage stacked four stories high in symmetrical, boxed precision. The structure oozed large-scale efficiency, a down payment on the internal workings of the institution.

Standing at the curb outside the building, Sarah could have described the floor plan—the offices, kitchen, dining hall, staff housing, and classrooms of the first floor. More classrooms occupied the second floor, and dormitories for more than four hundred children the top stories. Sarah saw the muslin curtain on a fourth-floor corner window flutter. That was the girls' side. For the last two years of her residency at St. Andrew's, Sarah had managed to situate her bed under that window. This had not been an easy achievement. The location was a popular niche, and other girls claimed they had more rights to the exclusive assignment, but Sarah had wormed her way in and held strong.

In reality, the curtain did little to diminish light or ensure privacy. Sarah supposed it was meant as a homey accent to mysteriously cheer the sixteen girls who slept in the room and kept their minimalist belongings in three narrow drawers each. The curtains never fooled Sarah. Muslin. She could think of no fabric more utilitarian. Certainly it was nothing like the gathered gingham or calico curtains her mother used to decorate the kitchen and bedrooms of their home, or the velvet drapes that adorned the dining room and front parlor. Muslin was nothing more than a lining, never meant to be seen.

Each day seemed a duplicate of the day before in regimented routine with hundreds of children going to classes and eating meals. In the static nights of the dormitory, Sarah used to kneel on her bed, push the useless curtain out of the way, and stare out.

It was not as if she could see much. The neighborhood around the south side orphanage included office buildings, a warehouse, a factory, and a row of stores with apartments above the shops, all limiting a view of the night sky. However, even watching the comings and goings on the streets below—and there was a surprising amount of activity given the hours of her vigil—reminded Sarah of where she had come from and that she was not, at heart, an abandoned orphan. She would never accept that identity. Not then. Not now.

She had stood in this same spot eight years ago. The exact spot.

As she remembered the day she arrived at St. Andrew's, Sarah's breath went shallow. She bustled home from school that afternoon with an elaborate tale to tell about Margaret Eddington, only to find a neighbor sitting stiffly in the kitchen. The fragrance of her mother's bread, a standard on Tuesday afternoons, was absent. The facts of the situation were bald and brief. Her parents' carriage had overturned in the street. They had been dead for nearly six hours. Arrangements had already been made for Sarah to go to St. Andrew's. There was no one else to take her, the neighbor explained. At the orphanage her needs would be taken care of and she would get a sound education. Within minutes Sarah had stood in this spot on the curb trying to imagine living inside the building before her. Without her parents. Without anyone.

Was it really only two days ago that she had sat across the table from Bradley Townsend? In the darkness, their faces lifted to the dazzling fireworks, he had whispered that he wanted to see her again. While hoping that she encouraged his interest, nevertheless she had declined his offer to escort her home. How could she accept? He wanted to see Serena Cuthbert, not Sarah Cummings.

In her mind, though, the two had already begun to blur.

⸙

Simon saw her through the window of his office and watched her while he tried to think of a replacement for the minister who had canceled for Sunday. He did not like the thought that the children might not have a church service if he did not find someone on short notice. Sarah Cummings, he remembered, was never fond of the Sunday services, but perhaps she had grown into them by now.

For the longest time, Sarah stood perfectly still, and Simon could only imagine what must be slicing through her. She was nearing twenty and had grown into a lovely young woman—at least, from what he could see. Clearly she took great care with her hair, which wound around her face with breathless luster. Even in this moment, when he could see bewilderment rising in her face, her shoulders were back and posture erect. Her form curved in all the right places, hardly a hint left of the bony girl she had been at thirteen, the first time he met her. Essentially she was a stranger now—but a captivating stranger.

By the time Simon arrived at St. Andrew's, Sarah was already sullen and obstinate, and he supposed she had been that way from her first day. He had come straight from earning his college degree at age twenty-one, not much older than Sarah was now. He knew little about large social institutions and even less about children, but Philip Emmett, the orphanage director, was eager to take on an assistant director to help manage the swelling number of orphans. When he stepped through the front door on the first day, Sarah Cummings dutifully had asked how she could help him. Although she could not have been less interested in why he was there, she escorted him to Philip Emmett's office and announced him as she had been trained to do. Something about her made Simon pay attention even then.

Sarah was a bright student, but a disinterested one, and eventually Philip Emmett was resigned that her progress was not satisfactory enough for the orphanage to continue to underwrite her education. At sixteen, it was time for her to leave. Lucy Banning Edwards, a frequent volunteer at St. Andrew's, suggested that Sarah work for her family while she sorted herself out, and Simon oversaw the transition. Lucy remained heavily involved with St. Andrew's, so Simon could ask after Sarah Cummings on a regular basis. Her obstinate edge had rounded off, according to Mrs. Edwards, and Flora Banning made sure Sarah had plenty of gowns to experiment with. Once her high spirits settled down, she could train with an established dressmaker.

Frankly, no one expected Sarah Cummings would remain three years at the Bannings'. Most of the domestic staff on Prairie Avenue barely lasted a year and a half before looking for a position that paid a bit more or offered slightly less taxing duties or more promising accommodations. Simon himself had planned to work only a couple of years in Chicago and move on. Yet here they both were, maybe for a reason.

Now Simon held the director position at St. Andrew's. Both his life and Sarah's had changed. Unquestionably, he was curious about what would transpire when she came through the door. She was no child anymore, and he was ready to consider a settled future.

A knock pulled his attention from the window to his office door. "Yes?"

"Mr. Tewell," fourteen-year-old Jane Porter said, "Mrs. Edwards said you wanted us to address some envelopes, but she does not have the address list."

Simon rummaged through a pile at the edge of the desk and extracted the fund-raising list. He flipped through the pages to double-check whether it was complete before handing it to the unsmiling girl.

"Did she show you which envelopes to use?" he asked.

"The large cream-colored ones," Jane said flatly. "For invitations."

"You're doing a very good job helping in the office, Jane," Simon said. "You always have. Mrs. Edwards depends on you heavily."

"Yes, Mr. Tewell." Jane turned to leave with the list. "I'll use the pen with the fine-point nib."

Jane reminded Simon of Sarah. The girl was one of the reasons he wanted to see Sarah and present his proposal.

Sarah finally pulled her feet out of the invisible cement that seemed to encase them and approached the red door. Unsure whether being a former resident meant she could simply walk in, she opted to pull the bell. Three years was a long time to presume.

A moment later, the door opened, and Sarah looked into a pair of dark, questioning eyes.

They stared at each other for a moment.

"Jane?" Sarah ventured.

The girl nodded and squinted as she examined the visitor. "I remember you. You used to live here. You were one of the older girls. You had your bed under the corner window."

Sarah managed a smile. "That's me. Sarah Cummings. I guess you're one of the older girls now. Are you going to high school?"

Jane nodded. "I'm going to finish no matter what."

"It's good to have a goal," Sarah said. "I've come to see Mr. Tewell. Is he available?"

"I'll tell him you're here." Jane turned on her heel. "Follow me, please."

Nothing in the main hall had changed, a fact that made Sarah cringe. One corridor led to the dining room, another to classrooms, and a third to the administrative offices. The same sorts of notices about rules and schedules were tacked to the walls at irregular intervals. Following Jane was like following herself. How many visitors had she led down this route?

They walked past the volunteer office where Lucy Banning Edwards organized a variety of tasks. Sarah had lost track of the schedule Lucy kept for her volunteer work and was relieved not to find her behind the desk just then. She wanted to attend to Simon's inquiry and leave as quickly as possible—preferably without obliging.

She did not want to be there.

Jane rapped lightly on the open office door and said, "Miss Sarah Cummings to see you, sir."

"Ah, Sarah, welcome." Simon stood and came around the desk to shake Sarah's hand. "Thank you, Jane."

"I'll work on the envelopes now." Jane meekly disappeared, closing the door behind her.

"I'm pleased you could come." Simon gestured to a chair.

She took a seat and removed her white gloves. The beadwork down the fingers had taken her every evening for two weeks, but she knew it was as skilled as any money could buy. She wore a deep scarlet chintz suit trimmed with a gray braid, having refused the notion that she should enter the halls of her past in a maid's uniform.

"It was delightful to run into you at the park," Simon said. "I was unsure whether I would recognize you after all this time. You have changed considerably."

Sarah moved slightly in her chair, not at all sure she liked the way Simon Tewell was looking at her. Surely he did not think she would be personally interested in him.

"Your notes did not say what you wanted to see me about," Sarah said.

Simon redirected his gaze, cleared his throat, and took his own chair behind his desk. "I would like to ask a favor. You've done well since leaving St. Andrew's, and I believe you can offer something we badly need."

Sarah refused to let her eyes widen, but could not quell the rush of blood to her head. Done well? Because she'd progressed from a kitchen maid to a parlor maid? Mr. Tewell's suggestion did not merit an answer.

"Mrs. Edwards tells me repeatedly that you do wonderful things with a swatch of fabric and spool of thread." Simon turned a palm up. "I'd like to explore whether some of the older girls might learn to sew, and I cannot think of anyone I'd be more pleased to have teach them."

"Teach them?" Sarah echoed vaguely.

"An organized class," he said, "perhaps once a week. You could come in and meet with a small group of girls. If it works well, we can consider what it might lead to."

"But Mr. Tewell—Simon—you know I am in service." She nearly choked on speaking those words aloud. "Surely you understand I have little time to call my own."

He nodded. "I'm asking a great deal of you. I would be willing to speak to the Bannings on your behalf and arrange their cooperation."

This was Lucy's idea, Sarah realized. Simon was far too confident it could be arranged.

Aloud she said calmly, "I do not want to prevail on the Bannings. Surely Mrs. Edwards could arrange a volunteer. Many of the women she knows dedicate long hours to needlework."

"Yes, many do take up needlework as a leisure activity, but I believe that's a different skill than constructing garments. Also, I'd like the girls to see an example of a girl from St. Andrew's who has achieved something commendable."

Had he dared to call her "a girl from St. Andrew's"? Sarah squirmed and resettled her hands.

Simon continued. "I'm told you are skilled enough that you could easily find employment in a dressmaker's shop, or even open your own shop one day."

Sarah remembered the way Bradley Townsend had smiled at her when they said good night after the last of the fireworks. A man like Brad would not notice a shop girl, but he had noticed Serena Cuthbert.

"I realize it's unlikely you've ever thought about teaching a sewing class, but I would ask you to seriously consider it now," Simon said. "It would be an opportunity for you to make a significant difference in the lives of these girls. You might use the gifts God gave you to inspire some of them to consider a future they haven't imagined before."

A future as a dressmaker was not the future Sarah imagined. And she had worked hard on her talent. What did God have to do with it?

"Mr. Tewell—Simon—I'm not sure this is a practical idea for the sake of the girls. I appreciate that you've thought of me, but—"

"May I show you the space?" Simon stood. "You would have full use of a classroom here on the first floor. You can leave sewing projects in process and I assure you they will not be disturbed. I'll personally ensure that the room stays locked."

"I appreciate the extent to which you've thought about this, but I'm afraid I cannot manage what you propose."

"At least let me show you the room." Simon gestured toward the door.

Sarah swallowed. "Perhaps on my way out." If she agreed to see the classroom, at least she would be out of this office.

Simon tucked one hand into a patch pocket on his jacket. "We'll go now. You'll remember the room, I'm sure. It used to be the library, but we've expanded the library into a larger space on the second floor."

Sarah stood up now as well. Simon opened the door, then stepped aside for Sarah to go through.

～∘≫⋄≪∘～

He led her across the main hall and down the side corridor that led to the classrooms.

"There's even a sewing machine," Simon said brightly as they walked. "It was donated to us just a month ago."

"Actually, I have never used a sewing machine," Sarah said.

"Then you might enjoy experimenting with this one."

Simon unlocked a door and stepped aside. Sarah entered the room slowly, and Simon had to admit to himself he had no idea what her movements meant. She might simply be polite and look around before reiterating that she would not teach the class. But he hoped not. This opportunity certainly would be good for the girls, perhaps even change their lives, but also it would guarantee he could see Sarah Cummings on a regular basis.

Sarah paced around the room, trailed her fingers on the long table, and opened a couple of cabinets.

"The cupboards would remain," Simon said. "We can bring in more storage if you require it."

"I don't know anything about teaching a class." Sarah closed a cabinet firmly.

"You know what it's like to live here and wonder what your future will be." Simon met the gaze of her brown eyes. "That will carry you far."

"I've been gone a long time now," Sarah said. "My life has moved on."

"How about one class?" Simon suggested. If she hoped he was going to give up easily, she would find out how stubborn he could be. "Just see how it feels."

Simon stood with both hands in his jacket pockets, waiting for the next excuse she would raise. He would answer every one.

Sarah pressed her lips together and twisted her mouth to one side. "I suppose I could show them some basic stitches." She looked around the room again. "What about fabric?"

"Donations." The door was open. She was going to do it.

5

Although Lillie had met Serena Cuthbert only a week ago, already she felt she had a best friend. Under the fireworks, she'd overheard Bradley Townsend invite Serena out for Thursday evening and jumped into action herself—inviting Serena to dinner on Wednesday evening. Serena had been coy before accepting Brad's invitation, acting as if she needed to check her social schedule, but she did not miss a beat in telling Lillie she would be glad to come to dinner.

Lillie sat in the Wagner parlor where she would be sure to hear the doorbell. The room's furniture was still new and unfamiliar. Frederic Wagner would have been content to move the old furniture from Cincinnati. Edith Wagner, on the other hand, would not concede for a moment that the sofa and chairs would be suitable for a parlor on Prairie Avenue—even if it were lower Prairie Avenue rather than the more prestigious upper end. Lillie had listened to her parents' polite but emphatic discussions for weeks before her father finally gave in to the expense of new furnishings for much of the Chicago house. Lillie rather missed the old sofa, but with a friend coming for dinner, she was glad her mother had prevailed.

Edith Wagner entered the parlor and raised her eyebrows. "Is your friend the sort who is on time?"

Lillie glanced at the mantel clock she had seen the housekeeper wind only a few hours ago. "I confess I don't know. She was on time for the picnic."

"I barely got to meet her," Edith said. "You whisked her off with Mr. Gunnison and Mr. Townsend before I could extend an appropriate welcome."

"I'm sorry, Mother. Tonight will make up for it. It's just the four of us for dinner, isn't it?"

"Yes. You know your father doesn't like to come home from his office and face a lot of company in the middle of the week. I persuaded him that one friend should not be taxing."

"Thank you. I think you'll both like Serena."

Before Lillie could sink back in the sofa, Frederic appeared with two long tubes in his arms.

"Are those the drawings?" Edith immediately snatched the tubes from her husband's grasp.

"I still don't understand why you insisted on two sets," Frederic said. "When we bought the house, I agreed to some renovations to make it our own, but you are getting carried away."

Edith unrolled the first set of drawings on a round ebony pedestal table at one end of the room. "You won't want to do this again, so we must make the right decision now."

Lillie rose to inspect the options. Leaning over her mother's shoulder, she saw an architect's drawing of their Italianate home, but with a mansard roof to bring it into the Second Empire. The roof in the drawing sloped on all four sides, with a gentler slope to the upper portion of the roof and a steeper slope below. The house looked less like a brick box and more imposing, more solid. Windows all around suggested the mansard was for more than show.

"If we add that roof, does that mean adding rooms underneath it?" Lillie asked.

"We might expand servants' quarters in that space," her mother murmured. "But I'm not sure Second Empire is the way to go." Edith unfurled the second set of drawings.

Lillie gasped. "Whose house is that?"

Frederic groaned. "Edith, I thought we agreed we were not going to build a new home."

"This is not a new home," Edith insisted. "It's a proposed renovation of this house."

Lillie looked more carefully, and gradually she recognized the main shape of the house but with an addition to one side for a sunny two-story conservatory. The original windows and doors were in all the right places on all three floors, but the drawing suggested a limestone façade be added over the red brick, allowing the design to incorporate pronounced arches over the windows and entrances. A matching arched portico jutted out from the main front entrance.

"It's Romanesque," Frederic said, "a complete departure. The Second Empire can be done with a reasonable budget. We'd just be raising the roof. But this—this is too much."

"Oh, but Second Empire is so passé," Edith protested. "It will be out of date by the time we finish construction. No one is doing that any longer. I rode past the Glessner house at Eighteenth Street a few days ago and I'm convinced Romanesque is the future."

"But the house is hardly recognizable," Frederic said. "Can we even live here during the renovations?"

"I'm sure we'll work something out." Edith began rolling the drawings again. "We'll have to sort this out later. Lillie's guest will be here any moment."

Frederic shook his head. "What you propose is going to require selling unprecedented amounts of candy."

Ten blocks. That was the distance from the Banning house to the Wagner home. The evening was already dimming, and though it was warm—July in Chicago never was cool—at least the day's heat was past its peak. Sarah paced herself so the walk did not make her perspire noticeably.

Almost at Twenty-eighth Street, she stood in front of the Wagner house for a moment. The home was not as ostentatious as the cluster of homes around Eighteenth and Prairie Avenue, but like all the homes on the lower stretch it still suggested wealth the ordinary person would never know.

But Serena Cuthbert was not ordinary.

If Sarah had come straight to the Wagner home when she left St. Andrew's three years ago, she might have fumbled her way through the dreamlike setting. As it was, though, she had plenty of experience in the Banning house and knew where the boundaries were in a home such as the Wagners'.

Only this time Serena would be on the other side of those boundaries. Sarah invited Serena to take the next step up the walk and slipped to the background.

She rang the bell. The housekeeper showed her into the parlor, where Serena chatted with Lillie and her parents until the housekeeper returned to announce that dinner was served.

Sarah had only known a household staff headed by a butler, but clearly here Mrs. Burnett was in charge, and she was not the cook or the parlor maid. Sarah smiled graciously as Edith Wagner led the way to the dining room. A round table awaited them, draped in a rich green damask tablecloth and laid with gold-rimmed white china. Each piece bore an intricate monogrammed W. Sarah's eyes soaked up the fresh variety of dishes, cutlery, and crystal—patterns she had never seen at the Bannings' or when she'd helped serve at one of the Pullmans' parties.

"What lovely stemware." Serena paused for Frederic Wagner to pull her chair out for her. Once seated, she arranged the yellow chiffon skirt of her gown around her knees, then touched the draping neckline discreetly to be sure it was not askew.

"It was my mother's." Edith lifted a goblet and turned it in the candlelight. "Not one piece was ever broken, not even during the war."

When the footman served the turnip soup, Sarah knew precisely how many turnips had been cleaned and peeled to produce it. Serena, though, nodded in pleasure and complimented Mrs. Wagner on what was sure to be a delicious menu. Sarah disliked fish in general because she hated to clean them, but when the trout was served, Serena inquired whether the scrumptious tarragon flavor had been Mrs. Wagner's suggestion.

"It was, actually." Edith Wagner's green eyes glowed. "I prefer to go over the menus with Cook in some detail."

"You seem to know a lot about food," Lillie observed from her place across the round table from Sarah. "I'm afraid I don't know my way around the kitchen very well."

"Nor I," Sarah said quickly. "Of course that would be unseemly. But the one servant I have with me this summer is an adventurous cook, and occasionally I'm curious enough to inquire about the seasonings."

"Lillie tells us your parents have gone off to Europe and left you on your own," Edith said. "Do you have any regrets about not going with them?"

"None at all." Serena responded before Sarah gave the question any thought. "I'm finding I quite enjoy being on my own for a time."

"What does your father do that takes him to Europe for such an extended stay?" Frederic asked.

"Dry goods," came the answer. "His firm is looking for fresh European suppliers for textiles. They prefer not to depend only on what comes through New York but to commission their own designs."

The roast lamb was tender beyond belief, and the vegetables platter colorfully presented. Sarah pictured the sharpened knives that must have been used to slice the peppers and beetroot at expert angles.

Serena made a pleasant inquiry about Mr. Wagner's business.

The salad boasted the best of what was in season at the greengrocer's shop. Sarah knew which bins the items came from.

Serena asked what Mrs. Wagner was finding to enjoy in Chicago.

"I hope you'll introduce me to your mother when she returns," Edith said.

"I'm sure she'll love to meet you." Serena gave her best smile. "I've already written about becoming friends with Lillie."

"How often do you hear from your mother?" Lillie asked.

"We write faithfully twice a week." Serena's answer was emphatic. "And I'm sure my aunt is reporting what she finds when she visits me."

Edith chuckled. "If your mother is anything like me, she has spies all over the city watching her little girl. Are you an only child?"

"Yes, I am. Lillie and I have that experience in common."

Lillie beamed from across the table. "We're sure to become sisters now."

"I hope you'll come to dinner again," Edith said. "We can invite Mr. Gunnison and Mr. Townsend as well. The four of you seemed to get on quite well the other day."

"I would be delighted." The yellow gown swished with Serena's graceful movement. "And I have a feeling Mr. Gunnison is smitten with Lillie and will easily oblige your request."

Lillie blushed.

The cheesecake arrived a few minutes later, rimmed with fresh raspberries. Sarah knew the stain the berries must have left on the cook's fingertips.

Serena savored the tart flavor as it melded into the sweet cheesecake in her mouth.

By the time the evening was over, Sarah Cummings knew a great deal about Serena Cuthbert. Serena had been tutored privately at home and attended a finishing school in Geneva, Switzerland, before touring the Continent two years ago. She liked the novels of Charles Dickens and the poems of Elizabeth Barrett Browning. Serena's favorite pastime at the lake house was sitting in a chair at the end of the pier and listening to Lake Michigan lap below her, and she found the Arts and Crafts movement in decorating a refreshing change, especially the work of William Morris. She saw no reason an item could not be both useful and exquisite at the same time. Despite her mother's repeated attempts, Serena had never mastered playing the piano, and her father tended to spend far too many hours absorbed with business, much to her mother's aggravation. Serena was woefully behind in embroidering napkins and tablecloths for her own trousseau, but since she did not have a steady gentleman caller, the task had not seemed urgent. She thought it would be a grand adventure to ride a train to Denver, Colorado, and see what life was like in a newer part of the country. Friends reported that hotels were more than adequate.

Sarah did not think twice about anything she said during the evening's conversation. Every question, every remark, provoked an automatic answer that lurked until it was time to spring forth fully formed.

Serena Cuthbert flushed with pleasure.

⌒

Sarah's heart beat wildly as she raced north on Prairie Avenue. What had she just done? She could never backtrack from the stories she told that night. She had barely escaped Mr. Wagner's insistence that he would have his coachman take her home by countering with the assurance that her own coach was waiting for her one short block west, on Indiana Avenue, and the evening was mild enough that she would enjoy the walk.

The State Street trolley line that ran for a stretch on Indiana Avenue rumbled out of her grasp just as she thought she might catch it. The hour was far too late and dark for her to be standing on the corner waiting for another, so she lifted her skirts and accelerated her step. She passed Twenty-seventh, then Twenty-sixth. The lots became smaller and less prestigious, but Sarah focused on the line of light the streetlamps created. When she sensed a carriage slowing on the street beside her, she broke into a run.

"Sarah!" a voice called. "Is that you?"

Sarah let out her breath and slowed down, turning to see Karl sitting atop the Bannings' open carriage. He pulled the carriage to the curb and reined in the horse.

"What are you doing out?" Sarah asked.

"I might ask you the same thing," Karl said. "Get in. You shouldn't be out alone at eleven o'clock at night."

"I don't suppose you brought a house key." Sarah climbed with relief into the carriage. "I'm sure Mrs. Fletcher has locked the doors and gone to bed by now."

"I know it's your day off," Karl said as he clicked his tongue for the horse, "but you don't usually stay out so late. Where were you that required you to be gussied up like that?"

"Were you out looking for me?" Realization dawned in Sarah.

"What if I were?" Karl retorted.

Sarah turned her head and stared at the home at Prairie and Twenty-second that marked the beginning of upper Prairie Avenue and more familiar territory. Grateful as she was for Karl's appearance, she could not tell him where she had been.

"Are you planning to make a habit of this?" Karl asked.

6

Sarah yanked on the sheet and stripped it from the bed in one practiced motion, then tossed it into the basket of dirty linens. The laundress would come Friday morning, so Thursday held the task of collecting the sheets, towels, and table linens throughout the house. Sarah was in Leo's room on the second floor. As she reached to unfasten the window, she was not sure whether it would hurt or help the temperature in the room to allow outside air in. The limestone construction of the house held some insulating value, and Leo's room was out of the sun at this time of day. The temperature in the room was not unbearable, but the humidity was another matter. It seeped through cracks and slits that held the sun at bay and saturated everything she touched. The curtains were muggy. The shirt Leo had left on the back of the chair could have been used as a damp dust cloth. Clammy bedding had to be changed on a daily basis.

At the moment, a train ride to Denver, Colorado, held great appeal. Sarah had heard that the air there was dry and temperatures moderate. She sat for a moment on the stripped bed and wiped the sweat from her forehead with the hem of her black work dress.

"I find it doesn't help much to rest." Mrs. Fletcher appeared in the doorway. "It just makes it harder to get up."

Sarah thrashed her arms against the mattress. "I'm swimming in humidity. I can't stand it!" She unfastened the button at one wrist and rolled the sleeve to her elbow.

"You could have gone to the lake." Mrs. Fletcher laid a pile of neatly ironed clean sheets on the end of the bed. "It's cooler there."

"Only if you're a Banning," Sarah retorted. "If you're working, it's still hot because you're always moving."

"Maybe the open window will get some air flowing. Finish up in here and you can have a glass of tea."

The cook disappeared down the hall, and Sarah reached for the sheets. She hated to admit it, but Mrs. Fletcher was right. Sitting down just made it harder to get up and move again.

And she had to move. This was the day she was meeting Bradley Townsend, and if she did not have her work done, Mrs. Fletcher would find a reason to keep her in for the evening. Sarah rolled up the other sleeve, stood up, and snapped open a fresh sheet.

In the distance, she heard the telephone in the foyer ring. She spread the sheet on the bed and began tucking in the corners. The phone continued to ring. At the fifth ring, Sarah abandoned the sheets and stepped out into the hall.

"Mrs. Fletcher?"

She had been there only a couple of minutes ago. Surely she heard the phone ring, and with the butler out of the house, it was Mrs. Fletcher's role to answer it.

The cook was nowhere in sight as the phone jangled for the sixth time, and the seventh. Sarah stood at the top of the wide marble stairs that led down from the family bedrooms to the foyer inside the front door. The thought of traipsing all the way down the hall, down the servants' back stairs, and across the house to the foyer was too much. With the family out of the house, Sarah saw no reason not to use the convenient front stairs.

By the time Sarah reached the bottom, the phone had rung ten times.

When she picked it up, though, no one was there. A fresh band of perspiration had broken out under her collar and begun to dribble down her back. Sarah lifted her eyes up the stairs and decided, before going back up, to find out why Mrs. Fletcher had not answered the phone. She stepped across the foyer and padded through the dining room with its one place setting awaiting Leo. Sarah reflexively adjusted the position of a goblet, then pushed through the door to the butler's pantry. A few steps took her into the kitchen.

"Mrs. Fletcher?" she called.

Finally she heard voices in the courtyard behind the kitchen. When she stepped outside, she saw the butcher's delivery cart pulled up near the door.

"Where's the beef roast?" Mrs. Fletcher's voice carried the demanding edge it always held when she dealt with merchants.

"I'll bring it tomorrow," the delivery man promised. "The butcher knew you would not be satisfied with the cuts we had on hand."

Mrs. Fletcher's reputation preceded her wherever she went. Sarah smiled involuntarily and flicked her eyes up. If there was anything to admire Mrs. Fletcher for, it was her insistence on having only the best in her kitchen.

Sarah stepped back inside the house and trudged back up to the second floor. She had finished in Leo's room except for dusting when Karl poked his head in.

"I forgot to tell Mrs. Fletcher this morning that when I dropped Mr. Leo at the office, he said he would not be home for dinner tonight," Karl said. "He's decided to go to the convention."

Sarah ran the feather duster across Leo's desk. "She'll be glad, I suppose. The butcher didn't bring the roast she wanted. Is he coming home at all before the convention?"

Karl shook his head. "He wants to hear the speeches, I suppose."

"But he's not a Democrat, is he?" Sarah asked. "I thought the Banning men voted Republican."

Karl shrugged. "He probably just wants to hear what they have to say. It's strange to think that the next president of the United States could be selected tonight."

"Only if the Democrats have their way," Sarah said. "The Republicans like to think their man will be elected." She picked up the basket of soiled linens. "Will you vote in the election, Karl?"

He tilted his head. "If I can ever make sense of this business about currency standards. The Democrats promise the common man will have more money in his pocket if things go their way, and the Republicans say the country will be in the ditch if we go away from the gold standard. It's a muddle to me. You should feel lucky women can't vote."

Sarah's mind drifted away from the Democratic Convention absorbing the energy of Chicago. She was meeting Bradley in six hours and still had not decided what to wear. He had not mentioned where they would go, so it was puzzling to know how to dress.

"Are you going out again tonight?" Karl took the basket from Sarah.

"What if I am?" Sarah met his eyes.

"It seems like you're developing a new habit. It will be hard to break a habit like that one when the family comes back—all this going out at night. The last two Wednesdays, Saturday in between, and now this."

"Well, the family is not here now." Sarah swiped at the dust on Leo's dresser. "As long as I get my work done, Mrs. Fletcher says she doesn't care. It doesn't take both of us to serve Leo his dinner, even when he is here. I'm going to ask her for the key to the back door."

"So you do expect to be out late."

"None of your business." Sarah snatched back the basket and stomped into the hall.

"If you do something to make tongues wag," Karl called after her, "it will get back to the Bannings!"

Sarah ignored him. She still had to dust the parlor and mop the marble stairs, daily tasks even if none of the family were home. If someone should turn up unexpectedly, the rooms downstairs must be spotless. The rug in the foyer needed a good sweeping, and the silver tea service used for breakfast every day had to be polished before it showed even a hint of tarnish.

As she moved through her tasks, Sarah's most difficult question was how Bradley Townsend would be able to communicate. She would do everything in her power tonight to ensure he would want to see her again, but he could hardly call on her, or send a message to the Banning house. Giving him the Banning telephone number was out of the question. If his intentions became serious, how long would Serena be persuasive about meeting him in public places?

7

Sarah tried to look as if she belonged in the exquisite lobby of the Lexington Hotel. Certainly the sky-blue georgette dress she wore could have hung in the closet of any of the guests at the Lexington. The square neckline showed enough skin to suggest she had selected it because of the warm weather, but the truth was she knew the way the diaphanous sleeves billowed at the shoulders would make her waist appear slender. Sarah had removed enough bulk from the original gown to create a matching shawl, which she had painstakingly embroidered with a silver leaf pattern along the main edge. She carried the folded shawl over her arm in the unlikely event the evening should turn cool. Her hair, pulled more tightly in back than usual, was snug under a hat with a flat brim and a silver ribbon on top.

Sarah hoped Mr. Townsend would be on time. She was not very practiced at sauntering around a hotel lobby as if she had business there.

"Sarah Cummings, is that you?"

Sarah forced her gaze to remain focused ahead of her and did not turn her head even slightly.

"Sarah!"

The tenor voice was oddly familiar, but she could not place it. She thought perhaps she should aim for the front door and altered her direction slightly. A man wearing a hotel uniform stepped out from behind the front desk.

"Sarah, it *is* you!" he said. "My goodness, I can't believe my eyes! I never saw you . . . dressed like this."

"I think you have mistaken me for someone else." Sarah refused to meet the man's eyes.

"I apologize." He stepped back. Immediately, though, he took his position in front of her again and said softly, "No, I do not think I am mistaken."

Sarah gave in. Kenny was not the sort to surrender easily. When he was a coachman for the Pullman family across the street from the Bannings, he had made a steady effort to attract her attention for more than a year, but she wanted nothing to do with him. She had no intention of getting involved with a coachman, even at sixteen, and had rebuffed him every time. Now, Sarah wished she had been a little more kind to Kenny. It was dangerous enough for someone to know her, much less someone who might carry a grudge. She had not seen Kenny in more than a year and had never even wondered where he disappeared to.

"So you're working here now," she said lightly.

"Yes, at the front desk."

"I trust you find the work agreeable." She tried to step past him.

"I have regular hours," he responded, touching her elbow to thwart her departure, "and better pay. It's good to see you."

"You've only moved a few blocks, Kenny." Going from Eighteenth and Prairie to Twenty-second and Michigan was not much of a journey. Sarah was wishing another hotel had sprung to mind when she was arranging a meeting place with Bradley Townsend. Clearly she had not ventured far enough. The convenience of the Lexington had been too compelling to ignore.

"I don't really see anyone from Prairie Avenue," Kenny answered, "and you don't look much like a parlor maid at the moment."

She glanced around. "Please keep your voice down."

"What's going on, Sarah?"

"Nothing's going on. I'm meeting someone, and this seemed to be a convenient location."

"I understand. He doesn't know you're a maid."

Sarah blew out her breath and let her shoulders sag. "Kenny, please." Why had she never realized Kenny was so smart?

"Don't worry. I won't tell him."

An idea dawned. "Actually, I'm glad I ran into you. A Miss Serena Cuthbert is traveling at the moment, and her arrival is uncertain. She wondered about using a hotel to take her messages. I could suggest the Lexington. I can easily come round to collect them so they don't become a nuisance. Then perhaps when she arrives she will choose to engage rooms here."

"How do you know Miss Serena Cuthbert?" Kenny sounded suspicious.

Sarah waved a hand vaguely. "A lot of people come through the Banning house. You know that. Will you help her?"

Kenny nodded slowly. "Yes, I suppose we can do that. Serena Cuthbert, you say? I'll watch for anything with her name. You can ask for me when you stop in to collect messages."

Sarah smiled. As much as she did not want to see Kenny again, it was probably better than dealing with anyone else at the desk. "Thank you. I'm sure Miss Cuthbert will express her own appreciation when she has the opportunity."

"I will look forward to meeting her."

Annoyed at the amusement crossing his face, Sarah glanced toward the door and saw a carriage pull up at the curb. "I'm sure my friend will be here soon. Perhaps I'll just wait outside."

Kenny stepped back behind the marble desk with the oak framing that seemed to cage in the desk clerks. A couple of guests appeared ready to check out and his attention was quickly diverted. Relieved, Sarah turned toward the exit.

Bradley Townsend met her at the door and offered his arm. His coachman held open the Quinby carriage, and Brad assisted her in. Sarah settled into the leather seat and silently admired the navy blue silk that lined the walls of the enclosure.

"I've been looking forward to our evening together, Miss Cuthbert." Brad leaned his head toward her.

"I have as well," Sarah replied. The carriage jostled into forward motion.

"I had hoped we might have an elegant evening, but I'm afraid I've had to change my plans."

"Oh?" Where was he taking her?

"I have some political interests," Brad explained. "The Democrats seem to have a chip on their shoulder toward anyone of means, and I suspect they are gaining ground."

"Are we going to a political meeting?" Sarah cringed inwardly.

"The meeting of all meetings. The Democratic National Convention."

Sitting beside Brad, Sarah was pretty sure he could not see her eyes widen. A political convention was not the evening she had in mind—and she was overdressed for such a setting.

"They're going to nominate their candidate before the convention closes," Brad said, "and I'd like to hear for myself what their final platform is."

"The papers are full of talk of gold standard or bimetallism," Sarah ventured. She had heard Samuel and Leo Banning debating the topic at breakfast on multiple occasions, though she never paid attention to the details. She was beginning to wish she had.

Brad nodded. "If we end up with a president who supports coining silver along with gold, the policies could seriously damage my business at the Chicago Stock Exchange. Too much money will be in circulation. The working class will get ideas."

Sarah swallowed hard, hoping Serena soon would say something clever.

"Coining silver will be a boon to the western states," Brad said, "where so many silver mines are located. It will completely change the financial landscape. The balance between credit and debt might never recover if farmers are able to pay off their loans because of the extra dollars circulating."

"It sounds complicated," Sarah said.

Brad turned and looked at her. "I'm sorry, Miss Cuthbert. I'm being rude. I don't expect a woman to understand the world of finance or politics. Nevertheless, I hope you will indulge me in hearing a few speeches tonight. I promise to share a late supper with you—perhaps back at the Lexington."

The convention. Leo did not come home for dinner because he was going to the convention. Sarah suppressed a grimace and hoped for a huge crowd and dim lighting. Simon Tewell had recognized her at the Fourth of July party. Kenny had recognized her at the Lexington. Leo saw her every day—how could he not know her? Serena was still too much like Sarah. Instinctively, she reached up and pulled the brim of her hat to an angle over her face.

Their carriage ride ended in front of the Chicago Coliseum at the western edge of Jackson Park. Sarah recognized the main entrance of the structure at Sixty-third and Stony Island, built for the world's fair three years earlier. As Bradley helped her out, he glanced up at the building. "Did you ever come to the Buffalo Bill show when it was here during the world's fair?" He started to laugh. "No, I don't suppose you would have done that. I didn't, either. But it was very popular and made a great deal of money."

"I've heard people say it was a mistake for the fair committee not to allow Buffalo Bill to be an official part of the exposition." To be precise, Samuel Banning, who served on the committee, had grudgingly admitted over the fish course one evening that royalties from Buffalo Bill's show would have earned the fair even more money than the Ferris wheel had. As an investor in the fair, he had come to regret his part in the decision to exclude the Wild West show.

Sarah stood on the sidewalk in front of the Chicago Coliseum, her hand resting in the crook of Bradley Townsend's arm. *I am Serena Cuthbert.*

The Coliseum was packed from floor to rafter. Brad consulted the notes he had written about where his friend would be saving seats and guided Sarah. One senator finished his speech and another rose. Sarah, who understood little of the political language because it did not interest her, smiled occasionally at Bradley Townsend, who listened intently to every word. Eventually Congressman William Jennings Bryan from Nebraska was introduced. He ran to the platform and took the steps two at a time, then stood, tall and slender, triumphantly behind the podium. His eyes flashed as he set his jaw firmly and thrust his right foot forward and waited for the applause to abate.

Brad leaned over and said, "Bryan has been building a following for weeks. What he has to say tonight could change everything."

"Does he support bimetallism?" Sarah hoped the question was remotely relevant.

Brad nodded. "Vigorously."

As Brad leaned forward in his seat, Sarah settled back in hers. Expecting that Brad was going to take her to dinner, she had not eaten all day. Now he seemed content to sit through speech after speech while her stomach rumbled. This was not the stellar evening Serena Cuthbert had imagined. Though she was not listening much to the words, Sarah realized Congressman Bryan's pitch was rising and the audience's response was palpable. Brad's hands gripped his knees.

"When you come before us and tell us that we shall disturb your business interests, we reply that you have disturbed our business interests by your action," Bryan thundered. "The man who is employed for wages is as much a businessman as his employer."

Sarah glanced at Brad, who was shaking his head. She scanned

the crowd and could not help but notice that Mr. Bryan was gar-
nering more rapt attention than any of the speechmakers who
preceded him. Neither the July heat nor the crowded assembly
seemed to deter him, though Sarah was tempted to remove her
hat and wished the air were circulating more freely. How much
longer was Mr. Bryan going to drone on? At the next change of
speakers she might devise an excuse to get up and move toward
some fresh air for a few moments. Brad seemed more intent than
ever on the proceedings.

Bryan continued with unflagging vigor. "Mr. Carlisle said in
1878 that this was a struggle between the idle holders of idle capital
and the struggling masses who produce the wealth and pay the
taxes of the country; and my friends, it is simply a question that
we shall decide upon which side shall the Democratic Party fight.
Upon the side of the idle holders of capital, or upon the side of
the struggling masses?"

Brad squirmed in his seat. "He's got it all wrong," he muttered.
"The economy flows from top to bottom. He proposes that it can
flow from bottom to top. That's contrary to nature. Have you ever
seen a stream flow uphill?"

Sarah had no idea what an appropriate response would be, so
she said nothing.

William Jennings Bryan raised his hands above his head, then
lowered his hands to his temples.

"Having behind us the commercial interests and the laboring
interests and all the toiling masses, we shall answer their demands
for a gold standard by saying to them, you shall not press down
upon the brow of labor this crown of thorns." He spread his arms
wide as if on a cross. "You shall not crucify mankind on a cross
of gold."

The crowd sucked in its collective breath. Jennings Bryan held his
pose for five hushed, pregnant seconds. When he stepped backward
and began to leave the podium, the crowd erupted. Sarah gasped as

men and women around them sprang to their feet screaming and cheering. Bryan was carried on shoulders back to the Nebraska delegation.

Brad remained in his seat, sullen. All around the Coliseum hats and canes waved in support of William Jennings Bryan. Having no other tangible way to express their enthusiasm, some flung their coats into the air and let them land haphazardly. Applause thundered until it shook the building.

Scowling, Brad grabbed Sarah's hand. "We have to leave." Abruptly, he shoved his way through the crowd, dragging Sarah behind him. The roar continued unabated, applause and cheers and stomping feet melding together at earsplitting levels.

Outside, Brad scanned the street looking for his coachman. "I am truly sorry, Miss Cuthbert," he said, "but I'm afraid I don't feel up to our supper. If they nominate that man for president, it will be disastrous for business and industry leaders. I would like to arrange another evening to give you my full attention."

"Of course." What else could Sarah say?

Brad calmed down. "How shall I reach you?"

"At the Lexington," she said without hesitation. "I'm not often in to take a telephone call, but if you would send a note, I will be sure to respond."

He nodded. "I will do so at my earliest convenience. Again, I'm sorry to disappoint you tonight."

"Not at all."

His carriage emerged from the glut of coaches along the streets. "Take Miss Cuthbert home to the Lexington," he instructed the driver. "I'll see my own way home."

8

On Friday afternoon, Sarah shed her uniform in favor of a straightforward dark printed cotton skirt and white blouse. The events of the previous evening rattled in her head, but the pieces refused to fall into a sequence that made sense. Sarah cared little about the political outcome of the convention except that it might affect Brad's attentions. Serena Cuthbert could hardly have made a memorable impression in a crowded Coliseum where Brad's interests were fixed on the stage. He had said he would like to see her again, but perhaps he was merely being polite. If William Jennings Bryan were nominated—something that could happen at any moment—Brad might forget all about Serena Cuthbert. Sarah only had five weeks before the Bannings would be back from the lake. After that, it would be far more difficult to arrange Serena's social life.

Sarah corralled her hair under a navy blue hat with white trim and inspected the resulting effect in a mirror. She doubted Brad had sent a message to Serena Cuthbert at the Lexington Hotel yet. Being seen going into the hotel lobby too often would only raise suspicions in the minds of Kenny and anyone else who might happen to spot her. Besides, it would not do for Serena to appear as overeager as Sarah felt. She resolved to make herself wait until Monday before inquiring at the hotel desk.

In the meantime she had to keep her word to Simon Tewell, although why she had ever promised she would teach this class was beyond her. She had not wanted to go to St. Andrew's in the first place, and she certainly did not relish going back—and so soon. Simon had wasted no time in arranging the first class only four days after their conversation. A telephone call on Friday morning had left her little option but to oblige that same afternoon.

He was afraid she would back out if she had time to think about it, she told herself. It was the truth. She had promised him one class on basic stitches. She would do it and be done with the whole business. Sarah smoothed the front of her skirt and descended the servants' stairs.

Mrs. Fletcher looked up from her breadboard when Sarah entered the kitchen.

"You look quite smart," the cook said.

Sarah straightened her hat. "It's nothing special."

Mrs. Fletcher leaned into the dough she was kneading. "You're doing something worthwhile, you know."

Sarah raised her eyebrows.

"Teaching those girls to sew," Mrs. Fletcher said. "It's a good thing."

"It's just a class on stitches. Anyone could do it."

"Obviously he wants *you* to do it."

Sarah touched her hat for a final adjustment. "I'd better go."

"I'll have supper for you when you get back. Leo is at the convention again tonight."

"Thank you, Mrs. Fletcher."

Sarah slipped out through the female servants' entrance, and walked up Prairie Avenue to Eighteenth and over to Michigan to catch the streetcar.

❧

Lillie turned her head to the left and to the right as she examined her reflection in the small mirror in the brougham. She would have preferred the open carriage, but her mother insisted she not risk having wind destroy her hairstyle while she made afternoon calls. As the driver pulled into traffic, Lillie leaned forward to the black leather carriage case and extracted the visiting list her mother had prepared. She was not sure what the point was for these calls. These women had called on Edith Wagner, not Lillie, and few of them had sons or daughters whom it was important for Lillie to meet. But her mother had given her an enthusiastic talk about putting a friendly face on her father's company for the sake of her own future and sent Lillie out with the list.

She put a check mark next to the name of the woman whose home she had left moments ago just north of Washington Park off Grand Boulevard. Lillie had two more calls to make, but they were to the north, closer to Prairie Avenue. She settled in to the brougham's sway as the horse trotted west and the driver scouted the best route to turn north.

Lillie could not help wondering what had happened between Serena and Brad the previous evening and chastised herself for not making a firm plan to see Serena and hear all about the outing. They should have arranged to have lunch or tea together. Lillie did not even know when Serena might be free again. Serena had mentioned she was hardly ever home in her suite but had promised to let Lillie know when she was available.

Lillie traced a finger along the bottom of the visit list. If only she had the independence of Serena Cuthbert.

Sarah approached the red door, but instead of reaching for the bellpull, she turned the knob. She heard an excited squeal from the dining hall where some of the children must have gathered for a few minutes of games—although Sarah knew from experience they would have assigned chores awaiting them and their diversion would soon be interrupted.

Glancing down the hall toward the classroom assigned to her,

Sarah turned in the other direction. She would have to let Simon know she had arrived so he could unlock the door. Then she would find out what supplies he had been able to arrange. She had asked only for simple cotton cloth—even the dreaded muslin. Contrasting cloth and thread would be the easiest way for Sarah to see the girls' practice stitches and assess what corrections were required.

A couple of younger children scuttled past her, and the stern voice of a teacher reminded them to walk, not run. Sarah did not recognize the teacher. While on the whole the orphanage remained the same, bits and pieces of it had shifted, and this was enough to keep Sarah slightly off balance as she went looking for Simon. The offices had been newly designed shortly before she left, and she had not quite gotten used to them.

A baby squalled, not an uncommon sound in an orphanage, but Sarah realized the noise had come from one of the offices, and instinctively she leaned her head forward to peer in the door.

"Hello, Sarah." Lucy Banning Edwards was behind her desk in the volunteers' office, leaning to one side to lift an infant from a basket. The child soothed instantly.

"Hello, Mrs. Edwards," Sarah said politely. "The baby seems well."

Lucy came to dinner at her parents' house regularly on Thursday evenings. She did not always bring her adopted son, Ben, and the baby, but when she did, she insisted on having the children with her in the dining room. Despite being raised on Prairie Avenue, Lucy made her own rules. At first Flora had scrunched her face in consternation, but Ben was polite and had learned not to prattle at the dinner table. The baby tended to get passed between Lucy, Will, Flora, and Violet Newcomb. No one took seriously any longer Flora's ceremonial protests about having children at the table.

Sarah had first seen Stella Edwards when she was two months old. How long ago had that been? The baby must be four or five months old by now, Sarah reasoned.

"Stella is doing marvelously." Lucy settled the child in her lap. The baby immediately reached for something on the desk. "She likes to help her mother with the piles of papers."

Sarah moved her mouth in the motion of a smile she did not feel.

"I keep her with me as much as I can," Lucy said. "Between my work here and my course at the university, I lose track of whether I'm coming or going."

"I had not heard if you were taking a university course this term," Sarah said.

"One or two classes at a time. Someday I'll have a degree. Benny is here today too," Lucy said casually. "He has some notion about attending your sewing class, but I told him it's only for the older girls."

"I might see him in the hall, ma'am," Sarah said.

Will and Lucy Edwards had adopted Benny out of the orphanage almost as soon as they'd returned from their honeymoon in Europe and set up housekeeping three years ago. He had attached himself to both of them long before that.

"How old is he now, ma'am?" Sarah asked.

"Almost ten. I can hardly believe it."

Benny had a home. Parents. A baby sister. He would not be put out to service when he turned sixteen. Sarah could not help the envy that made her heart wince.

"I've been thinking I might organize a group of women to sew clothing for some of the younger children." Lucy gave her daughter a knuckle to gnaw on.

"Yes, ma'am," Sarah responded automatically.

"Every little girl deserves a dress that is her own," Lucy continued. "Maybe one of the girls in your class will learn to do the wonders you do with old gowns. No one would ever guess your creations were not straight off the bolt. You can't imagine the conversation you stir up when we get a glimpse of what you've done. If you give her the slightest opening, Mary Catherine does go on about it."

"Thank you, ma'am." In Sarah's opinion, Mary Catherine, the kitchen maid, could learn a thing or two from Ben about not prattling on.

"Mr. Tewell tells me he's hoping you will come on a regular basis."

"He has asked me to," Sarah acknowledged guardedly.

"I imagine you're worried what my parents would think," Lucy said. "I'm more than happy to speak to them on your behalf. I'm sure we can come to an arrangement without adverse effects for you."

"Thank you, Mrs. Edwards," Sarah said, "but I'm not certain. Teaching a class seems a bit much for me."

"Please think about it, Sarah. It could be one of the most important things you do."

Sarah glanced toward Simon's office.

"I suppose you need to see Mr. Tewell," Lucy said.

Sarah nodded. "He said the room would be locked."

"I won't delay you. The girls are eager. I hope you enjoy the class."

———

Lillie saw the sign and urgently signaled the driver, who slowed and turned his head slightly for instructions.

"Please stop here for a moment," Lillie said.

"St. Andrew's Orphanage," the sign said. Lillie had heard of this institution. Though new to Chicago and Prairie Avenue, her parents had already been approached about making a financial contribution. They had been assured St. Andrew's was an upstanding institution and many of the wealthiest families supported it. A number of them even took in teenagers from the orphanage to train as servants. Hundreds of children lived at St. Andrew's. Thousands must have passed through its halls in the years since it opened.

But what really went on inside? So far Lillie had not run into anyone who had actually gone through the doors of St. Andrew's. She wondered what would happen if she went to the red door, tugged the bellpull, and asked to speak to the director.

The small clock in the carriage case confronted her. She still had two calls to make and limited time to accomplish them before she was expected home. In surrender, Lillie pulled a calling card from the case and signaled the driver to continue to the next address.

⎯⎯⎯⎯⎯

Jane bent over her swatch of dark calico and pushed her yellow thread through two layers.

"That's right," Sarah said, "nice and straight. Now stick the needle up from the bottom and make sure it's coming up right where you want it to be. If you need to, you can move it before you pull the thread through. Make sure your stitch is not too long."

Sarah glanced around the table to see if any of the other girls needed encouragement. She had demonstrated a straight stitch, a backstitch, and a hem stitch, then set them free to experiment for themselves while she looked over their shoulders. Eleven girls formed a long oval around the table. At one end of the room a cupboard stood open, revealing a rainbow of fabrics on the shelves along with two baskets of threads. Simon had kept his word to make sure she had supplies, but this was far more than she needed for one session on basic stitches.

"When do we get to use those fabrics?" Jane asked, looking at the cupboard as well.

The question caught Sarah off guard. "We're just learning basic stitches," she said. "Plain cottons are best to practice on."

"Can I at least feel the others?" Jane pleaded. "They look so shiny."

Sarah nodded. Simon really should not have raised anyone's hopes this way.

Jane scooted her chair back and padded across the room. Sarah tried to turn her attention back to the girls at the table, but her eyes kept lifting to Jane as the girl stroked the blue satin and green crepe.

What in the world was Simon thinking?

Jane looked at Sarah expectantly. "If we practice our stitches all week, can we try some of this next time?"

Despite her resolve that there would not be a next time, Sarah nodded.

9

She came back.

Simon hoped he sufficiently concealed his relief when he looked up to see Sarah Cummings standing in his doorframe for the second Friday in a row.

"I'm glad to see you again, Sarah." He stood and nervously jingled his keys in one hand. "The girls have been talking about the class all week. We may have one or two more who would like to join."

Was that a smile that crossed her face? Her glance would not meet his, but she had come back, and for today, that was enough.

"Jane seems to have her eye on something green," Simon continued. "She's been practicing her stitches every spare minute."

"I've told her she must master the stitches before she can manage that fabric," Sarah said. "Crepe snags easily. She must be confident in what she's doing."

"She seems quite determined." Simon gestured that Sarah should walk ahead of him into the hall.

"The fabrics are beautiful," she said, "but not all of them are suitable for beginners."

"It will give them something to look forward to," Simon said. "It was far easier than I imagined to get the donations. Just let me know what you need." A few notes, a few telephone calls—he would find whatever she asked for.

"Something sturdy," Sarah said. "Plain colors they could use to make skirts to begin with. Jane may be a little too . . . ambitious just now."

They walked to her classroom, and he put the key in the door. "I've kept everything locked up, just as we discussed."

She nodded. "Thank you."

Sarah stepped past him through the doorway, and Simon inhaled her lingering lilac scent.

"Have you experimented with the machine?" he asked.

"No." Sarah's answer was quick, final. But her tone relented. "I suppose I will have to, because the girls will want to learn in time."

She was planning ahead. She would come again.

"Perhaps you'll find it more useful than you suppose." He grasped for something substantial to say but found nothing.

Sarah carried a small bag the same beige shade as her dress. The thought flitted through his mind that the garment lacked the finesse of the ensembles he had seen her in previously, but he did not mind. His eyes fixed on her grace as she laid the bag on the table and glided to the cupboard. Opening it with one hand, she quickly reached in with the other and ran her fingertips down the ribbed stack. She was right, he could see now, about the fabrics. Although she could do wonders with any of them, they were not practical for the girls. Simon made a mental note to procure a wider selection of sensible choices for next week.

Would she have tea with him? he wondered.

She found a length of lightweight gray wool and unfolded it. A shock of hair escaped its pin at her left temple, and reflexively she reached to tuck it back in place.

"Do you have a regular day off?" Casually, he straightened a chair.

"Wednesdays," she answered, turning again to the cupboard, "as soon as breakfast is cleared, and every other Sunday for half a day."

Simon nodded. Was it too much to suggest dinner? He could afford a nice teashop with a simple menu. Sarah stooped to pull a basket of threads from the bottom shelf of the cupboard. Even her unadorned beige skirt moved in a graceful arc as she bent, then straightened with the basket in her hands.

"It must be just about time for the girls." Sarah looked at him, expectant brown eyes wide.

He did find her utterly lovely.

⁂

Jane was full of more questions than Sarah cared to answer. What was this fabric called? Why was this one so shiny? Why was this one so thick? Would Sarah show her some fancy stitches? Sarah remembered Jane as a quiet child and was surprised at her inquisitiveness. She was the last girl to leave the room, staying with Sarah until the final swatch of fabric was stored away and all the cupboards secured. Sarah barely heard anything Jane said, and she could not leave the orphanage fast enough.

It was not the girls who disturbed her, though one or two seemed incapable of making two straight stitches in a row. Her mind was full of Bradley Townsend—or more precisely, consumed with the fact that she had not heard from him since he'd dropped her off at the Lexington Hotel last Thursday night. Eight days had passed. She had made herself wait from Thursday until Tuesday before stopping at the hotel desk again, purposefully wearing her maid's uniform to put as much distance as possible between Kenny's memory of her and his unvoiced suspicions of the fictitious Serena Cuthbert. She had been planning all day Friday to stop in again. Although she was not wearing her uniform—she refused to wear it to St. Andrew's—she had selected a dull beige dress with no remarkable features. Anyone would have found it believable that Sarah Cummings owned such a garment.

Throughout the sewing lesson, her mind raced ahead to the Lexington Hotel desk. Finally she pushed open the hotel's front door and peered behind the glass at the desk. Kenny was there. She strode confidently across the lobby.

"Have you any messages for Miss Cuthbert?" she asked expectantly.

"Hello, Sarah."

"Hello, Kenny. The messages, please."

Kenny shook his head. "Not a word. Are you sure this was the hotel Miss Cuthbert meant to use as an address?"

"She was quite specific," Sarah insisted. "She knows it's difficult for me to get away from the house and was thoughtful enough to agree to a convenient location."

Kenny raised his shoulders and let them drop. "No one has been looking for her. When is she due to arrive in Chicago?"

"I told you," Sarah said, "her plans are indefinite."

"Then why would anyone be trying to reach her here?"

Sarah set her jaw and growled, "If you persist in this line of questioning, I shall report you to the hotel manager."

He smiled, unthreatened. "If anything does come in, I could have it sent over to the Banning house and save you the trouble of stopping in for nothing."

"No!" Sarah recovered her composure. "It's not necessary to go to that trouble. I'll stop in again."

She pivoted, glad her skirt was plain enough for the maneuver, and headed for the door. The Democrats had nominated William Jennings Bryan at their convention, just as Brad had feared. No doubt Brad had politics and business on his mind.

Sarah would just have to change that. In barely five weeks, the Bannings would be home. She stepped back out onto Michigan Avenue, undeterred.

Lillie fanned herself with the evening's program as the applause faded.

"It is a bit warm in here, isn't it?" Paul said from his seat next to her.

They sat at the front of the first balcony, toward the center, with a clear view of the stage and the sweeping series of beautifully lit arches that led to it. Even the breadth of the magnificent Auditorium Theatre could not combat the heat. The electric lights came on to signal the intermission.

"I have tickets to the orchestra's concerts in the fall," Paul said. "The temperatures are sure to be more comfortable then."

"That would be lovely." Lillie dipped her head and smiled. This was only July, and Paul was already thinking of what they might do together in the fall.

"Shall we go out to the lobby for some air?" Paul suggested.

Lillie took the hand he offered and stood. "It's a good turnout for an off-season amateur theater group," she said.

"It will be much fuller for the Chicago Orchestra. Theodore Thomas has a strong reputation as a conductor."

In the lobby a few minutes later, Lillie assessed the mingling concertgoers. Her parents were supposed to attend this event, but Edith had suggested that Paul and Lillie take the tickets instead. Lillie was not sure whom she should expect to see and only hoped she would remember the names of people she had met in recent weeks if she encountered them in this crowded public gathering. The women wore bright gowns and extravagant, colorful hats, and the men escorting them were in uniform black formal wear.

"Is that Miss Cuthbert?" Paul gestured discreetly across the lobby.

Lillie turned in delight and focused on Serena, who stood near a wall, draped in a spectacular silver gown that shimmered with even a slight movement.

"I really must remember to get her dressmaker's name," Lillie said.

"Shall we speak to her now?" Paul suggested.

Grateful for the opportunity to see Serena's gown up close, Lillie nodded. Paul put his hand on the small of her back and guided her across the lobby, stopping several times to greet friends and business associates. Lillie flushed with pleasure each time he introduced her, but she kept Serena in her peripheral vision as they gradually progressed toward her.

"She's talking with guests we met at the fireworks," Paul observed.

"From my father's office," Lillie said. "How kind of them to remember her."

"Who could forget Serena Cuthbert?"

Who indeed? They reached her at last.

"Lillie!" Serena exclaimed. "I wondered if I might see you here tonight."

"Where are your seats? Who are you with?" Lillie asked.

"I'm here with a friend," Serena said. "Our seats are rather high up, I'm afraid. It was a last-minute decision to come."

"The theater offers a wonderful view from any angle," Paul said.

"I quite agree. I've never been disappointed in any seat I've had here." Serena scanned the crowd from left to right. "Mr. Townsend mentioned he also had tickets for the evening. I haven't had an opportunity to greet him yet."

Lillie glanced around. "We haven't seen him, either." She leaned in close to Serena. "I've been dying to hear about your evening together. Shall we meet for lunch soon?"

Serena's eyes brightened. "Yes! Send me a note at the Lexington and we'll arrange something."

Lillie nested her hand in the crook of Paul's arm. "Lunch will be my treat, Serena. I insist. And if you have an extra card from your dressmaker, be sure to bring it."

Paul glanced at his pocket watch. "We should return to our seats in time for the next act. May we see you back to your seat, Miss Cuthbert?"

Serena shook her head. "No, thank you. I'm sure my friend will turn up momentarily. You go along."

———

Sarah had purposefully positioned herself against that wall because the location provided a panoramic view of the lobby. Getting past the ticket gate had been surprisingly easy, and she wondered why she had never attempted the ploy before. She did not actually require a ticket. It was not as if she intended to occupy a seat. She remained outside until she was certain intermission had begun and the lobby had started to fill. While concertgoers stepped outside for fresh air, Sarah slipped inside. When she ran into a couple of people she had met at the Fourth of July party, she smiled and chatted amiably. When she spotted the Kimballs, neighbors on Prairie Avenue, however, she subtly turned and dipped her head until she was sure they had passed. Sarah was becoming adept at hiding her face with the choice of a wider brim.

She was certain Brad held tickets for the evening and was determined to see him, even if just long enough to say hello and remind him of her existence—and even if he were with another woman. Sarah knew just how the silver gown flattered her and had no doubt what its effect would be on any man.

Sarah held vigil during the entire intermission and finally surrendered to defeat when she stood alone in the lobby and sensed an usher was going to ask if she required assistance finding her seat. Brad was not there.

She slipped out a side door. Bradley Townsend was the first man she had ever met who could give her what she wanted. She was not going to give up easily.

Eighteenth and Prairie was not far, but the streets were congested with theater traffic. Sluggish, Sarah aimed her reluctant steps toward the Banning mansion.

10

*N*early three weeks and not a word out of Mr. Bradley Townsend. Sarah mopped her frustration into the floors of the Banning house. She scrubbed her agitation into the pots, stitched her irritation into the household mending. She folded her resolve into the sheets and towels, pounded her aggravation into innocent cuts of meat. She snatched up Leo's newspapers from the abandoned breakfast table so she could read the political articles before Mrs. Fletcher used the paper to wrap meat scraps, and gradually her understanding of the party platforms came into focus. Samuel Banning spent three days sleeping in his own bed, eating at his own dining room table, and going back and forth from his office. Sarah tended to his routine needs, making the poached eggs he preferred and freshening his room, but her mind thought of nothing but Brad.

And Serena Cuthbert. Sarah began to have internal conversations with Serena in which the young woman revealed a great deal about herself. Serena had traveled, Sarah discovered, and would rather be with people every minute of the day than at home with a book. She disliked potatoes and preferred her vegetables to be green. Earl Grey was her favorite tea. She thought Theodore Thomas was a brilliant conductor for the Chicago Orchestra and Susan B. Anthony made too much fuss about women's rights. But what did it matter what Serena thought if no one else knew?

The first time Kenny handed Sarah an envelope addressed in florid script, she looked him straight in the eye and thanked him for collecting Miss Cuthbert's mail. The second time, he looked sheepish and she did nothing to take the edge off her contempt. Kenny had gone out of his way to imply Serena Cuthbert would not receive mail at the Lexington, and Sarah had no sympathy for his embarrassment now. Sarah waited until she was safely outside the hotel to open the envelopes—a note from Lillie about how sorry she was that they had not seen each other recently, and later an invitation to a dinner party Lillie was giving. Sarah breathed relief when she saw the invitation was for a Wednesday night. She would not even have to connive to be away from the house.

When Sarah arrived at the Wagner home on the final Wednesday in July, the housekeeper let her in, and immediately the ladies' maid collected Serena's silk shawl and inquired whether the guest would like to freshen up before dinner. Sarah had seen the protocol many times when the Bannings welcomed guests and Elsie, the ladies' maid, offered assistance to all the women. Lillie's maid led her to a room down the hall, where Sarah removed her hat and allowed the young woman to rearrange a few hair pins. Then she was ready for her entrance in the parlor. A pale seafoam moiré dress fitted to her form with darts and tucks and drew the eye to the ruffles floating about her shoulders. Although the fabric was several years old, a cast-off length Flora Banning had never had made up by her own dressmaker, Sarah had patterned the gown after an illustration she'd seen in *Harper's Bazaar* only six months ago.

There he was.

She had been sure without asking that Lillie would invite Bradley Townsend. It could well be that the occasion for the dinner was to bring Serena and Brad together. But Sarah could not have been sure he would accept, and Lillie could hardly cancel the entire engagement because one guest declined.

But there he was. Tall. A trim beard. A dark suit. Standing at the end of the room with one hand on the back of the sofa.

Sarah paused in the doorway and smiled. Paul and Lillie were there, as well as two other couples she had not met before. She was sure—fairly sure, at least—none of them were from Prairie Avenue families.

"The Colts seem to be in for a winning season. I do love a good base ball game." Brad thumped the back of the sofa.

Sarah moved into the room, hoping to capture his gaze.

"They certainly ought to rout the St. Louis Browns next week." Paul, standing behind the side chair where Lillie sat, twisted his torso slightly toward Brad.

"Still, several teams are ahead of the Colts in the standings. I'd love to see them at least catch the Boston Beaneaters, or Cincinnati."

Sarah delicately cleared her throat.

Brad looked up and straightened his posture. "Oh, Miss Cuthbert, forgive my lack of manners. There you are, a countenance of beauty, and I'm mumbling on about base ball."

Sarah stepped into the room. "It's lovely to see you again, Mr. Townsend." She moved toward him and held out a gloved hand. Brad took it, catching her eye as he let her hand rest in his palm.

Lillie jumped up from the side chair and latched on to Sarah's arm. "Serena! I'm so glad you could come. Why has it been so difficult for us to find a time to see each other? We'll have to rectify that in the near future."

"I hope so." Sarah glanced at the other guests. "Hello. I'm Serena Cuthbert. I don't believe we've met."

"My etiquette teacher would be dismayed." Lillie laughed. "I'm delighted to present my friend, Miss Serena Cuthbert. This is Mr. David Butler, Miss Laura Anderson, Mr. Christopher Trapp, and Miss Diana Prescott."

The group exchanged nods and handshakes around the room.

Sarah was pleased to see everyone paired off. Clearly Lillie had intended that Brad attend to Serena tonight.

"So Mr. Townsend," Sarah said, "you're an avid base ball fan, I gather."

He nodded. "I try to get out to West Side Park to see the Colts whenever I can. Are you a fan, Miss Cuthbert?"

"An afternoon at the ball park does make a pleasant outing." Sarah had never been to a base ball game, but it seemed like something Serena would find adventure in.

"Perhaps we can take in a game together sometime," Brad suggested.

"I would be delighted." Would he really call for her, or was he just being polite? Just in case, she would have to discover what Karl knew about the game.

The housekeeper announced that dinner was served. Brad offered his arm and Sarah took it as the group ambled toward the dining room.

"Lillie," Brad said, "are your parents not joining us tonight?"

"They're out for the evening." Lillie's hand waved through the air in a relaxed gesture.

Sarah saw the pleasure Lillie took in hosting her own dinner party rather than merely adding a friend or two to her parents' table. The place cards assigned Mr. Bradley Townsend to the left of Miss Serena Cuthbert. He held her chair while she arranged the drape of her dress, then he took his own seat.

Conversation flowed easily, and Sarah soaked up the information about Lillie's guests—whom Lillie did not know well, either. David Butler's family had come to Chicago from Philadelphia when he was a boy. While he had returned to Philadelphia for his college years, he considered Chicago home. Anyone could see in his face that it was Laura Anderson who had pulled him back to Chicago. Their eyes met frequently and lingered, although both were careful to speak in a manner that included everyone. David had recently passed the bar and joined a Chicago law firm. A few casual questions assured Sarah he had never met Samuel Banning in the legal circles, so he would have no reason to recognize a maid from the Banning house. Diana Prescott had made her European tour at age eighteen and decided to stay for an extended time, choosing the unlikely Madrid, Spain, as her favorite locale. The Spanish phrases that slipped off her tongue sounded authentic to Sarah.

"Miss Cuthbert, did you work on your French while you were in France?" Diana asked Sarah.

Sarah shook her head without missing a beat. "One learns enough to order coquille Saint-Jacques or filet aux deux poivres, of course," she said, "but my circle of friends were Americans or citizens of the British Empire. I'm afraid I was not a very devoted student to my French lessons. I rather regret that I did not make a better effort." Mrs. Fletcher had a cookbook featuring French dishes, the only reason Sarah knew any French food labels. The French class at St. Andrew's did little more than teach students to count in the language.

"Perhaps when you return to France," Diana suggested, "you will find time to study the language."

"Serena's parents are in France right now," Lillie said.

"Ask your mother to write to you in French," Diana said.

Sarah smiled at Diana, then turned her attention to the man on her right. "What do you do, Mr. Trapp?" If Sarah changed the subject often enough, Serena would not have to answer so many questions.

Christopher Trapp launched into more explanation than anyone was interested in about his structural engineering work and the soil qualifications for bridge supports. Sarah nodded and smiled her way through the meat and vegetable courses.

"Have you traveled in the East, Miss Cuthbert?" Brad asked when the salad came.

Sarah nodded. "We had an estate in New Hampshire when I

was young." Flora Banning's persistent envy of John and Frances Glessners' property in New Hampshire had provided ample fodder over the last three years. Mrs. Banning came home from ladies' luncheons with stories of how the Glessners had entertained themselves through the summer months on their estate—croquet on the rolling lawns, picnics, walks along the bluffs. The older Banning sons, Oliver and Leo, had plenty of stories from their years in Princeton, New Jersey, and Lucy's husband was from New Jersey as well. Meal after meal, for three years, Sarah had stood by, mute, listening, and now she found the details flooded her mind and tripped off her tongue. She had little trouble mentioning the right locations and train lines to be credible. No one around the table could doubt the travel experience of Serena Cuthbert.

The group took dessert and coffee in the parlor, where Lillie begged Diana to play the piano and Laura to grace them with her trained soprano voice. Sarah felt Brad's eyes on her repeatedly, though for the most part she managed to avoid staring at him and outwardly absorbed herself in the music. Nevertheless, she was aware of his every movement, and when he stood to stretch his long legs during a break in the music, Sarah followed the impulse. With unspoken agreement, they drifted to the same corner of the parlor.

"I've been hoping for a private moment," Brad said at last. "You have been much on my mind, despite my neglect since our last meeting."

"I imagine your time has been consumed with politics and your business interests," Sarah said offhandedly, as if she had not begun to harbor resentment at his lack of attention.

"Yes, the presidential election is causing a stir," he said. "I'm resolved to do my part to make sure William McKinley is elected. Mr. Bryan would be an unsuitable president and cause an economic crisis of a scale this country has never seen. He's far too concerned about the 'masses' for his own good—or anyone's."

"I'm glad you have confidence in Mr. McKinley." If Sarah accomplished her goal, she would not have to be among the masses any longer.

"There is more to life than politics, Miss Cuthbert, and I promise to make up for my neglect. I have been invited to a ball at the Palmer House on Saturday evening, and it would give me great pleasure to escort you."

A ball!

"May I call for you at the Lexington at eight o'clock?" Brad asked.

"I would be delighted," Sarah said.

"I apologize for the short notice," Brad said. "Your dressmaker may scowl at you."

Sarah smiled. "My dressmaker is most agreeable, I assure you."

11

The door burst open and Sarah gasped. She had not even heard the clomping on the narrow wooden stairs or the approaching sound in the hall.

"Please knock!" Sarah jumped off her bed and pushed the mound of fabric aside.

"I did knock." Mrs. Fletcher's reply had an edge Sarah had not heard recently. "Your own dinner has gone cold and it's nearly time to serve Mr. Leo. You've had too much freedom this summer after all, if this is the thanks I get for allowing it."

Sarah pushed out a breath. "I'm sorry, Mrs. Fletcher. I got caught up in my project."

"Clearly."

"I said I was sorry."

Mrs. Fletcher stepped farther into the room. "Every spare minute you've had today, you dashed up the stairs. What are you working on?"

"I had an idea. I wanted to see if it would work." Sarah plunged a needle into the pin cushion and quickly wrapped the pale pink—almost white—thread that had unrolled. The gown had been Flora Banning's. Sarah remembered when it was new and the gallery opening for which it had been created. Right from the start she was smitten with the generous folds of whispery pink satin. Patiently she waited two years for Mrs. Banning to decide she could not be seen in the gown again. For her own design, Sarah had made the bodice more fitted than the original gown and lowered the neckline. She had also shortened the train, leaving ample fabric for another project. However, she still struggled with the sleeves. Her sketches had been inspired by the feathery pale pink clouds of a summer dawn, the ones she saw from the courtyard behind the Banning house. So far, though, the sleeves hung too heavily.

"You'll have to put it away for now," Mrs. Fletcher admonished, "and get dressed to serve."

"I'll be right down."

"You have seven minutes." Mrs. Fletcher turned and left the room.

Sarah surveyed the state of things. Brad had only invited her to the ball the evening before, but trying to make a gown while also doing enough work to placate Mrs. Fletcher was proving to be a challenge. She only had two more days. Vaguely she wondered what it would be like if she had a sewing machine.

She groaned aloud. Simon was expecting her at St. Andrew's the next afternoon, the last thing she had time for when she had a ball to prepare for.

A ball!

Sarah still could not believe she had been invited to a ball at the Palmer House. Undoubtedly she would rub elbows with some of the most prominent people in Chicago. Despite their physical resemblance, Sarah Cummings and Serena Cuthbert were nothing alike. No one paid any attention to the face of a maid. As long as she did not encounter another Prairie Avenue servant, Serena would have no trouble.

The dress, however, would keep her up all night.

—◦◦—

Sarah carefully removed Leo's soup bowl and carried it through the butler's pantry and into the kitchen. She was grateful to see

Mrs. Fletcher had simplified the meal somewhat by eliminating the fish course and combining the vegetables and salad.

"Don't skimp," Mrs. Fletcher admonished Sarah as the maid picked up the meat tray of braised pork chops and rare roast beef. "Behave as if the entire family were here."

In the butler's pantry, out of sight, Sarah rolled her eyes. It would have made much more sense for Leo to ask for a tray in the parlor or his own room than for her to pretend she was serving a seven-course dinner to a roomful of people. She pushed through the door and offered the tray to Leo, who nodded with pleasure.

"Both pork and beef, I think," Leo said.

"Yes, sir." Sarah watched as Leo put a generous portion of each meat on his plate.

"Sarah," Leo said, "would you give Mrs. Fletcher a message for me?"

"Of course, sir."

"Let her know I want to invite a few people for dinner on Saturday night—three guests, I would imagine. I'll let her know the final number no later than breakfast on Saturday."

Sarah felt the color swirl out of her skin. "Saturday, sir?"

Leo nodded. "That's right. Some people from the department at the university." He paused to look at her. "Are you all right, Sarah? You look pale."

"I'm fine, sir." Sarah recovered and stood up straight. "Mrs. Fletcher will want to know if you have any special menu requests."

He shook his head. "Whatever she thinks best. Roast lamb would do well."

"Yes, sir."

Sarah stepped away from the table, set the meat tray on the sideboard along the wall, and took her position to wait for Leo to finish the course. As he chewed, she could see his mind was buzzing and he was barely aware of her presence.

He was rarely home on a Saturday night, and he had to choose this Saturday night to host a dinner party.

Finally, Leo finished his meat and put his hands in his lap. Sarah stepped forward to remove his meat plate. With lips pressed together, she shuffled into the butler's pantry and paused there to let her shoulders sag. It was difficult to imagine under what conditions Mrs. Fletcher would allow her to leave the house on Saturday night when even one Banning was eating at home, much less bringing guests.

The plain fact was there were no such conditions. Sarah could suggest that Karl might serve, and Mrs. Fletcher would scoff. Karl was a driver. He helped with table service only in situations of household duress. Certainly he was not qualified to serve a dinner party on his own. Panic welled in Sarah's chest.

Mrs. Fletcher pushed open the door from the kitchen. "Why are you standing in here looking so stricken?"

"No reason." Sarah pushed past Mrs. Fletcher. "He's ready for the vegetables."

—⁓∽⁓—

The corners of Lillie's mouth turned up at the sight of the baked asparagus in a butter sauce. If her mother were as fond of the dish as Lillie was, perhaps they would eat it more often. The housekeeper lifted four spears from the tray and laid them on Lillie's plate, then spooned carrots alongside them.

Edith Wagner picked up her fork, and her husband and daughter followed her cue.

"I met some of the neighbors from upper Prairie Avenue today," Edith reported.

Lillie bit into the asparagus and let the flavor seep into her taste buds before swallowing. "Whom did you meet, Mother?"

"Mrs. Keith," Edith responded. "She gave a small tea."

"Aren't there several Keiths on the Avenue?" Frederic Wagner asked.

"Yes, Elbridge and Edson are brothers. They run the family millinery business together. I believe there's a third brother, as well."

"Do they have a hat shop nearby?" Lillie asked. "I must say, though, the shop I discovered on Michigan Avenue has the most delicious hand-sewn creations."

"This was Mrs. Elbridge Keith," Edith clarified. "I was afraid to ask about a shop for fear of sounding ignorant. I believe Mr. Keith is also president of the Metropolitan National Bank. I understand he's quite successful."

"Whom else did you meet?"

"Let's see, Mrs. Wheeler and Mrs. Bissell. I was rather hoping to meet Mrs. Field, but she sent her regrets."

"How about Mrs. Glessner or Mrs. Banning?" Lillie took another bite of asparagus and nearly moaned with the salivary pleasure.

"Mrs. Glessner is in New Hampshire." Edith frowned at the asparagus on her plate. "Why did I agree to this weed?"

"Because you know I love it." Lillie batted her eyes at her mother. "What about Mrs. Banning?"

"The Bannings are at their house in Lake Forest."

Lillie's face brightened. "The Cuthberts have a home in Lake Forest. I wonder if it's near the Bannings'. And they used to have an estate in New Hampshire. What a curious coincidence."

"Not really." Frederic reached for his water goblet. "I gather it's rather common for families in the neighborhood to have summer homes in Lake Forest or elsewhere, even New Hampshire."

"We should visit Lake Forest and consider a lot," Edith said.

Frederic scowled. "Not unless you've changed your mind about the Romanesque façade."

"We must do the renovations, Frederic," Edith said. "We agreed."

"I wonder if Serena might invite me to her home in Lake Forest." Lillie's eyebrows pushed up.

"I hope you know better than to suggest that to her!"

"Of course, Mother. But I feel Serena and I are going to become great friends. If she should invite me, it would be rude to decline."

"I would like to meet Mrs. Banning," Edith mused. "At tea today, I heard the most curious things about her daughter, Lucy Edwards. She works at an orphanage."

"She works?" Lillie asked. "You mean she is employed? But she's married."

"I believe it's all volunteer, and her husband is understanding." Edith pushed aside the last of her vegetables. "She's heavily involved and has been for several years. They have quite come to depend on her."

"What's the name of the orphanage?"

"Saint something. St. John's? No, St. Andrew's, that's it. Somewhere south of here."

"Oh, I saw St. Andrew's! The driver went by it once while I was making calls. I confess I'm curious about those places," Lillie said. "If we ever meet the Bannings, perhaps I'll have an opportunity to ask some questions."

"It's hardly dinner conversation." Edith signaled to the maid that she was finished with her vegetables. "I also heard that the Bannings have a maid who is quite handy with needle and thread. There was talk that she could easily work in a dressmaker's shop."

Lillie touched three fingers to her forehead. "That reminds me, I really must remember to get the name of Serena Cuthbert's dressmaker. Every time I start to, something interferes."

Sarah pulled open another kitchen drawer and riffled through the contents, sure she had seen the butler lay a stack of stationery in one of them. So far she had found three sheets of cream-colored paper and six pale green envelopes. It would have to do. Sarah shoved the final drawer closed, took her mismatched stash to the kitchen table, and sat.

Nothing had changed between the meat course and dessert. Sarah had passed Leo's message along to Mrs. Fletcher, who took it in stride and began to make notes for the menu. Sarah slammed her way through clearing the dining room and scrubbing down the kitchen, frantic for any glimmer of a solution. None came. She would have to find a way to break her date with Brad and had settled on sending a carefully worded note that would reach him on Saturday after the midday meal.

The note had to be perfect. She would claim sudden illness. Or Serena's aunt would unreasonably insist that she must spend the evening with her. Sarah drummed her fingers on the table as she pondered the options.

Absorbed in her problem, she did not hear Karl come in to find her staring at the blank paper and pursing her lips. Only when he sat directly across from her did she acknowledge his presence.

"Do you need something, Karl?" Sarah asked. "Mrs. Fletcher has already gone upstairs for the night."

"That's all right," Karl said. "It's you I'm curious about."

"What in the world are you talking about?" Sarah stacked her three sheets of paper precisely.

"What are you up to?" Karl asked.

"Up to?"

He pointed at the paper. "You look like you're writing a fancy note."

Sarah eyed him. "How is that your business?"

"I suppose it's not," he admitted. "But you have been acting strangely the last few weeks."

"I don't know what you mean."

"Yes, you do."

Sarah straightened the papers again.

"You're up to something, Sarah Cummings," Karl said. "I don't want to see you get hurt."

"I don't intend to." Sarah stood up and shoved the paper and envelopes back in a drawer. "I think I'll just go to bed."

"Sarah, if you want to talk—"

"I don't. Good night, Karl."

12

"Miss Cummings, there's a lump in the bottom of my bag." Twelve-year-old Virginia fingered the knot between her thumb and forefinger. "Right here in the corner."

Sarah reached for her scissors. "You probably need to trim the seam. Turn the bag inside out."

Virginia complied, and Sarah saw how wide the seam had become at the bottom of the bag, creating a glut of fabric at the fold. She handed the scissors to the girl and explained to the whole group the importance of keeping the seam an even narrow width. A minute later Virginia had trimmed her seam and turned her bag again, this time in satisfaction.

"Can I really use this for a purse?" the girl asked.

"Of course," Sarah answered.

Around the table, other girls had lifted their eyes for the answer. Before each one was a small bag with the top turned and stitched down to create a casing. The project had consumed the sewing class for the last two weeks. The bags ranged from heavy satin to corduroy to tweed, and Sarah was confident they would all be serviceable. She had been careful not to allow any girl to get too far into the project without acceptable stitching that would hold up under use.

"We're going to use a thin cord for the drawstring," Sarah explained and began to distribute lengths of ivory braided cord likely left over from dining room drapes or reupholstering a parlor settee. Sarah did not much care where it had come from, only that it was thin enough and neutral enough in color to be paired with the variety of fabrics the girls had chosen for their bags.

"Won't it fray?" Melissa asked.

"We'll tie a knot on each end and stitch down the end in a ball," Sarah answered. "You can practice your tiniest catch stitches."

"It looks so plain," Mary Margaret observed.

"You can add a row of lace around the top of the bag if you like," Sarah said. "We have several laces to choose from." She demonstrated how to feed the cording through the casing at the top of the bag and pull it through so that both ends hung out the same small opening. When the ends were pulled tight, the bag drew closed.

Most of the girls were eagerly positioning their strings. Jane's hands had slowed down to doing almost nothing.

Something was wrong with Jane, Sarah thought. The week before she could not wait to work on her bag, and today she had hardly touched her project. Jane's dark head bent over her bag, which lay flat on the table, but her fingers did little more than stroke the gray tweed. Sarah turned her attention to the other end of the table. If Jane was unhappy about something, let Simon Tewell deal with it. Sarah had bigger problems to sort out. In her mind, she had two carefully crafted and deliberately understated versions of the note she would send to Bradley Townsend the following afternoon, but she still could not make up her mind which one would be the most persuasive and leave the greatest opening for him to invite her out again.

The girls chattered among themselves as they wrestled with their drawstrings and unwound unnecessary lengths of lace, but Sarah did not interfere. She was grateful for the time to think. She was surprised, a few minutes later though, to hear the patter of a small child's feet.

"Henry, slow down," a mother's voice admonished.

Sarah looked up to see Charlotte Shepard standing just inside the door. She nudged herself into politeness and stood to cross the room. "Hello, Charlotte."

"Hello, Sarah." Henry worked loose from Charlotte's grasp, and her eyes tracked his progress as he ventured into the room. "I stopped in to pick up Stella from Lucy's office and take her home with me. Lucy plans to stay late. She told me about your classes, so I thought Henry and I would drop in and say hello."

Sarah gestured around. "This is it. We haven't done anything complicated yet, but the girls seem to like it."

"Henry, no, don't touch that," Charlotte called to her son, whose hand was raised over his head and poised over the latch to the cupboard that held the fabrics and thread. He turned his attention instead to running his fingers along the length of one wall and humming to himself, his blue eyes bright as ever.

"I've lost track of how old Henry is." Sarah made the mild inquiry out of politeness. She never paid much attention to children, but she was surprised to see Henry looking more like a little boy than a toddler.

"He'll be four in September," Charlotte answered with a mother's pride.

It seemed a lifetime ago that Charlotte Farrow, a kitchen maid herself, had hidden the existence of her son from the entire Banning household. Sarah had been in the courtyard that August afternoon when the woman caring for Henry had deposited him abruptly. For a time, Charlotte had let everyone think he was an orphan left for Lucy Banning Edwards to find. Sarah had fed and bathed him herself. It had seemed to her that being a nanny was better than working in the kitchen. When the truth had finally come out, Charlotte had survived the scandal by moving out of the mansion and marrying a man eager to adopt the baby.

"Marriage seems to suit you." Sarah grasped for something to be polite about. Serena would know what to say. "How is Archie? Still working for Mr. Glessner?"

"Yes, and he loves it," Charlotte answered.

Archie Shepard had escaped—sort of. He had successfully exchanged being a footman and coachman for the Bannings for being a clerk in the office of their neighbor's farm machinery company. What Archie saw in Charlotte, Sarah never understood. But he had married her without judgment of her past, embraced her son, and taken them both away from the Bannings.

"If you're here for Stella, you must still be working for Lucy," Sarah remarked.

Charlotte nodded. "Just a few hours during the day. We don't live in. You know how independent Lucy likes to be. And Archie is saving so we can have a bungalow of our own someday."

A bungalow. Sarah forced her eyes not to roll. Charlotte had settled so easily—a husband happy to be a clerk, a day job as a maid, and the dream of a bungalow. That was not good enough for Sarah. Not when she had Bradley Townsend within reach. Not when she had Serena Cuthbert.

"I have some happy news," Charlotte said.

"Oh?"

"Archie and I are having a baby!" Charlotte grinned.

Sarah smiled because she knew she was supposed to. "Congratulations."

"The new little one should come around the middle of February. Archie is so pleased."

"Tell him I said hello."

"I will. I suppose Henry and I should get out of your way and go find little Stella. She'll be looking for something to eat soon."

Sarah nodded. "It was nice to see you, Charlotte."

The maid's life would never be good enough for Sarah—especially now that Serena Cuthbert had arrived.

Simon Tewell opened the door to the classroom and inhaled the mingled scents of textiles. Just as he had hoped, the girls were gone and Sarah was alone at one end of the table.

"Ah, Miss Cummings," he said. "Finished for the day?"

Sarah nodded. "The girls have each completed a small drawstring purse."

"I suppose they'll be showing them off at dinner." Standing opposite Sarah, Simon tucked a chair under the table.

"Yes, I suppose so." Sarah folded a length of cotton. "Melissa got this out. I asked her to put it away."

"If the girls are not listening to you, I'll have a word with them," Simon offered.

"No, don't bother. They're just excited."

"They know better than to leave a mess behind. We have clear expectations about that sort of behavior."

"Don't worry about it." Sarah tucked the folded fabric into the cupboard. "If she does it again, I'll mention it myself."

Simon nodded. "Yes, that's better, no doubt. They need to respect your authority." He was suddenly aware that he was staring at her—did she have any idea how beautiful she was?—and made himself glance around the room. "Have you tried out the sewing machine yet?"

Sarah turned toward the machine in the corner. "Not yet. A couple of the girls have asked about it."

"You're welcome to use it anytime," Simon said, "even for your own projects. Perhaps you'd like to come early some day and experiment."

"Perhaps." Sarah picked up her hat from the table and arranged it on her head.

She was trying to leave, Simon realized. He wished he could come up with a reason why she should stay. Why she would want to stay.

"The girls would probably enjoy it if you shared a meal with them sometime," Simon said. "Come for lunch, or stay for supper. The children eat early. I eat with them myself from time to time."

Sarah picked up a tapestry bag she had begun carrying to class and her white gloves.

"You set a marvelous example for the girls by wearing the clothes you create," Simon said. "Surely it's an inspiration to them."

"I must catch the streetcar, Mr. Tewell," Sarah said. "Maybe I'll see you next Friday."

She swept out of the room with a new posture Simon had not seen before, an air about her he did not quite recognize.

~~~

Sarah got off the streetcar at Michigan and Eighteenth and sauntered toward the Banning mansion. It was still early. She had already freshened Leo's room, dusted the parlor, and sorted the vegetables for tomorrow night's dinner party. What was there to make her rush home only to write a note to Brad and put away the nearly finished gown? Now she would have all the time she needed to add the perfect finishing touches while she awaited another reason to wear the dress.

A few minutes later, Sarah entered the kitchen through the back door.

"Oh good, you're back." Mrs. Fletcher stirred a pot on the stove. "Mr. Leo is out tonight, but he sent word that tomorrow's dinner party has become a luncheon party instead."

"Lunch? Not dinner?"

"Didn't I just say that? Are your ears stopped up?"

"No, of course not, Mrs. Fletcher." Sarah fumbled. "It's just that now we've lost half a day getting ready."

"We'll be ready. Change your clothes and let's get to work."

Sarah flew up the back stairs and burst into her room. The pink silk beckoned from its hook across the room, and Sarah answered the call, stepping around her narrow bed to finger the fabric once again, to let its cool shimmer slide through her hands, to close her eyes and hold her breath and imagine what the inside of the Palmer House ballroom must be like.

13

When the doorbell rang, Sarah looked up from the sideboard in the dining room, where she was arranging silver serving spoons for lunch. She intended to answer the bell, but across the foyer, Leo emerged from the parlor to welcome his lunch guests himself. Three men of various ages and builds entered, and Leo shook their hands and clapped their backs. Camaraderie swelled in their voices as they lingered in the foyer.

Sarah leaned against the wall, blew out her breath, and peered at them. The guests brought far more noise and enthusiasm into the house than she felt up to coping with. She was dead on her feet as it was. Dawn had nearly arrived before she put the final exquisite touches on the gown. At moments throughout the night, she wished Flora Banning were as generous with jewelry as she was with old dresses. In six hours Sarah had to step aside for Serena Cuthbert and be at the Lexington Hotel looking leisurely and gracious—and with a bare neck. Sarah had only one necklace, and it was glass, so she did not dare wear it to a ballroom full of women who would know the difference at a glance. The dress was perfect, however. She persuaded herself jewelry would have detracted from her precise stitching, the flawless fit, the exactness of the drape of the sleeves brushing off her shoulders.

Leo had confirmed his intention to dine out on Saturday evening, as he usually did. Nothing would keep her from being ready. All she had to do was get through serving lunch and cleaning up. Then Mrs. Fletcher was sure to want to put her own feet up for the evening and have an early night. Sarah could bathe and dress without interference.

The men drifted into the parlor and Sarah roused herself to return to the kitchen.

"Everyone is here?" Mrs. Fletcher asked.

Sarah nodded.

"The table is ready?"

Another nod.

"The artichoke soup has been chilling in the icebox all morning," Mrs. Fletcher said. "You can announce lunch and serve the soup while I slice the lamb."

In the butler's pantry on the way to the dining room, Sarah paused to splash cold water on her face and smooth her skirt.

Six hours.

They were certainly in no hurry. Sarah reprimanded herself for foolishly supposing they might be. It was not the problem of Leo Banning and his guests that the maid had an engagement with a young man. Table conversation settled into commentary on events in the university department in which they all worked. It was clear even to Sarah that if they strayed from shared employment, they had little in common. One seemed to be quick to offer opinions, while the other two were less outgoing. Leo was pleasant to everyone, as he always was. Sarah did not care what they talked about, though, if only they would eat a little faster. Thirty minutes into the meal, and they were still toying with the lamb. Vegetables. Salad. Dessert and coffee. Sarah's impatience did nothing to speed the service of the meal.

With a stifled sigh, she stepped forward to refill the water goblet of the best-dressed guest. He had already emptied it twice. If he did again, she would have to refill the pitcher as well. No one seemed as interested in what he said as he was himself. Sarah glanced at the other two guests. When one of them caught her eye for a fraction of a second, she turned away immediately. Admonishing words of Mr. Penard, the Banning butler, rang in her ears. Fraternizing with the guests in any way would not be tolerated.

"I appreciate your changing this dinner to lunch," the thirsty guest said as he cut his lamb.

"It's no problem, Thom," Leo assured him. "I know the ball tonight is important to you."

Ball? Sarah's boredom rolled away, and she examined the guest more carefully while counting on being a faceless maid to him. In the pink silk gown, Serena Cuthbert would be nothing like Sarah Cummings. Still, she inventoried his features to avoid later if necessary.

"It's my wife's father's event," Thom said. "Amanda would never forgive me if we did not attend."

"Is your father-in-law giving the ball?" Leo asked.

Thom nodded. "He's one of several organizers. My father is in on it as well. Their hope is to rally a strong Republican contingent in the weeks ahead. Fortunately the Palmer House could accommodate them."

"Ah," Leo said, "this is a reaction to Mr. Bryan's nomination by the Democrats."

"My father-in-law would prefer to say it's proactive," Thom said, "a positive step toward making sure William McKinley is the next president. We like to think of it as a gathering of like-minded men."

I should have known, Sarah thought. Brad was so perturbed when William Jennings Bryan was nominated. This was just the sort of affair he would be involved in. Considering his silence over the last few weeks, she would not have been surprised to learn that the Townsends were one of the other families behind a ball meant to be a political fund-raiser.

Everyone finished their lamb at last, and Sarah approached the table to remove the meat plates. Holding the stack with both hands, she leaned into the door to the butler's pantry.

"Some important people will be there," Thom said. "If you would like to attend, I would be happy to introduce you."

Sarah froze. Even if Leo's guests overlooked the features of the young woman who served their meal, Leo knew her face.

"Thank you, Thom," Leo said, "but it's rather late to change my plans for the evening."

Sarah breathed relief as she set the plates in the sink in the butler's pantry, then proceeded to the kitchen for the vegetables tray.

Mrs. Fletcher looked up from the counter where she was arranging the beets and cauliflower. "You look like you've seen a ghost."

"It's nothing," Sarah muttered. "Are the vegetables ready?"

"I hope you're not showing that face to the guests," Mrs. Fletcher cautioned.

Sarah would have been glad not to be showing any face to the guests.

"I'm fine. I'll take the next course." Sarah picked up the vegetables tray and turned her back on the cook.

In the dining room again, Sarah moved smoothly to the table to continue serving.

"That Mr. Bryan gives a good speech," Leo commented. "Out of curiosity, I was there the night he gave the Cross of Gold speech."

Thom huffed. "One speech. The man gave one good speech."

"It was electrifying," Leo said, "whether or not you agree with him. When he pulled down that imaginary crown of thorns to his temples, you could have heard a pin drop. He'll give the Republicans a run for their money."

"You sound as if you think he has a chance."

"He might." Leo nodded for an extra serving of vegetables on his plate. "He's courting the working class and succeeding. They like the sound of more widespread prosperity. That's a lot of popular votes."

Sarah held the tray firmly, willing it not to shake in her hands as she served another guest.

"They don't understand the issues," Thom insisted. "The Democrats are promising a better economy, but they'll never be able to deliver if they introduce silver as a monetary standard."

"The so-called 'Silver Republicans' would disagree with you," Leo pointed out, "and plenty of Democrats would argue to adhere to the gold standard. It's a mixed bag across the country."

"Mr. Bryan is quite clear on where he stands, and he's the official candidate," Thom said. "The Democrats adopted his platform. That's what we have to fight against."

Leo waved a hand. "Well, gentlemen, that is not the problem we gathered here to solve. Why don't we get down to business?"

Sarah stepped to the sideboard and put the vegetables tray down. Gold standard, silver standard—what did it matter? If she married someone like Bradley Townsend, she would not have need to wonder about it, and if she did not marry someone like Brad, she would be so busy working she would never have time to wonder about it.

The conversation turned to industrial uses for the field of mechanical engineering and the particular technical dilemma Leo had gathered the group to discuss. Sarah made no attempt to follow the train of thought, instead letting her mind drift to the evening ahead. She cared not one whit about the politics that apparently inspired the occasion. Her challenge was to be utterly captivating, irresistibly beautiful—to be Serena Cuthbert.

It was past three-thirty by the time Leo suggested the group take their coffee and dessert in the parlor to continue their conversation. Sarah pushed the tea cart across the foyer and into the parlor as efficiently as she could and dispensed the apple pie. Back in the kitchen a few minutes later, she filled the sink with water and began to scrub dishes.

"Don't be so rough," Mrs. Fletcher cautioned. "Those are china plates, not tin cans. If Mr. Penard comes back from the lake to discover you've chipped something, he'll chip your head."

Sarah pursed her lips. It was true the Bannings' butler could give a serious dressing down. But she needed every minute she could scrape up to be ready for the night.

Mary Catherine should have been there washing dishes, she thought. This was not even her job anymore.

Sarah knew better than to speak such a sentiment aloud. She slowed her pace just enough to placate Mrs. Fletcher's caution. She washed, dried, stacked, and put away far more dishes than it seemed to her four people ought to need. As she did, she imagined her hair put up with a twist on the side. The cool, sleek silk of the dress. The turning heads as she entered the grand ballroom at the Palmer House on the arm of Bradley Townsend.

Mrs. Fletcher fractured Sarah's reverie at ten minutes to five.

"I have some things that need mending." The cook stood with table linens draped over one arm. "I thought you could do them tonight."

Sarah blanched. "Must they be done tonight?"

"It's still very early," Mrs. Fletcher countered, hanging the linens on the back of a chair. "You can rest a bit first if you like."

"Monday would be soon enough, wouldn't it?" Sarah said.

Mrs. Fletcher halted her progress across the kitchen and pivoted to examine Sarah. "Did you think you were going out again tonight?"

"A friend invited me out. I did not see any reason not to accept."

"This is the first I've heard of it," Mrs. Fletcher said.

Must Mrs. Fletcher know all her business? "I rather imagined you would want to relax this evening."

"You should not presume," Mrs. Fletcher said. "You're drawing a full salary while the family is away. You should expect to put in a full day's work a little more often. I'm beginning to think you're taking advantage of the family's absence."

"It's only the mending," Sarah pointed out calmly.

"The mending is not the issue, as you well know. I'm no fool." Mrs. Fletcher turned toward the stairs again. "I suppose it can wait a day or two, but don't let your imagination get the best of you. You've still got a job to do."

14

*S*arah sat in the corner of the Lexington Hotel lobby clos-
est to the door and with her back to Kenny, who eyed
her from behind the main desk. A steady stream of hotel guests
prevented him from leaving his post, and Sarah refused to grant
him the satisfaction of eye contact. Instead, her eyes monitored
activity outside the door. While she bathed and dressed for the evening, adrenaline had kicked in. The fatigue of a few hours ago had
dissipated in anticipation of an evening with Bradley Townsend,
even if it was a political occasion. Sarah Cummings may have been
weary from stitching until dawn, but Serena Cuthbert was fresh
and primped for the occasion.

Brad's carriage finally rolled up just after eight o'clock. When
he stepped out, Sarah forgot to breathe. In evening formal wear,
he was even more stunning than in the dark suits she had seen
him in before this. A white vest sparkled under his dark tails, and
at his neck was a white bow tie. It was all Sarah could do not to
jump up and dash toward him, instead making herself wait with
no visage of eagerness. She turned her head to glance casually
across the lobby as if she had not even noticed his carriage arrive.
In her peripheral vision, she watched him pull open the lobby
door and step inside.

Tall, dark, and handsome. And rich. Perfect.

"I'm sorry if I kept you waiting, Serena," Bradley crooned, bowing slightly to offer her his arm.

"No trouble at all." Sarah slipped a gloved hand into the crook of his arm and rose from her seat. "You're right on time."

He led her to the carriage with the luscious blue silk interior, and Sarah arranged herself as she was sure Serena would—graceful and erect.

"I'm looking forward to a delightful evening," Sarah said as the horse began to trot.

"As am I," Brad said. "I should mention that you may hear some political conversation, but pay it no mind."

So it was the same event that Leo's friend was attending. Sarah doubted the guest—Thom something—had even noticed the color of her hair, much less the features of her face.

"I hope there won't be any long speeches." Sarah coyly gestured with one hand.

Brad shook his head. "Not tonight. Just a few conversations here and there about how to proceed in the face of what the Democrats have done."

"You mean Mr. Bryan's nomination?"

"I don't believe he has a serious chance at election, but we have to be sure."

"Of course."

"The working class, you know," Brad said. "They get ideas in their heads. In the end it doesn't help anyone, least of all them."

Sarah looked away and pressed her lips together. She was going to a ball at the Palmer House on the arm of one of the most eligible bachelors in Chicago. A smattering of political discussion about the working class would be of no consequence. Certainly she did not have to involve herself in it.

"You might think I have no imagination," Brad said. "All I seem to do is invite you to political events. I promise you'll enjoy the evening, though. After the election we'll have plenty of time for outings more to your liking."

"No apology is necessary," Sarah said. "One can hardly go wrong with a ball."

After the election, he had said. Brad Townsend was thinking of seeing Serena Cuthbert in the future. Sarah leaned back slightly and smiled. Whatever the evening held, it was a down payment on better prospects.

When they entered the ballroom, Sarah felt dozens of eyes on her—men and women alike. Serena Cuthbert made a striking impression, the whispering pink silk swirling around her slender form and draping flawlessly from strategic points. Heads turned when Brad and Serena were announced. Sarah confidently lifted her chin and met the many gazes.

Though she had never been to the Palmer House, ballroom protocol was not foreign to her. The Pullmans on Prairie Avenue gave balls for two hundred people in their home, and nearly every time, Sarah was conscripted to join the expanded staff of servants. From simple observation she had learned what to expect in the guests' behavior. And now Serena knew what to do.

Brad patted the hand that rested inside his elbow. "You look ravishing and they all know it. It would not surprise me to learn that every woman in this room is jealous at this moment."

Pleasure pulled at her lips.

"Let me introduce you to a few people." Brad led her toward a table on the perimeter of the dance floor. "I must pay my respects to some of the organizers. I can't let them think I did not accept their kind invitation."

"I'd love to meet your friends," Sarah said.

At the table, two men stood and greeted Brad enthusiastically, their eyes wandering to Sarah.

"May I present Miss Serena Cuthbert," Brad said. "Mr. and Mrs. Hayden Powell, and Mr. and Mrs. Timothy Pearce."

"I'm very pleased to meet you." Sarah nodded at the foursome with restrained pleasure.

"Emma and I have heard Mr. Townsend's kind remarks about you before," Timothy Pearce said.

With Serena's grace, Sarah smiled at the compliment.

"Miss Cuthbert, your dress is divine," Emma Pearce commented. "Such a flattering color."

"Thank you, Mrs. Pearce." Sarah turned up the corners of her mouth with poise.

"I had no idea Bradley was acquainted with anyone as delightful as you," Mr. Powell said.

Mrs. Powell slapped her husband's elbow. "Hayden! I'm surprised Brad wants anything to do with you, the way you harass him."

Sarah smiled and turned her attention to Mrs. Powell. "Your husband is most kind."

"Pay no attention to him. When Brad's around, Hayden likes to imagine he's still a young man himself."

"He cuts a fine figure." Sarah aimed Serena's smile at both the Powells.

"The truth is we have a son older than Brad," Mrs. Powell said. "I hope you'll meet him before the evening is over."

"Where is Thom?" Brad asked, swiveling his head to scan the room.

"He'll turn up," Hayden Powell said. "Brad, I hope the business deal we discussed a few days ago will sort itself out soon."

"First thing Monday morning," Brad promised. "Diamond Matches is going to make a tidy profit for both of us. I've spoken with the Moore brothers personally and made all the arrangements. We're just waiting for the exchange to open on Monday."

Powell nodded. "Good, good. I appreciate your tipping me off to it."

"It's my pleasure," Brad said. "This is going to be a deal to remember. I certainly intend to make a considerable return."

Sarah felt the slight blush rise in her cheeks. This was just the kind of outlook she wanted in the man she would marry. Confidence. Business expertise. Visions of wealth.

"Oh, let's not talk business now," Mrs. Powell said. "I want to dance. They're playing a waltz."

"Your favorite, Mildred." Hayden Powell dutifully offered his hand and led his wife to the dance floor. Emma and Timothy Pearce followed.

Brad looked at Sarah. "May I?" He held out his hand, palm up.

"I'd be delighted." She laid her hand in his and wondered if he felt the tingling.

He waltzed her out to the center of the floor. Sarah's father had taught her to waltz when she was young, and buried grief shivered through her for a fraction of a moment. Brad led their steps confidently and all she had to do was follow, her feet reprising girlhood practice. She shyly turned her eyes down much of the time, her right hand resting in his left. Her left hand on his shoulder. His right hand at the small of her back. Sensation looped from one point of contact to the next as she breathed in his scent and wondered what the soft curls of his beard would feel like against her face.

"We seem to be good dance partners," Brad observed.

"One always needs a reliable partner," Sarah answered quickly.

"I can think of other partnerships we might explore as well."

"I'm most eager to hear what you have in mind." She hoped he might bend his face toward hers.

Brad raised an eyebrow and smiled, but said nothing more. Instead he began to step more briskly through the dance, brushing up against other pairs until he had cut a swath where he and Sarah danced freely and others slowed their own steps to watch the finesse of the swirling couple.

"I fear people are gawking." Sarah flushed with pleasure and kept up with every fluid step.

"Only at your beauty," Brad responded.

"We seem to be taking over the dance floor."

"They stand back because they find they cannot breathe in your presence."

"Perhaps you exaggerate, Mr. Townsend."

"Not an iota."

"You're a marvelous partner," Sarah said, "and the orchestra is spectacular."

"You deserve the best."

You deserve the best. No one had said that to Sarah Cummings in more than ten years. Her father had made it a habit, but no one since had seemed to agree with him. The years she had spent nevertheless believing it were coming to fruition at last. Tears glistened in the eyes that Sarah now hid from Brad.

Around and around they spun in one great circle.

When the waltz ended, Brad smiled. "Something to drink, Serena?"

"I do seem to have worked up a thirst."

He led her to a table and pulled out a chair for her before signaling a waiter.

"Oh, there's Peter Sattler," Brad said as the waiter set drinks before them. He waved his hand above his head. The burly man for whom the gesture was intended made his way toward their table. Brad made the introductions.

"Forgive me, Miss Cuthbert," Mr. Sattler said. "I wish only a moment of Brad's time for a small matter."

"Of course," she responded.

Sattler turned to Brad. "I presume you've heard the news from our friend in Ohio?"

Brad nodded. "Mark Hanna will get the job done."

"William McKinley has the political weight, and Mark Hanna

has the business know-how," Sattler said. "What he proposes seems like a reasonable precaution."

"Five dollars a head does not seem too much to ensure we win the election," Brad said. "I'm sure the donations made tonight will go a long way toward that end."

"I quite agree." Sattler turned toward Sarah, bowed slowly, and took a step back. "It was delightful to meet you, Miss Cuthbert. I'm not at all sure Mr. Townsend deserves you."

"You're most kind." Sarah batted her eyes above a smile.

Sattler wandered off.

"Donations?" Sarah asked Brad.

"The price of tickets to the ball," he answered.

"But five dollars a head? After the expenses of the ball, how will they have anything left for the campaign?" Even a parlor maid could appreciate the cost of the extravagance she saw tonight—the hotel, the food, the orchestra.

Half of Brad's mouth twisted into a smile. "No need to worry about it, Serena. I assure you the ticket price was far more than five dollars a person. That figure refers to a certain level of enticement to be offered at a later date."

"Enticement?"

"You have many questions tonight," Brad said. "I don't expect you to understand the ins and outs of how political deals are done. Shall we dance again?"

Sarah nodded, and they returned to the dance floor, this time for a slower, four-step dance. They had barely begun when a man about Brad's age tapped his shoulder.

"Will you permit me to cut in?" the man asked.

Brad paused. "Only with the greatest reluctance."

"My father was adamant that I should meet your guest."

Sarah looked the man in the eye.

"May I present Miss Serena Cuthbert," Brad said, "and this is Thom Powell. We chatted with his parents earlier."

"I remember," Sarah said.

Thom. Leo had called his friend Thom. Unquestionably this was the same man. His eyes betrayed no glimmer of recognition.

Brad stepped away and Thom Powell led Sarah back into the dance.

"How is it that Brad Townsend met you before I did?" he asked.

Sarah raised her eyes to look him square in the face. "Perhaps we have met and the moment escapes you."

He shook his head. "I'm sure I would remember being introduced to you, Miss Cuthbert."

"I suppose our paths simply have not crossed."

"I hope we will see each other again," Thom said. "It would be my pleasure to introduce you to my wife."

Sarah permitted herself one of Serena's most encouraging smiles and gave herself over to her success.

15

$\mathscr{S}$arah did not often go to church.

The plain fact was that the Banning household staff, like all the domestics on Prairie Avenue, was routinely occupied with their responsibilities on Sunday mornings. But the family was gone, and even Leo had left early on Sunday morning to spend the day at the lake with his parents and stay overnight. Sarah had not slept after the ball, instead lying in bed savoring the minutiae of the evening. Now she was in the courtyard leaning against a rounded stone ledge in the morning sun. Her mind continued to replay every dance step with Brad, the delicious morsels of conversation, the promise of more times together in the weeks to come. Daydreaming was almost as invigorating as sleep.

Karl popped out of the kitchen. "Let's go to church," he said.

Sarah scoffed. "I haven't been in ages."

"So why not go today?"

"I had a late night." Sarah closed her eyes and turned her face to the sun.

"You're already up." Karl put his hands out, palms up. "Admit it, you don't have anything better to do."

Sarah looked Karl in the eye. "Is that really why you want to go to church? You're bored?"

"I love the hymns," Karl said. "But I don't like to sit by myself. Come with me."

"Maybe I have something better to do."

He nudged her elbow. "Go put on one of those suits you're always making."

An hour later Sarah stood in the balcony at Second Presbyterian Church, on the left side of the sanctuary, looking down on the main floor while the congregation sang a hymn. Karl sang with gusto, but Sarah had quit singing after the first stanza.

I belong down there.

The Banning pew was empty. Every year Samuel Banning donated slightly more money than the year before for the privilege of his family's reserved seating on the main floor. Other Prairie Avenue families had pews scattered around the sanctuary, while domestics and day workers climbed the stairs to the balcony that ran around three sides.

As the fourth stanza of the hymn began, Sarah saw Serena Cuthbert materialize in the vacant Banning pew, wearing a rose crepe dress that outshone anything around her and a hat fashioned from matching fabric. Serena held a hymnal and sang. Sarah watched. When the hymn ended, Serena gracefully lowered herself into the pew and arranged her skirt. Sarah sat next to Karl and sighed. When Sarah moved her eyes, Serena faded.

The pastor stood to preach and announced his theme—belonging to God above all else. He held an open Bible in one hand and preached to the main floor, rarely lifting his eyes for a glance at the balcony.

I belong down there.

Karl leaned over and nudged Sarah. "I can tell you're not listening to a word he says."

Sarah shrugged. What did the pastor know about what she needed?

Two rows in front of her sat Charlotte and Archie Shepard, with Henry nuzzled in Archie's lap. Charlotte leaned a contented shoulder against her husband. Sarah supposed they were happy enough, but to her they were a drab reminder of her own ambitions. What made them happy would never be enough for her. And why should she settle, when Bradley Townsend clearly found delight in her presence?

Sarah looked down at the main floor again, her eyes drifting toward the rear of the sanctuary.

She gasped.

Lillie Wagner sat between her parents.

"I have to go," Sarah whispered to Karl.

"Are you ill? I'll walk you home."

"No, you stay. You love the hymns, remember?" Sarah could not risk being spotted in the balcony, nor in the company of a driver. If she did not leave now, she might be trapped in the departing crowd after the benediction. Stepping as quietly as she could, Sarah found the stairs and was out the side door of the church before the minister gathered his full preaching steam. Lillie was expecting Serena Cuthbert for tea in five hours. Sarah chided herself for letting Karl persuade her to go to church. She should have known that a family like the Wagners would attend Second Presbyterian.

<hr />

"I want a full report." Lillie handed a teacup to her friend. "Don't spare a single detail."

Serena Cuthbert sipped delicately. "But weren't you out with Paul last night? You must have a story to tell as well."

Lillie smiled at the warmth that rose in her chest. She had the attentions of Paul Gunnison and the confidence of Serena Cuthbert, a blissful combination.

"You first," Lillie urged. This was such a pleasant way to spend a Sunday afternoon. She took up the embroidery project in her lap, a square white tablecloth with copper-colored stitching meandering around the edges. She could stitch, remember her evening with Paul, and be regaled by Serena's story all at the same time. As Lillie aimed a fresh length of thread at the eye of her needle, Serena launched into her account. Several times Lillie let her hands lie idle in her lap while she leaned forward to soak up the details Serena offered.

"You tell it so beautifully!" Lillie said at last. "I can picture the Palmer House in my mind's eye and imagine the orchestra and the servants and the dancing and the flowers. It all sounds fabulous."

"It was a spectacular evening," her friend assured her. "Some of the most important people in Chicago were there, and Brad seems to know them all."

"Of course he does. He's very well connected. That's why my father likes to invite him to business events. Having a seat at the board of trade makes him quite popular."

"Yes, I heard him telling someone about an important deal that is supposed to happen tomorrow morning. Of course I don't know details, but it seems Brad expects to make money personally as well as on behalf of his clients. He has already asked me to tea tomorrow afternoon, so no doubt I'll hear about it then."

Brad probably was more wealthy than Paul Gunnison, Lillie realized. He was more ambitious and charismatic. Paul had gone into the family candy business, and while the company had been growing steadily in the last few years despite the recession, it would not likely lead to sudden enormous profits. But Lillie was content with that prospect. The early signs of Paul's affections were more satisfying than she had dared dream, and Lillie was confident he would always provide a comfortable home.

"Has Paul spoken to your father yet?" Serena asked.

Lillie loved the conspiratorial hint she heard in Serena's voice. "Not yet, but I feel it will be soon."

———❧———

"I'm so glad things are going well with you and Paul," Sarah told Lillie. "You seem very well suited to each other."

"We are!" Lillie poured more tea into Sarah's china cup on a saucer and handed it to her.

"Surely your parents would be thrilled with the match, since your fathers are in business together."

"Paul wants to prove himself," Lillie said. "If the future of the company is to be in his hands, he wants both our fathers to be confident he can do the job."

"No doubt he's already proved himself," Sarah said. "It's only a matter of finding the right moment to speak to your father, and then you can see Paul as much as you both like. Before you know it, he'll propose!"

"I hope so!"

Sarah smiled into Lillie's eyes. She meant everything she said. Paul and Lillie did seem like a good match, and Frederic and Edith would find little to object to. Serena Cuthbert could be the bride's attendant at a society wedding. A pale peach gown took form in Sarah's mind.

If—when—things progressed to that point with Brad, Serena's mother would become too ill to travel home from Europe and both parents would give their blessing for Serena to marry Bradley Townsend in their absence. Sarah would produce the elegant letter. Later, the Cuthberts would be tragically lost at sea. Or some such story. Perhaps it would not have to be as dreadful as all that. Sarah would sort everything out as the need arose.

Lillie picked up her embroidery project. "I had the oddest sensation in church today. We visited Second Presbyterian Church for the first time. Mother and Father have heard that many Prairie Avenue families attend there."

"Yes, I've heard that as well." Sarah swallowed and set the teacup on a side table. "What did you find odd?"

"They say everyone has a double somewhere in the world. Yours was in the balcony at Second Presbyterian."

Sarah narrowed her eyes and tilted her head. "That *is* odd."

"She was dressed nicely enough," Lillie conceded, "but she seemed haggard, overworked."

Sarah gestured to the project in Lillie's lap. "What are you working on there?"

Lillie took the cue. "It's for my hope chest," Lillie said. "Mother insists."

"Have you sewn many things for your hope chest?" Sarah took note that once again she had little trouble distracting Lillie from a subject she preferred not to discuss.

In all the time Sarah had spent making gowns, it had not occurred to her she ought to work on linens. Now she could see clearly that a woman of Serena Cuthbert's standing would have followed the tradition of embellishing linens for her future home. Sarah was going to have to find time to work on a few pieces so she would be ready when Brad proposed.

"I have a few tablecloths in various sizes," Lillie said, "twelve napkins, three sets of pillowcases, and two sets of towels. Of course, I can't monogram them yet."

"I'm sure you'll know the right initials soon," Sarah said.

Lillie let her project drop in her lap. "Every now and then I wish I could stitch something that mattered. I heard that Lucy Banning Edwards works with the orphans at St. Andrew's. I'd like to do something meaningful like that."

"I thought you had not met Mrs. Edwards—or any of the Bannings."

"I haven't," Lillie responded, "but everyone up and down the Avenue seems to know about her work. I'm eager to meet her."

"Prairie Avenue families contribute to many charities. You could choose any worthy cause for your donation."

Lillie tilted her head. "I suppose so. But Mrs. Edwards inspires me. I want to do more than give a donation. It wouldn't even be my own money, after all. If I could arrange to meet Mrs. Edwards, I could ask if there is anything I would be qualified to do. It might be simplest to just stop in at St. Andrew's, rather than wait for a formal introduction."

"There must be a score of charities you could volunteer for." Sarah's heart rate jumped. If ever there was a time to distract Lillie, this was it. "Jane Addams, for instance, has opened a settlement house."

"Mother would object to that, I'm sure. Don't the workers live in the settlement house?" Lillie resumed stitching. "I can just see Mother getting squeamish about the squalor and fearful that I would catch some dread disease. I confess I have a great deal to learn about their work myself."

"Then the Chicago Orchestra." Sarah forced even breaths as she stood up and casually wandered toward the front window. "The Glessners have been instrumental in organizing the orchestra. Mrs. Glessner might have a suggestion for how you could help. I'm sure your mother will meet her as soon as the Glessners come home from New Hampshire."

"I enjoy going to concerts," Lillie said. "Paul has promised to take me when the orchestra begins their new season. But that's not the sort of thing I'm after. I want to help someone who really needs it."

"You'll want to find something appropriate to your standing," Sarah said. "Fund-raising, then."

"Oh, I don't care about that," Lillie said. "Anyone can raise money. I've never had the opportunity to truly help someone in need, but I think I would like to do it."

"What would your parents think?" Sarah clasped her hands behind her back, her fingers a tight web of nerves.

"Mother might not allow me to volunteer at St. Andrew's, but surely she could not object if I were to sew for the children. Mrs. Edwards might suggest what they need."

Sarah let out her breath and returned to her seat on the settee. "That's a wonderful idea. I'd like to help you!"

"Really, Serena?"

"Yes. We could make dresses for the little girls. And shirts for the boys. I would imagine children in the orphanage wear a lot of castoffs and hand-me-downs. Imagine how delighted a little girl would be to get a new dress!"

"Yes!" Lillie was on her feet now. "Do you know how to make a dress? I've never done anything but linens."

"I'm sure we could figure something out," Sarah said. "I'm certain my dressmaker would draw us a pattern."

"That's perfect!" Lillie put the embroidery down and began to pace. "If I had a pattern to follow, I'm sure I could manage the seams and hems."

"I'm sure you could. We both could. We can both gather some fabrics."

"Mother has a wardrobe full of textiles she never had made up. Father thought she should have given them away in Cincinnati before we moved, but she brought them. She'll let me use them."

"Then we're off to a wonderful start."

Lillie halted her pacing. "But how will we get the dresses to the orphanage? How will we know what sizes to make them? Which girls need them the most?"

Sarah twisted on the settee to look at Lillie. "You handle getting some fabric from your mother. I'll handle contacting St. Andrew's."

"You would do that?" Lillie's eyes widened.

"I'll take care of it," Sarah assured her. "Your social calendar is so full, and with my parents out of the country I have much more freedom."

"I envy you, Serena," Lillie said. "You're full of ideas and not afraid to try anything."

"You're the one who said you wanted to help," Sarah pointed out. "I'm just sorting out the best way to do it."

And the best way to keep Lillie Wagner away from St. Andrew's.

16

$\mathscr{S}$arah checked the tilt of her hat in the mirror on Monday afternoon, then gracefully descended the servants' stairs.

"Where are you off to this time?" Mrs. Fletcher made no effort to disguise her irritation.

Looking at the cook sitting in the chair under the kitchen window, her feet up on a stool, Sarah felt no compunction about going out. The slower pace of work during the family's absence benefited everyone.

"A friend asked me to tea," Sarah said.

"Did you mend the linens?"

"Mended, ironed, and put away."

"You're dressed in rather a fine manner."

"I'm meeting rather a fine friend."

"Just be back in time to serve. Leo will be home for dinner tonight."

Sarah slipped out the female servants' entrance, put her shoulders back and her chin high, and walked elegantly toward Michigan Avenue. Her eyes remained focused on her path, not turning to catch the glances of a scattering of other Prairie Avenue servants outside.

At the Lexington Hotel a few minutes later, Sarah hesitated long enough for the doorman to perform his responsibilities. She had her eye on the chair that she had decided would become her usual place to wait for Brad. From this position, she could easily see out the front of the hotel. However, she had barely settled in when she felt a tap on her shoulder. Sarah turned to see Kenny standing just behind her.

"Hello, Sarah," Kenny said.

"You've mistaken me for someone else."

"Oh, pardon me, Miss *Cuthbert*." Kenny bowed slightly and rolled his eyes. "I had not heard that you had arrived in Chicago."

"Oh, all right," Sarah said. "What do you want, Kenny?"

He held out a silver tray, on which was laid a thick envelope. "This arrived a few minutes ago. The messenger said it was urgent Miss Cuthbert receive it immediately."

Sarah picked up the envelope and quickly ripped open one end.

Kenny chuckled. "Sarah, are you sure you should be reading Miss Cuthbert's mail?"

"I do what Miss Cuthbert asks me to do."

"I know there's no Miss Cuthbert."

"Mind your own business, Kenny." A card unfolded in Sarah's hands, and a small pin slipped into her palm. Still she scowled.

"What's the matter?" Kenny asked.

"He's not coming," Sarah muttered.

"Who is not coming?"

"Oh, never mind, Kenny."

"What fell out of the card?"

Sarah clutched the pin in a closed hand. "You did your job and delivered the message. Thank you. I'm sure they need you back at the desk."

"Sarah, if something—"

"Thank you, Kenny." Sarah gathered her skirts and walked back out to the sidewalk before reading the note again, more carefully.

My dearest Serena,

With deep regret I must inform you that urgent business matters have interfered with our plans for today. I am uncertain when the

issue will be resolved. In the meantime, I hope you will accept this
offering of my attentions.

Kindly yours,
Bradley Townsend

Brad had been so confident about this business deal with Diamond Matches. What could have gone so wrong that he could not take time for a cup of tea to celebrate? Sarah opened her fingers and inspected the pin, a slender silver rose. She had polished enough silver around the Banning house to know this piece was genuine silver through and through.

She would wear it the next time she saw Brad, and she would never forget the first gift from him. Sarah closed her hand around the pin again.

⤜⤚

The next morning, Sarah laid the dining room table for Leo's breakfast and positioned the newspaper to the right of his place setting, where he would reach for it out of habit. She routinely extracted the business section and placed it on top.

There it was. The headline in the business section.

The Chicago Stock Exchange was closed. Indefinitely.

This explained why Brad had broken their date. Sarah scanned the article, recognizing key words. Diamond Matches. Moore brothers. Wealthy investors. She picked up the paper to read more carefully.

As far as she could make out, the article conjectured that W. H. and J. H. Moore had been involved in speculative deals related to the stock of Diamond Matches. The moment had come when they could no longer meet the margin call, and their brokerage firm collapsed. Members of the exchange voted to close down trading out of the belief that an open market would only result in sharp decline in the value of stocks across the board and bring harm to many members of the board of trade. The Moore brothers had risked their own funds as well as money from investors. Both brothers were officers in Diamond Matches. The stock had been trading at extremely high levels, and the brothers were thought to be engaging in short-selling to maximize their profits.

Sarah puzzled over the paper. What was short-selling? Why would it lead to collapse? What did it mean when a firm could not meet the margin call? She did not understand most of it, but she understood that the collapse of this deal would hit the pocket of Bradley Townsend.

When she heard Leo's footsteps progressing across the foyer, Sarah straightened the paper and determined to go back to the Lexington in search of another message from Brad that afternoon. She could put up with Kenny mocking her if only she would hear from Brad.

Sarah heard nothing from Brad on Tuesday. Nothing on Wednesday. Nothing on Thursday. She followed the scandal in the newspaper as best she could. George Pullman and John Doane, both of whom lived in the same block of Prairie Avenue as the Bannings, were expected to become involved in sorting out the failure of the Moore brothers' firm. Both were large lenders on the stock exchange and were expected to underwrite the Diamond Matches stock being held in escrow by the exchange.

Sarah blew out her breath when she read of George Pullman's arrival. No doubt he would find a way to get even richer out of this fiasco. He was not known for his compassion. But what about Brad? Would he survive?

"The girls are excited about starting their skirts," Simon said. He hoped someday he would think of a way to greet Sarah Cummings that would spark her interest, but for now he seemed unable not to utter whatever trivia sprang to his mind. He reached into a desk drawer. "Let me get the key and we'll open the door."

"I wanted to speak to you about a related matter," Sarah said, "before the girls interrupt."

Simon gestured that she should sit opposite his desk. If Sarah Cummings wanted to speak to him rather than find the fastest way out of the room, he would certainly give his attention. "What can I help you with?"

"It's more how I can help you," Sarah replied. "I have a friend interested in sewing some clothes for a few of the children."

"If she's half as talented as you are, it will be a wonderful gift."

"Actually, we'll be working together. I don't have a lot of time of course, with my duties for the Bannings, but my friend has more time. Obviously we can't help all of the children, so we wonder where the greatest need is."

Simon nodded. This was a side of Sarah he had always hoped to see more of. The wall around her began to come down the day she agreed to teach a class. Perhaps being back at the orphanage had kindled hidden compassion. He refused to believe she was as thoughtless as she often seemed. "The older girls are learning for themselves, thanks to you," he said. "The littlest girls outgrow things before the clothes wear out."

"Then the girls in between need new things," Sarah said. "That makes sense."

The way she tilted her head. The gesture she made with her hand as she spoke. The smoothness of her voice. The sheen of her hair. How could she not know how appealing she was? And now—to see her willing to use her time and skill to help other girls. Simon had hoped the sewing class would penetrate the fortress around Sarah's heart, but this was more—and sooner—than he had expected.

"Will you draw the patterns yourself?" Simon found his lapsed composure.

"Something simple." Sarah smoothed her skirt. "My friend will want it to be pretty, but I realize it must also be sturdy."

"Do you need anything from me?" Simon asked.

"I'll bring the clothes here as we finish them." Sarah crossed her ankles and held her hands together in her lap. "We would be most appreciative if you could be sure they go to the girls who need them most."

"Of course." Simon leaned forward in his desk chair. "Thank you for your generosity, and I hope to be able to express my gratitude to your friend as well."

"And she would love to meet you. However, her schedule is complicated, so that may not be possible. That's one of the reasons I offered to be in touch with you about the project."

"Then perhaps at some point in the future." Simon took a breath, deciding whether to proceed. "As long as you're here, Sarah, I wonder if I might ask you something as well."

"What is it?"

"A kind donor has given us a batch of tickets for the Chicago Colts game next Wednesday. I need help chaperoning a couple dozen children. I would love to have you come with us."

"To a base ball game?"

"Have you ever been to a base ball game?"

"No, never."

She was thinking about it, Simon could see. He said, "Here's your first chance! It will be an adventure."

"I've never been a chaperone before, either," Sarah pointed out.

"Another first. You just have to keep an eye on them and use your good sense. Please come. You did mention that Wednesday was your day off."

At last she nodded, and Simon breathed relief.

"Perhaps we'll have the opportunity to chat a bit," he said. "I would welcome the chance to get to know you better."

Her face seemed to change color. Simon swallowed hard.

Jane missed the sewing class.

Normally she was one of the most enthusiastic students, so Sarah found it odd that she was not there and none of the other girls seemed to know why. As the girls took turns selecting fabric and finding matching threads in the basket, Sarah's thoughts were on Jane. Sarah managed to slide the green crepe to the back of the cupboard, knowing that if Jane were there she would select that length of fabric. Sarah had drawn a pattern for a loose-fitting skirt that would suit all the girls. All they had to do was gather the top edge under a waistband cut to their own measurement. The girls chattered while they took turns laying their fabric on the table, smoothing the pattern on top of it, and cutting out the pieces of their skirts. The more Sarah watched them, the more she thought it peculiar that Jane would miss class. Of all the girls, Jane had been the most eager to sew her first garment.

They would begin sewing next week, Sarah assured the girls. When everything was put away securely and the room empty, she pulled the door locked behind her.

Sarah hesitated. She ought to walk out the front door and mind her own business. Jane was old enough to decide if she wanted to come to a sewing class. Why should it matter to Sarah?

Then she remembered. She remembered what it felt like to have two parents one moment and none the next. She remembered the intense little girl Jane had always been.

She walked down the hall, away from the front door, to the foot of the back stairs. From what Jane had described in the last few weeks, Sarah was fairly certain where the girl's bed was. It was next to impossible to find a private moment at St. Andrew's. Sarah had not been the only girl to retreat to her bed and pull the covers up over her head in search of solitude.

But would Jane do that now, when she loved the class so much?

Sarah began to climb the stairs and continued to the fourth floor. A smattering of children scampered past her going up or down but seemed not to find her presence of concern. Sarah did not see a single member of the staff as she stepped softly down the hall to the room where the fourteen-year-old girls had always slept.

There she was, on the third bed from the window. Sarah had occupied that spot herself before she captured the coveted corner under the window. Jane did have the covers pulled up over her face, but enough of her hair hung out that Sarah was sure it was Jane. Sarah let her weight sink into the end of the thin mattress and waited for Jane to respond to her presence.

The blanket came down soon and Jane bolted up. "Sarah! What are you doing here?"

"I missed you," Sarah answered. "We cut out our skirts today."

"I'm sorry I couldn't come." Jane's voice was barely audible.

She had been crying. That was clear. Sarah did not allow herself tears, and she did not know what to do for Jane's.

"I saved the green crepe for you." Sarah said the only thing she thought might make Jane happy.

"Thank you." Jane wiped one eye with the back of her hand.

"Jane, what's wrong?" Sarah reached over and put a tentative hand on the knob she supposed was Jane's knee under the blanket. "You can tell me."

Jane's dark eyes met Sarah's, and the girl seemed to make several attempts to speak. Finally sobbing overwhelmed her.

Sarah scooted up on the bed and put her arms around Jane—hardly believing her own actions. How long had it been since anyone had done that for her? Years.

"I lost it," Jane finally mumbled.

"Lost what?"

"My . . . book."

"I'll help you look," Sarah offered. "It can't have gone far. What's it called?"

"I've looked everywhere!" Jane wailed. "It has been gone for more than a week. Someone took it."

Sarah chewed on a lip. Petty thievery was endemic to orphanage life. As soon as you had a morsel of happiness to call your own, it was gone. Sarah once built up her collection of hair ribbons to five different colors, and one afternoon they disappeared. Her fury had done nothing to turn them up.

"I'm sorry about your book." Sarah resolved at that moment to have the girls in her class mark the insides of their new waistbands with their names so there could be no question. Sarah smoothed Jane's dark hair, a nervous pulse she had not expected running through her as she did so.

Jane pulled away. "I just want to sleep now."

Sarah had left the girl with the blanket over her face once again. Whether she was actually sleeping, Sarah could not say.

She hopped off the streetcar in front of the Lexington, and only then was she able to push Jane out of her mind. A carriage down the block stopped, and the driver lowered himself from his bench to the sidewalk.

That's Brad's driver! Sarah stopped her mindless forward progress and tilted her hat down to hide her face. She never wore her maid's uniform to St. Andrew's, but she certainly did not put on her finest clothes. Turning her back to the carriage, Sarah reached to lower the brim of her hat even farther. The driver went inside the hotel but returned a moment later, hoisted himself up in the driver's seat, and nudged the horse away from the curb.

Sarah waited until he was two blocks away before she entered the lobby and went directly to the desk.

"Good morning, Miss Cummings," Kenny said, "or should I say Miss Cuthbert?"

"Knock it off, Kenny," Sarah said.

"You've been in here every day this week."

"You must have a note for me."

He had it in his hand and now waved it in the air. "Haven't even had a chance to put it away yet. You're not stalking the driver, are you?"

Sarah snatched the envelope from Kenny and moved to a secluded seat before tearing it open.

My dear Serena,

How rude of me to break our date on Monday and keep you waiting. I'm afraid my business concerns have been particularly demanding this week, and it may be some time before matters are resolved. Can you meet me next Wednesday at six o'clock? I'll explain in more detail at that time.

Yours,
Bradley Townsend

In a postscript, he named a restaurant. Sarah knew where it was but had never been inside.

She had promised Simon she would go with him to the base ball game that afternoon—primarily because the experience might prove useful in discussing the sport with Brad at a later opportunity. How long did a base ball game last, she wondered. She had to get Karl to sit down and explain this game and make sure it would finish in time to dress for the evening.

17

$\mathcal{S}$arah followed Simon into the row of bleacher seats along the right field line.

"If we sit here," he said, gesturing to her spot, "we have all the children either next to us or in front of us where we can keep an eye on them."

"Why can't we sit behind home plate?" one of the boys moaned.

"Our tickets don't allow that, Alonzo," Simon said calmly. "Remember how we discussed being grateful for the generous gift and the privilege of coming today?"

Alonzo crossed his arms on his chest in a pout, but he sat down in the row in front of Sarah and Simon.

Sarah shaded her eyes and peered across the playing field. Uncovered bleachers extended along both foul lines and along the outfield. The right field bleachers were less than ten rows deep to accommodate the billboard and the scoreboard on the extreme right. Beyond the outfield, brick apartment buildings hemmed in West Side Park.

Following her gaze, Simon commented, "Just wait a few minutes. The roofs of those buildings will be full of people watching the game."

"That's a lucky location," Sarah said. "Do you go to many games?"

Simon shook his head. "No, hardly ever. None of these children have ever been before. They worked hard to earn the privilege of coming—even if Alonzo is complaining."

"I confess I don't really follow the game," Sarah said. Leo did. Every morning after he finished with the business section, he turned to the sports, but Sarah had never paid much attention to his random comments about pitchers and third basemen with strong arms. From Karl she had learned the names of the positions players occupied on the field, but most of the rules had gone in one ear and out the other.

"A month ago, an outfielder from the Phillies knocked four in-the-park home runs in one game," Simon said. "Wish I could have seen that one!"

"That sounds exciting."

"I'm sure it was. But today's game should be a good contest as well."

"Will the Colts win?"

Simon tilted his head. "After four losing seasons in a row, the Colts are finally on a winning streak, but Cincinnati is still ahead of them in the standings." Simon leaned forward and poked a finger into the shoulder of a boy. "Keep your hands to yourself, Frank."

She scanned the bleachers in both directions, hoping that Brad had not decided to take in a ball game to distract himself from his troubles.

~~~

Simon thought Sarah Cummings looked stunning in a sporting navy-blue suit and a coordinating mannish-style hat. But mannish was the last thing she was.

"Even if you've never played," Simon said, "you'll pick up the rules of the game quickly."

"I'm sure the boys will be eager to explain if I miss something."

She was smiling, and it seemed genuine. Simon cleared his throat softly. "Base ball is good for what ails you. Democrats and

Republicans may not agree on the gold standard, but they agree on base ball. And Diamond Matches may have sunk the Chicago Stock Exchange, but a few good strikeouts can make anyone forget all about it."

"It sounds as if you keep up on current events," Sarah said.

"Don't you?" Simon asked.

She looked flustered. "No one calls for the opinion of a woman."

"You must have one nevertheless."

"I can't vote," Sarah said. "I don't think too much about politics."

"Someday you'll vote," Simon said. "The suffragettes are right. Why should women not have all the rights of citizenship?"

Her eyes widened. "Is that your true opinion?"

He nodded. "Of course. I do not hold to the prevailing judgment that women are somehow less able than men to comprehend challenging subjects. Consider Lucy Edwards. She's determined to have a university degree. She's not afraid to take on challenges, and she certainly has strong views."

"She is a Banning. No one cares what a parlor maid thinks," Sarah said softly.

"I do." His gentle response was staunch. "A maid is not everything you are."

Her brown eyes met his gaze fully, perhaps for the first time ever.

Sarah realized that she'd seldom truly looked at Simon Tewell. He was shorter than Brad and his coloring bland, but he was not unattractive. His roundish face was gentle, his pale green eyes welcoming, and he seemed quite earnest in his opinions about the virtues of a woman's mind.

Sarah broke the gaze and looked down at the playing field again. Though kind and thoughtful, Simon Tewell had nothing to offer her. What would be the point of having an opinion and no money? She was only at the game with Simon so she could learn enough not to sound like an idiot if Brad should invite her to another game before the end of the season. Distracting thoughts of what it might be like to go to dinner with Simon Tewell had no place in her plan.

When the skirts were finished, she could stop going to St. Andrew's.

"It looks like they're ready for the first pitch," Simon said.

The children cheered.

~

Would the constant calling cease if she became engaged to Paul Gunnison? Lillie hoped so. On the other hand, an engagement would only spur her mother on. With a list of three calls still to make, Lillie was reaching her social threshold for the day. Her mother was supposed to be with her but had claimed a headache at the last minute and left the task to Lillie. As they became more settled in their home, more and more people had stopped in to welcome the Wagners to Chicago, and the visits had to be reciprocated.

There was that sign again. "St. Andrew's Orphanage." This time curiosity got the best of Lillie, and she signaled the driver to stop. At first she intended only to study the building, but her hand had a mind of its own and reached for the handle on the inside of the carriage door. Sensing her wish, the driver jumped down and held the door open for her. Lillie crossed the street and stood on the walk leading toward the orphanage's red door. And then she was walking toward the door. Knocking on the door. Stepping through the doorway.

"My name is Jane," the girl said. "Mr. Tewell is not here, but I can take a message."

"Mr. Tewell?"

"The director, miss," Jane said. "Aren't you here to see him?"

Lillie was not sure what she was there for, but she could hardly say that to Jane.

"Actually," Lillie said, "I'm interested in exploring how I might help here at St. Andrew's. Is there someone else I might speak to about volunteering?"

"You'll want Mrs. Edwards, miss."

Lucy Banning Edwards. Lillie relaxed. "Yes, I suppose I do. Is Mrs. Edwards here just now?"

Jane nodded. "Follow me. I'll see if she can receive you. Whom shall I say is calling?"

"Miss Lillie Wagner of Prairie Avenue."

Lillie followed the girl's stooped shoulders down the hall that led to the orphanage's offices and lingered discreetly in the hall while Jane inquired on her behalf.

"Show her in, please, Jane." Mrs. Edwards's voice came from an inner office. By the time Lillie entered the room, Lucy Edwards had stood up to greet her.

"Thank you for seeing me without an appointment." Lillie extended a gloved hand for Lucy to shake. "I'm afraid I'm here on a whim because I was passing by, but I have thought of stopping in for some time now."

"We're always happy to have visitors." Lucy waved her hand toward a wooden chair and sat behind her desk. "We're especially grateful if they want to help."

"Oh, I do want to help. I just haven't known how to go about it," Lillie said. "I've begun gathering some textiles. A friend and I thought we might sew some clothes. Dresses. For the girls."

"We always need clothing," Lucy said. "Even when the older children leave, we want to provide something to send with them."

"Sewing a few dresses is not much," Lillie said, "but it's a start. Perhaps I'll be suited to do something more later on."

"Sewing is important both for the clothes, but also for girls to learn skills," Lucy said. "In fact, we've recently begun offering a class to teach a few of the older girls. We have a talented seamstress working with them, but I'm sure she could always use an extra pair of hands in the class."

A knock on the door interrupted them. Lucy's face lit up and she was on her feet again. She stepped across the room and took an infant from a young woman's arms. Two young boys pushed their way past the woman's skirts.

"This is my daughter, Stella," Lucy explained, "and my son, Ben. This angel of mercy is Charlotte Shepard and her son, Henry."

"I'm pleased to meet you all," Lillie said. "I'm Lillie Wagner."

"No, Henry, leave the papers alone." Charlotte nudged her son's shoulder, then turned to Lillie and smiled. "He likes to touch everything."

The young woman clearly was a maid, but Lillie sensed an unusual degree of equality between Lucy and Charlotte.

"I would be lost without Charlotte," Lucy explained. "Her work in caring for my family makes my work possible."

"I'm a little early," Charlotte said. "I could keep the children in the hall if you like."

Lucy shook her head. "Thank you, no. Will should be here any minute to take us all home."

"Then if you don't mind, I'll go," Charlotte said. "I don't want to miss the streetcar. Archie will be home soon."

"I should go as well." Lillie stood up. "I have several calls still to make today, and I don't want to hold you up."

"I hope you will stop in again, Miss Wagner," Lucy said. "I'm sure we can find a way for you to fit in at St. Andrew's. Let's both think about it, shall we?"

—◦◦◦—

Four boys were in a tussle at the end of the row in front of Sarah, and Simon had taken three others for a stroll down the baseline. The boys giggled conspiratorially, and Sarah knew the situation could not wait for Simon's return. After all, this was why he had asked her to come—though she suspected he had ulterior motives as well. She pressed her lips together and tried to recall the names of the boys, who were getting more aggressive by the second.

"Boys!" she said, standing and pressing toward them. "What are you fighting about?"

"Nothing," came the unanimous answer—too quickly.

One boy shoved his hands behind his back. Sarah remembered him from her days at St. Andrew's. Michael O'Brien. He had been boisterous from the first day he entered the orphanage as a toddler.

"What do you have behind your back, Michael?" Sarah asked.

"Nothing."

"Somehow I don't believe you." Sarah put out her hand. "Let me have it."

The other three boys fell away from Michael, leaving him little option but to surrender.

A book. Brown with a red stripe down the cover. Sarah flipped it open. Handwritten pages. A journal.

Jane's lost book.

A player cracked a bat against a ball, and the heads of all the boys cranked to follow the spinning white arc.

18

*S*arah surveyed the parlor. If she didn't pay strict attention, she would see only the collection of picture frames, vases, and small statues. None of that really mattered. What was important for the parlor maid to see were the deposits of dust and incipient spider webs. Sarah systematically had pulled her feather duster through the niches and ridges in the room and now hoped she had not missed even one. If she had, Mrs. Banning would be sure to spot it as soon as she entered the room.

"Aren't you finished in here yet?" Mrs. Fletcher's voice came from the foyer. "This table needs polishing."

"I'll just go get the tin of vegetable soap." Sarah was too tired to protest the accusing tone the cook's words carried. She had been up half the night as it was. Between the base ball game with Simon and the restaurant with Brad, Sarah had spent precious little time at home on Wednesday, even though she knew the Bannings were due to arrive on Thursday. She had reasoned Wednesday was her designated day off, so Mrs. Fletcher could not forbid her to go out. But it was true enough that she had left tasks from earlier in the week to the last minute. She had not gotten home from seeing Brad until nearly eleven in the evening, and she had put in several hours of work before finally going to bed well after three in the morning.

Sarah walked through the dining room and the butler's pantry to the kitchen, where she rummaged around in a cabinet until she came up with the tin of vegetable soap and a clean cotton rag. The rich, round mahogany table in the foyer had to gleam from every angle, or the butler, Mr. Penard, would make her polish it again. Sarah had not missed Penard these last seven weeks. She had grown to tolerate him during the previous three years, because most of the time his threats amounted to little consequence, but the routine was so much easier when he was not there to inspect and criticize at every opportunity.

Life would be more complicated with the family back—that much was certain. Serena Cuthbert would have to make some adjustments.

Rubbing oil into the table in the foyer, Sarah went over the restaurant conversation from the night before. In his note, Brad had promised to explain more, but he hadn't, not really. He said only that the stock exchange might be closed for some time. The Moore brothers were cooperating with turning over their records for investigation, but the directors of the exchange expected it would take time to sort matters out and they did not intend to be giving public updates. After all, the exchange was a voluntary association of brokers. They did not owe explanations to anyone. Brad had heard some talk of remaining closed until after the presidential election so that the markets would not be subject to the speculation of how either candidate would affect trading.

However, Brad had said all this in a passing manner as if he did not expect Sarah to understand, and he revealed nothing about how the matter affected him personally. She knew he had funds tied up in Diamond Matches stock. How much of his fortune had he risked? Would his holdings be worth anything at all after the election?

The questions that trundled through her mind reminded her of Simon. It was true she did not understand the inner workings of the stock market, or the implications of adopting a silver standard for currency, or why it mattered whom the men of the country elected president. But at least Simon believed her gender was not the reason she did not understand—nor even her status as a domestic.

Sarah scooped out more oil and rubbed harder. The restaurant itself had been exquisite, a setting Sarah could not dream of revisiting except with a man like Bradley Townsend. If she had any hope of bringing an end to her table-polishing days, she had to focus on Brad. Or rather, Serena Cuthbert had to focus on Brad.

Sarah was laying the table for a late lunch—the family was expected home around two—when she heard the commotion in the kitchen.

Penard.

Sarah used a dish towel to rub a smudge off a silver spoon, then slung the towel over her shoulder. As much as she did not want to make one, an appearance in the kitchen was mandatory. She ducked into one corner and stood quietly watching the entourage divest themselves of traveling capes and baskets. Along with Penard, the carriage had carried home Elsie, the ladies' maid; Mary Catherine, the kitchen maid; and Willard, the footman who also had served as driver for the journey. All of them were in the kitchen now, clamoring for refreshment and competing to tell stories of the weeks at the lake. Karl sauntered in and took up a position beside Sarah, leaning against the wall.

"So much for peace and quiet," Karl muttered.

"We knew it would happen." Sarah puffed her cheeks and blew out a breath.

"I suppose this will bring an end to your fancy gallivanting."

"You're jealous that I have something to do with my time off."

Karl shook his head. "You're going to have a lot less time off now."

Mr. Penard clapped his hands sharply and the room silenced. "Harry will be only two hours behind us with the family," he said. "We must be ready. Unload your personal things and put them away promptly. I will inspect the house and be sure everything is in order."

"We're ready." Mrs. Fletcher jabbed a finger at the butler.

"It's prudent to be sure," Penard responded. "Mary Catherine, find out what Mrs. Fletcher needs you to do for luncheon. Karl and Willard, make sure the horses are properly cooled. Elsie, lay out a change of clothing for Mrs. Banning. She will want to refresh herself before the meal. Sarah, come with me to be sure everything is as it should be."

"Why does he think he needs to tell us our jobs?" Karl murmured so that only Sarah could hear.

"Makes him feel important," she muttered in return.

Mr. Penard clapped his hands again. "The Bannings have a full social calendar beginning immediately, and there is much to do to send off Mr. Richard to Princeton. I expect the household to resume normal disciplines immediately. Is that clear?"

The staff mumbled responses.

"Two hours, people," Mr. Penard said. "Dismissed!"

⁓ↄ⌇ↄ⌇⁓

Two hours and twelve minutes later, the largest of the Banning carriages clattered to a stop in front of the house on Prairie Avenue. Sarah watched out the dining room window, standing at the edge of the claret velvet curtains under blue swags, as Harry held open the door and offered his hand to Flora Banning. Flora emerged wearing an orange shade from head to toe.

It was a hideous color, Sarah thought. If Flora ever tried to give her that dress, Sarah would burn it.

Behind Flora came Richard Banning. Was it possible he had grown even more in the last seven weeks? At eighteen, Richard threatened to be the tallest of the three Banning brothers, already easily half a head taller than his father. Richard wore a pale blue seersucker suit and a straw boating hat. Politely, he offered his arm to his mother to escort her up the walk to the front door. Samuel Banning trailed a few steps behind them in his chronic black suit, ever the lawyer.

As the trio progressed up the walk, Sarah stepped away from the window and took up her position in the foyer, ready for whatever request might arrive with the Bannings. Mr. Penard opened the front door so the family could enter without breaking stride.

"Thank you, Penard," Flora Banning said. "Hello, Sarah. We'd like some refreshment in the parlor. And make sure Elsie knows I'm home. I shall require her as soon as I've had a cold drink."

"Yes, ma'am." Sarah curtseyed, a gesture that grated every time she supplied it.

"I think I'll go straight to my room," Richard said. "You can bring me a tray."

"Yes, sir," Sarah answered.

Mr. Penard caught her eye and nodded his head almost imperceptibly, discharging her to fulfill the requests.

In the kitchen, Mrs. Fletcher had a pitcher of lemonade ready and was arranging pastries on a plate. Sarah rolled the tea cart from the corner where it was parked and transferred the refreshments from the counter to the tray atop the cart. On the shelf below, she arranged goblets and small china plates.

"Mr. Richard asked for a tray in his room," Sarah said.

"I'll send Mary Catherine up," Mrs. Fletcher said. "Go on with the cart."

As Sarah rolled the cart through the dining room and across the foyer, she heard the sounds of another carriage. Penard turned his head toward the sound as well and looked out the narrow window alongside the front door.

"It's Miss Lucy," he announced. "You'll need more dishes." He pulled the front door open again.

Sarah returned to the kitchen, added a plate and glass for Lucy, and a child's tin cup for Benny—the same cup they always used when Benny visited the Bannings.

By the time Sarah reached the parlor, Lucy was settled on the settee with Stella on her lap and Ben beside her. Samuel and Flora had taken their favorite side chairs. Sarah rolled the tea cart in and began pouring lemonade.

"Hello, Sarah," Lucy said. "I hear wonderful things about your class."

"Thank you, ma'am." Sarah felt Penard's eyes on her, but as long as a family member had addressed her, she was permitted—even obliged—to respond.

"Class?" Flora queried. Sarah handed her a glass of lemonade and a pastry on a plate.

"While you were gone, Sarah began teaching a sewing class to some of the girls at St. Andrew's." Lucy straightened her daughter's white cotton dress. "She's doing a wonderful job. I promised Simon I would prevail on you to allow her to continue."

Flora Banning looked from daughter to maid before setting her refreshments on the side table. "Why do I have the feeling the matter is settled already?"

Lucy laughed.

"May I have some lemonade?" Benny asked.

"Wait your turn, Ben," Lucy said. "Sarah is pouring as fast as she can."

Sarah handed a glass to Samuel Banning.

"Seriously, Mother," Lucy said, removing the baby's bonnet, "I hope you'll let Sarah keep up with the class. It meets on Friday afternoons."

Flora pressed her lips together with an inconsequential huff, then said, "I suppose we can see that it does not interfere with the household routine."

Sarah served Lucy and made sure Benny had a good grip on his cup before she released hers. Did she not get a vote in this decision, either? No one seemed to consider that she might not wish to keep up with the class.

After offering everyone refreshment, Sarah left the cart in the parlor. Penard was there to pour if anyone wanted another glass. When she pushed through the door to the kitchen, she was surprised to see Charlotte Shepard sitting at the kitchen table with Mrs. Fletcher. Henry looked small in the chair next to her. Clearly bored, he rested his chin in his arms on the table.

"Hello, Sarah," Charlotte said. "We dropped in with Miss Lucy and I thought I'd chat with Mrs. Fletcher while I waited."

Sarah only nodded, refusing to say something welcoming when she did not mean it.

"Charlotte just told me something interesting," Mrs. Fletcher said. "She mentioned a new Prairie Avenue neighbor came by the orphanage yesterday."

Sarah perked up. "Oh?"

"A Miss Lillie Wagner," Charlotte said.

"I've heard mention of them around the neighborhood," Sarah said cautiously. "I believe they are down on lower Prairie Avenue."

"Miss Wagner wants to help at the orphanage," Charlotte said.

Sarah's heart nearly stopped, but her conversation did not miss a beat. "I suppose Mrs. Edwards will find something for her to do, then."

"She's interested in sewing," Charlotte said. "Lucy told her about your class. Wouldn't it be nice to have someone to help you?"

"That is not necessary." Sarah picked up a dish towel and flipped it over one shoulder.

"They haven't made any final arrangements yet," Charlotte said. "It was just something Lucy mentioned to Miss Wagner."

"I have the class well in hand." Sarah absently opened the icebox and peered in. "Is everything ready for lunch?"

"Lunch is something I have well in hand." Mrs. Fletcher scraped her chair back and rose. "Is the table laid?"

"I was not sure which napkins Mr. Penard would want."

"I'm sure white linen will be fine. Finish the table, Sarah."

"There's time," Sarah answered. "Mrs. Banning will want to change before she comes to the table."

"I'm thirsty." Henry lifted his head off the table.

"There's more lemonade in the icebox." Mrs. Fletcher gestured with her head as she picked up a bread knife and began slicing a loaf baked that morning.

Charlotte stood up and moved to a cupboard.

"I just gave Ben the only tin cup," Sarah said.

Charlotte extracted a squat blue glass. "Henry will have to be careful, then."

"Perhaps you'd better see if they're ready for you to clear the parlor," Mrs. Fletcher suggested.

"Yes, that's a good idea." Sarah was glad for the excuse to push out of the kitchen and pause in the solitude of the butler's pantry.

Lillie at St. Andrew's. Sarah had to make sure that did not happen again. Ever.

19

*B*ut it's my half-day off," Sarah protested.

"The family has just come home," Mr. Penard replied. "The routine of the household has resumed."

Sarah stood in the kitchen, dressed in a skirt and blouse and holding her tapestry valise. The day was scheduled to be an every other Sunday half-day off for her. She had served lunch to the Bannings after church and tidied the parlor, and she saw no reason why she should not have her time off.

"I am scheduled for a half-day off," Sarah repeated, "and I made plans."

Penard eyed the valise. "Why do you require a bag?"

Sarah stared him down. It was none of his business.

"All right." The butler relented. "But we expect you back by nine."

"I'll be here." Sarah scooted into the hall and out the female servants' entrance before Penard could think of another reason to delay her.

Her ultimate destination lay ten blocks to the south, but Sarah headed west to Michigan Avenue and turned north for a few blocks. Outside the Illinois Central's Twelfth Street Station, she paused to catch her breath. All day long, every day, trains thundered in and out of the enormous train shed, taking people far away and bringing them home again. Sarah had never been on a train that went anywhere but another Chicago neighborhood. But someday. For the moment, the train station was the easiest place to find a room where women could refresh themselves. She needed only a few minutes to change her blouse, add a wide belt to the top of the skirt, arrange her hair in a less taut manner, and put on a hat sure to impress Lillie Wagner. The ordinary blouse and hat soon were scrunched at the bottom of the bag beneath assorted lengths of fabric Sarah judged to be sufficient for girls' dresses.

Southbound streetcars were abundant outside the station.

"Thank you, Mrs. Davis."

Simon took the scratched tray and set it on the table. His quarters—a bedroom and a shadowy sitting room at the rear of the first floor of St. Andrew's—were modest, even lacking, but he never thought to complain. He enjoyed his privacy when he needed it, and Mrs. Davis not only oversaw the housekeeping regimen of the entire orphanage, but also she kept his rooms tidy and made sure he ate. She had been with St. Andrew's since the day the doors opened.

"Don't you have something better to do than hide out in your rooms on a Sunday afternoon?" Mrs. Davis pushed the drapes open wider.

Simon glanced at his head housekeeper, reached for a sugar cube, and dropped it in the coffee she had brought him. "I have matters on my mind."

"Some fresh air would do you good."

"I think better in here. Thank you for the coffee."

"Just ring if you need something before supper."

When she had gone, Simon smoothed the page against the scarred table and read the letter again. Dozens of orphanages cared for thousands of children in Chicago, but the difficult economic times had taken their toll. An orphanage on the city's far south side was forced to close its doors. Charitable contributions simply were not keeping up with expenses, and if the institution tried to stay open more than another few weeks, the children would be reduced to squalor. The director had surrendered to the inevitable and now was trying to find placements for the orphans. The letter asked Simon to take in an additional forty-eight children.

Simon did not see how he could. Every bed in St. Andrew's was full, and he barely had floor space for the beds he had. Contributions swung up and down, giving the orphanage good months and bad months. Feeding and clothing another four dozen children would stretch his budget past the point of ever hoping it would balance. Out of habit, Simon turned and looked out his window. He lived on the ground floor, and so did Mrs. Davis and the handful of other staff who did not leave every day for their own homes. But the children were all housed on upper floors, and only one side of the building had fire escapes. The first floor had been electrified, but gas lines still ran through the rest of the building. The thought of what could happen in a fire already terrified him. Extra children crowding the rooms would magnify a horrific scenario.

Then there was the other letter. Simon reached into his coat pocket and pulled it out. He had been carrying it around for more than two weeks. When he came to Chicago, his intention was to return to Philadelphia eventually, but after settling into the director's job at St. Andrew's he thought about his home city with decreasing frequency. Now he had an offer of employment—with a firm whose purpose was to make money. Simon had not been looking for a new job. When a college friend contacted him, he thought it must have been a mistake and very nearly wrote to decline immediately.

Then he began to think. Such a position might change the way Sarah Cummings looked at him. He was no fool. He knew she wanted to shed her past, and he was part of the past. But if he could take her out of Chicago, she might have a fresh perspective. She might be willing to take a chance on Philadelphia. And him.

His coffee went cold.

"But it's Sunday afternoon," Edith Wagner remarked. "You girls should be receiving callers or visiting in the parlor."

"Mother," Lillie said, "it's already been decided. Serena and I are going to start on the dresses today."

"What if Mr. Gunnison calls for you?"

Warmth oozed over Lillie's face. "We're just going upstairs to the guest suite, not across an ocean to Europe."

"It doesn't seem like a proper Sabbath observance."

"We're trying to take care of orphans," Lillie said. "If that is not God's work, then I don't know what is." She turned to her friend. "Come on, Serena. I have everything set up."

Lillie led the way up to the second floor and down the wide hall to a spacious suite. The furniture had been pushed to the walls to make room for a long narrow table.

"Will this work?" Lillie asked.

Her guest nodded, set her bag on one end of the table, then paced around it. "It looks perfect for cutting. I brought a few lengths of fabric."

"I have some too," Lillie said brightly. "Mother said I could use whatever I liked." She strode to a chair at the end of the room where the fabric was folded and stacked.

"I made a simple pattern." Serena pulled sheets of thin paper from her bag. "Just a round neckline, and the dress falls loosely from there. We should be able to adjust for several sizes without too much trouble. The girls can always add a belt or a ribbon around the waist."

"I can't wait to get started. Let's see what you brought." Lillie reached into her friend's bag with both hands and pulled out a pile of fabric. From within the folds, a book shook loose and tumbled to the floor. Reflexively, Lillie stooped to pick it up. "What's this?" She turned the brown leather book with a red stripe on the cover in her hands. "There's no title."

"Oh, I didn't realize that was in the bag." Serena reached for the book.

Instead of surrendering it, Lillie opened the book and rifled through a few pages. "It's a journal!"

"It must have been caught up in the fabric my dressmaker gave me." Serena pressed a piece of a pattern flat on the table. "Just drop it back in the bag. I'll make sure to return it."

"Remind me to get your dressmaker's name before you leave today," Lillie muttered as she settled on a page to read. "This looks like a girl's diary."

"Perhaps we should just put it away."

But Lillie was caught up in what she was reading. "Listen to this. 'Today was my birthday and Mother arranged the most spectacular party with a Japanese theme. No expense was spared. The music, the food, and the costumes were authentic in every detail. It was one of the happiest days of my life.'"

Serena took two lengths of fabric from Lillie's pile. "Which material would you like to start with?"

How her friend could be so disinterested in the journal baffled Lillie. "Serena, does your dressmaker have a daughter?"

"I don't believe so. The diary must belong to someone else. A client's daughter, perhaps. I'll take care of returning it."

Lillie turned away slightly, keeping the book out of her friend's reach. She scanned and flipped several pages. "Here's something more. 'I'm so lucky my family never has to worry about anything. Today Mother let me choose the menu and said Cook would go out and buy anything I wanted. I asked for scallops and artichoke.'" Lillie turned a few more pages. "'I'll go to my first ball soon. Father's friends from New York will be visiting, and he's giving a party in their honor.' Serena, the pages are full of descriptions like this."

"Obviously the girl leads a busy life. I brought some extra scissors. I wasn't sure what you had."

Lillie still turned pages. "This is not realistic. It doesn't sound like someone's actual life."

"Everyone likes to dream."

Lillie looked up at last. "Every entry is about wonderful parties and trips and exotic food. There's never a sad thought. Even a girl of privilege would know life is not trouble-free."

"It's harmless imagination." Serena held out her hand. "Let's just put it away and get on with the dresses."

Lillie finally surrendered the book to her friend's grasp. "I'm sure whoever wrote it thought it was private. I shouldn't have read it. You're right. Let's get to work."

———— ❧ ————

Sarah had not read any of Jane's diary. The girl had missed Friday's sewing class for the second time, and Sarah had not had time to go hunting for her to return the book. Now she realized what the boys at the ball game were smirking about. Jane was devastated at losing what was probably her only personal belonging, and no doubt she was horrified to think someone had read it. Haunted by the excerpts Lillie had voiced, Sarah tucked the book in the bottom of her bag. She would have to find Jane. What she would say, she had no idea, but at least she could give Jane the book.

"You'll have to tell me what to do," Lillie said. "I've never cut out a dress before."

"It's simple enough," Sarah said. "Just lay the pattern along the grain on top of the fabric and cut around the edges."

"Where did you learn so much about making dresses?"

"My mother always thought I should understand where things come from, including dresses." Sarah spoke the truth. Her mother had sewn her girlhood dresses not because she had to but because she loved to. Sarah unfolded blue calico fabric.

"I stopped by St. Andrew's this week," Lillie said, watching carefully what Sarah was doing.

Sarah smoothed the fabric, turning her face away from Lillie. "Oh? What prompted you to do that? I thought we were going to make some dresses first."

"I know. I just couldn't wait. I was passing by between calls, and curiosity got the best of me. The director was not there, but I was able to meet Mrs. Edwards."

"Oh?" Sarah pressed a pattern across the calico fabric. "And what is your impression?"

"I admire her. She seems to have taken things in hand. She even has an office of her own."

"Yes, I've heard that."

"She mentioned that a woman comes in and gives a sewing class. She thought I might like to help with that."

"Would you like to try cutting?" Sarah handed scissors to Lillie.

Lillie took the scissors, but they hung limply from her fingers. "I know many of the Prairie Avenue families donate to St. Andrew's, but I think I'd like to get involved in a more personal way. Mrs. Edwards's example is inspiring."

"We shouldn't make a nuisance of ourselves," Sarah said. "People do that, you know. They say they want to help, but in the end they cause more work for the director because he has to organize something they actually can do for an hour or two a week instead of things that really need to be done every day."

"I hadn't thought of it that way," Lillie said. "I didn't get that sense from Mrs. Edwards."

"Of course not. They are not in the habit of discouraging people of means. I spoke to the director, after all, so he knows we want to help. I do think it would be better to wait until we have some dresses made."

"Well, all right," Lillie conceded, "but I am going to sew for a while every day. I don't want to just talk about helping. I want to *do* something."

Sarah asked Lillie about Paul Gunnison, what Lillie's favorite part of Chicago was, what she missed about Cincinnati, her most treasured memories—anything to turn the conversation away from St. Andrew's. They cut out ten dresses in various sizes, and Sarah made sure Lillie understood how to put the pieces together. Lillie said nothing more about visiting St. Andrew's.

As the formal dining hour approached, Sarah excused herself, assured Lillie she would find a cab easily enough, and headed over to Michigan Avenue to hop a streetcar. She got off at the Lexington. Kenny was at the desk and shook his head when he saw her.

"Nothing? Are you sure?" Sarah asked.

Kenny raised both eyebrows and shrugged.

"Well, it's only been four days," Sarah said.

"Who is this man?" Kenny asked. "You hardly even let him get his head in the door here."

"Surely you appreciate my circumstance." A thin, neat pile of paper on the desk caught Sara's eye. "Kenny, I'd like to borrow some of this stationery. Are there matching envelopes?"

"That stationery is for guests of the Lexington," Kenny said.

"I've informed you that Miss Serena Cuthbert *intends* to be a guest at the Lexington." Sarah planted her elbows on the desk and leaned toward Kenny.

"You're stretching it, Sarah."

"Just a few sheets, and a few envelopes." Her fingers pulled a few sheets loose from the stack.

Kenny looked around. Sarah followed his glance across the lobby, which was unusually empty. The only guests were an older couple looking at newspapers and a young woman—probably a nanny—buckling a child's shoe. No other employees of the hotel were in sight.

"I suppose it wouldn't cause any harm," Kenny finally said.

Sarah flashed a grin. Stationery imprinted with the Lexington's name would be perfect. Serena Cuthbert owed Bradley Townsend a proper thank-you for the lovely times they had shared.

20

We need two more place settings," Mr. Penard announced at the staff supper Thursday evening of the following week. "Mr. Leo invited a guest, and Miss Lucy has as well."

Mrs. Fletcher ticked off the evening's diners on her fingers. "That's eleven. Twelve if Lucy brings Benny."

Penard nodded. "Surely you planned for extra food."

Mrs. Fletcher scowled and passed a basket of bread. "I've been cooking dinner for this family for close to twenty years. Nothing catches me by surprise."

"Why an odd number?" Sarah asked. "Mrs. Banning usually tries to even things out. Who's coming?" She pushed boiled potatoes to the edge of her plate, wondering why the staff were not having the stuffed baked potatoes Mrs. Fletcher had made for the family.

"I did not inquire," Mr. Penard said. "It makes no difference to the quality of our service."

"I was just curious," Sarah muttered.

"I'll set the extra places," Mary Catherine offered.

Mrs. Fletcher shook her head. "Let Sarah do it. I need you in the kitchen. The cake still needs frosting."

"Leo has been seeing a young woman, you know," Karl said. "I've driven them together several times. A Miss Christina Hansen."

"It's about time." Mrs. Fletcher raised her napkin to wipe her chin.

"Is she pretty?" Mary Catherine leaned toward Karl, eyes wide.

"Stop gossiping," Mr. Penard said. "We all have work to do. Finish eating and do it."

Sarah tapped a foot under the hem of her dress. In her estimation, Penard treated the staff like a bunch of children. She never understood why everyone put up with it. No one said much more. Instead the room filled with the sounds of scraping forks and chinking knives. Sarah finished her meal, dutifully carried her plate to the sink, and went into the butler's pantry to take from the shelves the elements of two more formal place settings. The china hand-painted with blue flowers was her favorite of the three sets of china Flora Banning kept. In the dining room, the white damask tablecloth was flawlessly starched beneath a long, narrow arrangement of summer flowers, and the blue in the napkins perfectly matched the blue in the china.

Sarah paused to put her hand in the pocket of her dress, under her apron. The note from Brad had come yesterday after a week of silence. It looked like more silence lay ahead. Brad's note said only that he expected to be occupied for some time with political and business engagements. He promised to think of Serena often and begged her not to doubt his affection during this busy time. Under her apron, Sarah wore the silver rose fastened to the front of her dress.

Affection. Sarah smiled involuntarily when she thought of Brad Townsend using that word. She just had to be patient. The board of trade would sort out their problems, and the election would be over in a couple of months. Then Brad would turn his attentions back to what mattered.

Affection. Then why hadn't he tried to kiss her yet?

⸺ ⸰⸻

Sarah stood at the sideboard in the dining room. Mr. Penard had just passed through looking as if he were tied to a plank in his evening tails. He would say simply, "Dinner is served," and the family and their guests would interrupt their polite conversation, rise from their seats in the parlor, and proceed to the dining room. The scene played out every Thursday evening, when the Bannings assembled for a family dinner with no absences.

Flora and Samuel Banning led the pageantry, followed closely by their son Oliver and his wife, Pamela. Behind them was young Richard, looking grown-up with his Aunt Violet on his arm. In another couple of weeks, he would be in New Jersey, where he could choose to escort any young woman he liked.

Leo did in fact have an attractive young woman beside him, the rumored Christina Hansen. She looked nervous to Sarah, and perhaps that was a sign that she and Leo were considering a serious relationship. Why else would she be uncertain about having dinner with his parents for the first time?

Sarah patted her pocket again. She knew nothing about Brad's parents. How long would it be before he invited Serena Cuthbert to dinner with his family?

Lagging at the rear of the procession were Will and Lucy Edwards. Sarah was glad to see they had opted to leave the children with Charlotte for the evening—but instead they were with Simon Tewell! They strode across the foyer three abreast in somber conversation. No doubt they were talking about the orphanage.

So Simon was the eleventh person, the unattached gentleman.

Flora and Samuel Banning had long ago made their peace with their daughter's proclivity to test the unwritten rules of Prairie Avenue. Sarah had not realized, however, that their indulgence had stretched to the point of welcoming the orphanage director to their table.

Sarah supposed Lucy had not even asked her parents about Simon. What could they say once he arrived? She also suspected that the suit Simon wore had once belonged to Will Edwards. It did not fit quite right in the shoulders. Simon drew a salary for his work, but certainly not on a Prairie Avenue scale.

Simon caught her eye as he entered the dining room. Sarah looked away.

Samuel Banning intoned a prayer of formal gratitude for God's provision. Sarah suffered through it, wondering why, if God was in the business of providing, he did not spread it around a little more evenly. What was there to keep the Bannings from being grateful, after all? After "amens" were murmured around the table, the footman stepped forward to swirl butternut squash soup into the waiting bowls. Without even glancing at the butler, Sarah knew Mr. Penard's eyes watched every move the young man made.

And she felt Simon's eyes on her.

As she cleared the soup bowls a few minutes later.

As Penard served the curry lobster, something Sarah was certain Simon had never eaten before.

As she removed the fish plates.

While Simon politely inquired about Richard's plans, his eyes flickered toward Sarah. In the middle of Leo's story of where he had first met Christina, Simon's eyes—and a vague smile—wafted toward the place at the sideboard where Sarah waited to deftly reach between the diners and make the remains of the roast goose with stuffing and red cabbage disappear.

Sarah did her best not to look at Simon, hoping fervently that he knew better than to speak to a servant during the meal.

When she carried the meat plates into the butler's pantry and quietly set them in the sink, Penard noiselessly followed her. He stood beside her and spoke almost inaudibly.

"You will stop making eyes at Mr. Tewell."

"But I'm not!" Sarah whispered back.

"Whatever your relationship is with this man, it is not appropriate to flaunt it at the Bannings' dinner table."

"We have no relationship!"

"The look on his face would suggest otherwise. Anyone can see how he regards you. And the blush in your face is unconvincing of your protests."

Penard pivoted and returned to the dining room to present a platter laden with stuffed baked potatoes, Brussels sprouts, green beans, and cauliflower.

Sarah put a hand to her cheek, willing the blush to subside.

Simon breathed in her hanging scent when she took his vegetable plate. Even serving a meal and clearing dishes, Sarah was captivating. As hard as he tried to keep his eyes on one of his many dinner companions, inevitably they wavered and drifted, even if only for a split second at a time. He simply could not pretend she was not in the room.

"I wanted Simon to be here for a reason," Lucy finally said when Penard placed a hefty slice of red velvet cake in front of her. "I have an idea for which I would like your support."

"Something to do with the orphanage, I suppose," Samuel said.

"Yes, as a matter of fact. I have arranged to hold a luncheon and invite the young women of Prairie Avenue," Lucy said. "Just recently I had the pleasure of conversing with the daughter of one of the newer families. She's keen to do something practical for the children, to be personally involved. I find myself wondering if others might feel the same way. A luncheon will give us opportunity to discuss the matter. It's all arranged for Tuesday."

Samuel Banning cleared his throat. "If I may be direct, Mr. Tewell, what sort of condition is the orphanage in?"

"Of course the difficult economic times have had some effect," Simon answered—though as he looked around the Banning house he could not help but wonder if the recession had touched them at all. "The number of children who need help continues to climb. They're not all orphans, strictly speaking. More and more parents simply cannot care for their children. For now our financial picture is satisfactory—barely—but if the need continues to grow at the current rate, we will face uncertainty."

Simon gave this talk often in his fund-raising efforts, though not usually in the opulence of a Prairie Avenue dining room.

Richard spoke up. "I've read in the newspaper that Jane Addams believes the orphanages should be done away with. Children should go into foster care—placed with families rather than be herded into institutions. She likens them to warehouses for children."

Simon nodded. "I like to think that description is rather severe for what we're trying to do at St. Andrew's. One can certainly make a compelling argument for foster care and even adoption. Such arrangements take time, however. The system cannot be changed overnight. The children must be cared for in the meantime."

"Mr. Tewell," Flora Banning said, "what is your opinion of the orphan trains? Children from New York and Boston are riding them. Many children even end up here in Illinois, as I understand it."

"You understand correctly," Simon answered. "Institutions in the East are sending children to the farms of southern Illinois, along with other destinations farther west. One might think that clearly it is better for a child to be placed with a family, but we must remember that many of the families are merely looking for help with the labor of running a farm."

"Even still, the children are housed and fed, are they not?"

"It's difficult to say," Simon replied. "I have heard stories of children being malnourished and mistreated, but I would like to believe that for many, it is a better life than what they left behind."

"We're talking about real *children*," Flora's sister Violet said. "Mr. Tewell has informed us that many of them are not truly orphans. Their parents are just unable to care for them. Surely there is a better answer than loading them into boxcars like cattle and shipping them to unknown circumstances."

"Thank you, Aunt Violet," Lucy said. "That's precisely my point."

"And that brings us back to the orphanages," Leo said. "Simon, if you could do one thing for St. Andrew's right now, what would it be?"

"Fire escapes." The answer came quickly. "We only have them on one side of the building, and we're at maximum capacity. I hate to think what would happen in a fire."

"Lucy was born in the middle of the Great Fire," Flora said.

"Yes, Mother," Lucy said, "but our home was not burning at the time."

"Do you have fire drills?" Violet asked.

"Of course we could institute fire drills," Simon said. "The children are routinely reminded where to assemble if they need to leave the building in an emergency. However, without fire escapes, we're avoiding the true issue."

"Isn't it true that very few large institutional buildings have fire escapes?" Leo asked.

Simon nodded. "Unfortunately, that's true. Nevertheless, I would love to see St. Andrew's equipped."

"Fire is a constant danger," Lucy said. "Just look at what happened to the world's fair buildings. So many of them burned, either during the fair or right after."

"But that was a problem with tramps," Samuel said. "They were squatting in the empty structures and building fires where they had no business being."

"They were just trying to keep warm," Lucy countered. "They had no place else to go."

"Fires are in the headlines on a regular basis," Leo acknowledged.

"Let's return to my idea to host a luncheon and get people involved," Lucy said. "I don't think the young ladies of Prairie Avenue can build a fire escape, but they can raise money for one. It will help if they know their parents approve." Lucy turned from one parent to the other. "That's where you can help."

"We've been contributing to the orphanage for years," Samuel Banning pointed out.

"And we're deeply grateful," Simon said quickly.

"We can do more," Lucy said, "help in different ways. Use your personal influence."

Simon nodded his head toward Sarah. "Sarah is doing a wonderful job with the sewing class. The girls are working on their skirts and dreaming of blouses."

"Yes, thank you, Sarah," Lucy said enthusiastically. "That's the kind of thing I'm talking about. Doing something practical. Something personal. Giving these children something to dream about. Sarah is setting an example many others should follow."

—⁓❦⁓—

Sarah wished a crack in the polished floor would open wide enough to swallow her. Lucy Edwards pressed her mother to promise she would speak to other Prairie Avenue women and help stir up interest to do something personally. Simon clarified that financial contributions were still needed as well. Will Edwards, an architect, offered to draw sketches of how a network of fire escapes could be constructed around the orphanage. Simon, thankfully, had the good sense not to look at Sarah again.

Finally the dinner party agreed to retire to the parlor, where Lucy would play the piano for them. Everyone stood up and began to drift across the foyer.

Simon hung back. "May I have a word, Sarah?"

She glanced around. Simon was the last guest to leave the dining room, but almost certainly Mr. Penard was within earshot.

"I didn't mean to embarrass you," Simon said. "I suppose I have become accustomed to Lucy's manner of being direct about orphanage concerns. I know the Bannings can be influential with other families. But I can see I disturbed you by drawing attention to you."

"It's all right, Simon." Sarah picked up a stack of dessert plates. "Let's just forget it."

"I am so pleased at what you're doing. You deserve recognition."

Sarah saw the door to the butler's pantry open and Mr. Penard's head peek out. She added to her stack of dishes. "Perhaps you should join the others."

Simon nodded and left, to Sarah's relief. To her consternation, however, Penard emerged from the pantry.

"I have warned you about this behavior. You should know better than to fraternize with a dinner guest, even someone you see in his own setting."

"He approached me," Sarah said. "I did nothing to encourage him."

"You will prepare the cart with coffee and serve in the parlor," Mr. Penard admonished. "Don't fool yourself, though. I will be watching. Send Mary Catherine in to finish clearing."

He moved away from her dismissively and busied himself with the serving dishes at the sideboard.

Sarah pressed her lips together and blew air out her nose. The Bannings' butler did not think a maid was worthy even of the attentions of a man who directed the orphanage she grew up in. Someday she would disappear to marry a man who had a seat on the board of trade, and Penard would be left mumbling to himself.

21

For the third Friday in a row, Sarah ran her hand along the cool green crepe, then positioned it in the back of the cupboard.

"Melissa," she said to the nearest girl, "I haven't seen Jane for some time now. Is she all right?"

Melissa rolled her eyes. "She always says she doesn't feel well and goes back to bed."

Mary Margaret entered the conversation. "It's getting annoying. Even if she's not hungry, she's supposed to come down and help when our group has duty in the dining hall."

"But she doesn't come down?" Sarah probed.

Both girls shook their heads. "She doesn't work in the garden when she's supposed to, either," Mary Margaret said.

"She doesn't do anything anymore," Melissa said. "When school classes start again, she's going to get into a lot of trouble."

"If she doesn't study, they'll make her leave school and go into service," Mary Margaret added.

Sarah knew that full well.

"Jane wants to stay in school," Sarah said. "She told me that herself."

"She can't stay if she doesn't work," Mary Margaret said flatly.

"Mrs. Davis says plenty of other orphans would be happy to take Jane's place."

"Is Mr. Tewell aware?" Sarah asked.

"He's too busy," Melissa said. "I think I made my waistband too long. Can you help me fix it?"

At the end of class, Sarah pulled the door closed behind her and made sure it was locked. Then she went in search of Jane.

The girl was right where Sarah expected her to be, on her bed in the middle of the afternoon. Jane looked up as Sarah entered the dormitory room.

Sarah moved slowly toward Jane, her eyes drifting to a narrow runner between the rows of beds. "Is the tile still cracked under that old rug?"

Jane nodded, mute.

"And does that cupboard door still come off its hinges?"

Another nod.

"May I sit down?" Sarah asked, gesturing to the end of Jane's bed.

"I'm sorry I haven't been coming to the sewing class," Jane muttered, slinging her legs over the side of the bed and sitting up.

She looked thinner than the last time Sarah had seen her. Pallid. "You don't have to come if you don't want to. I've been saving the green crepe in case you change your mind, though."

"Really?" Jane's posture straightened. "It's still there?"

"Yes. Waiting for you."

"It's too late. I'll be so far behind." The girl's shoulders slumped as quickly as they had risen.

"I'll help you catch up." Sarah reached into the bag she carried to every class now. "I have something for you."

Jane's eyes settled on the journal and widened. "Where did you find it?" She grabbed the book and clutched it with both hands.

"You were right, I'm afraid. I'm not sure how they got hold of it, but some of the boys had it."

"Boys! Oh no. Did they read it?"

Sarah grimaced. "I'm not sure how much." The boys had certainly read enough to make them giggle.

"Did *you* read it?" Jane asked.

Sarah rubbed one earlobe. "Only enough to realize what it was."

"Then you know. Everybody must know. I'll bet it was Michael O'Brien. He never keeps a secret." Jane made no effort to suppress tears as she shoved the book under her pillow and buried her face.

Simon would have known what to say, Sarah thought. Or Lucy. Or even Charlotte. But Sarah had no words. She let the girl sob for a few moments.

"You're unhappy," Sarah said finally, "and you wrote something you thought would make you feel better."

Jane nodded into the pillow.

"You haven't done anything wrong," Sarah said. "The boys had no business with your private book, and whoever snuck it out of this room had no business either. You wrote your private thoughts."

Jane sat up again "But they aren't true! Everyone will laugh."

"I think the boys have forgotten all about it," Sarah said.

"But you haven't."

"I'm not laughing, Jane. You're imagining the life you want to have someday. There's nothing wrong with that."

Jane scoffed. "I'll never have that life. Now I can't even imagine, because everyone knows."

Jane flopped back on the bed. Sarah saw herself doing the same thing, in the same room, right before she claimed the niche under the window and began to stare out at the night.

<hr>

"May I have a word with you?"

Simon looked up, grateful for the visage in the doorframe. "Of course. Come in and sit down."

Sarah curved into a chair on the other side of his desk and distributed her skirt. Even in the automatic gesture, Simon saw grace and elegance.

"I'm glad you stopped in," Simon said. "I wanted to say again I'm sorry if I caused distress for you last night at dinner. The butler seemed to have a peculiar expression."

"Penard always has a peculiar expression," Sarah responded, "but it's true he was disturbed. He thought I was . . . encouraging your attentions."

She did not have to encourage anything. Simon owned how he felt about her.

"I didn't mean to be the source of difficulty for you," Simon said. "The butler must read faces better than I give him credit for."

Sarah did not speak, but her eyes widened.

"You were the epitome of control," he said, "whereas I fear I could not hide my feelings."

Sarah shifted in her chair. "I . . . I . . . I came to talk about Jane."

"I've made you uncomfortable. I'm sorry."

"Please stop apologizing." Sarah gripped her bag in her lap.

Simon nodded, then riffled through some papers on his desk and pulled out a newspaper clipping. "I wonder if you saw this notice. There is to be a textile display downtown and it's open to the public."

"A textile display?"

"They promise everything—fabrics for clothing of all styles, home decorating. I wondered if you might like to go on your Wednesday evening off."

"Together?" Sarah asked.

Simon nodded. Yes, of course, together. He could not quite make himself say the words aloud.

Sarah inhaled. "That does rather sound like something I would enjoy seeing."

"I thought of you as soon as I saw the advertisement."

"I'm not sure what my plans are," she said hesitantly. "I could let you know later."

"Certainly."

"In the meantime, we do need to talk about Jane. I'm concerned."

"Oh?"

"I realize there are four hundred children here, and you can't know what each one is doing every minute of the day."

"I trust the staff to be where I can't be."

Sarah nodded. "I think Jane is slipping through the cracks."

"I'll have someone speak to her."

"She needs more than that, Simon. She needs someone to really care about her welfare."

"Of course we care—"

"You have a good heart, Simon," Sarah said. "I know that. Most of the children are happy enough, I suppose, considering their circumstances. But Jane is different."

"You seem genuinely worried."

"I am."

Her beauty was more than skin deep whether she would admit it or not.

"Why don't you tell me specifically what your concern is?" Simon said.

"She needs someone to talk to."

"Will she not talk to you?"

"I've tried. But I don't know what I'm doing."

"You've been in her position," Simon pointed out. "You can understand her feelings better than anyone."

"I do. But I'm not the right person to help her."

"I rather suspect you are."

Simon's eyes turned to the door again in response to a rap.

Lucy Edwards stuck her head in. "I'm sorry to interrupt, Simon, but you're scheduled to go to the orphanage board of advisors meeting. Are you going to be able to attend?"

Simon slapped his forehead. "I completely forgot."

Sarah stood up. "I won't delay you further. I merely wanted to express my concern."

"Thank you for doing so. Please think about what I said."

Sarah's steps out of the office were quick. Simon turned his attention to Lucy.

"Would you be available to accompany me to this meeting?" he asked. "Your advice on these decisions would be immensely helpful."

Sarah just barely caught the streetcar under a bulging gray sky. She collapsed into a seat and set her bag next to her.

She could not admit to Simon she had read Jane's diary. She could not even tell him there was a diary without risking more distress for Jane. Simon might decide he needed to read it for himself to discover what was troubling Jane.

Sarah believed what she told Jane. Nothing was wrong with imagining a life she wanted. Sarah had done the same thing, and now she was making it happen. The last thing Sarah would do was squelch that girl's imagination—her only hope.

Yet Jane's face haunted her. Despair was winning. And Melissa and Mary Margaret were right—if Jane did not earn a chance at high school, the staff would recommend something else. At fourteen, she was old enough to work.

Sarah looked down at the copper crepe skirt. She had been wearing that skirt the day in the hat shop, the day Serena Cuthbert surfaced. The day her own imagination found wings.

But she was older than Jane. She had met Lillie Wagner, who opened the crack into higher society. Brad Townsend was offering his affection. What she imagined was becoming real.

How could Simon possibly believe she was the right person to help Jane?

———⁓———

Simon and Lucy emerged from the conference room together.

"Do you feel any closer to a decision?" Lucy asked.

With one finger, Simon rubbed the middle of his forehead. "I'm afraid not."

"You did the right thing in taking the question to the board," Lucy said.

"They don't appear to want to make the choice, either," Simon said. "Their answer was to say they would abide by my recommendation. Nothing changes the reality that we don't have space or money for those extra children."

"But how can we turn our backs on them?"

Simon covered his eyes with a hand. "I honestly don't know what to do."

"Simon," Lucy said, "come back to my parents' house again tomorrow afternoon. They're hosting a small private concert by a visiting vocalist."

A concert? How was that supposed to help anything?

"I'm not sure what you're saying, Lucy," Simon said.

"After the performance I can introduce you to some people. We do need people to get involved personally, but we also need funding. My parents' guests are well situated. If you felt you had the financial resources, you might find inspiration about how to proceed with finding space."

Simon tilted his head and smiled. "Your parents were gracious enough last night, but I hardly think they are expecting me to become a regular guest, especially to beseech their friends for funding."

"I'll handle my parents," Lucy answered. "Just say you'll come at five o'clock."

They stepped outside together. Simon studied the looming sky. "This storm is going to be a bad one."

"The concert, Simon," Lucy prodded.

"Yes, I'll come. But if there's any sign of a storm in your parents' parlor, we will run for cover."

22

The black sky collided against itself and cleaved, spilling electricity into the night.

The thunderous smite was immediate. The window of Sarah's third floor room clattered in feeble resistance. Despite the rain earlier, when she went to bed she had left the window open in the faint hope of a breeze. Now she gasped and sat bolt upright in bed.

The sky split again.

And again.

Sarah felt the spray of rain through the open window. She pushed back the clammy sheet and stepped tentatively across the small room. Outside, rain dropped in a torrent and thrust down the Avenue. Already branches tumbled in the wind and rolled into the street. In the respite between outbursts of the storm, Sarah listened to the slush and splash of water seeking lower ground.

When the sky lit again, she slammed the window shut and jumped back all in one motion. Now she was wide awake.

Her sleep had been fitful anyway, mired in images of Simon and Jane. Simon losing the battle not to stare at her while he sat at the Banning table. Jane's brown eyes looming on the brink of misery. Simon noticing Sarah's every movement, even the purely ordinary. Jane's slight form under a threadbare sheet. Simon at his desk, thoughtful with the end of a pen between his lips in that illuminated instant before he realized she was in the doorway. Jane's fingers sliding on the green crepe. Simon's words saying one thing, and his eyes pleading something else.

The storm was almost a relief.

Sarah was not the only one up. Shuffling footsteps and murmuring voices drifted in from the hall. With another crack of lightning came the sensation that Sarah did not like being on the top floor of the house during an electrical storm. She stepped to the door, opened it, and saw Mrs. Fletcher, Mary Catherine, and Elsie huddled.

"So we're all up," Mrs. Fletcher said.

"Yes, at three o'clock in the morning!" Mary Catherine wailed.

"We might as well go have some warm milk," the cook said. "This storm is nowhere near finished. Find a shawl or something, all of you."

No one argued. The three maids ducked back into their rooms and returned with the robes and summer shawls of modesty. Mrs. Fletcher led the way down to the kitchen with an old kerosene lamp. No one was eager to touch an electric switch.

Sarah lit the gas stove while Mrs. Fletcher poured milk in a pan. They all jumped at the sound of footsteps in the back hall.

"It's only Karl." Sarah let her breath out and lifted the lamp.

"Are the grooms and coachmen all up as well?" Mary Catherine asked.

Karl nodded. "One of the horses spooked and made a racket. We got him soothed, but now everyone's awake."

"The whole city is probably awake," Sarah said.

"There are sure to be fires," Karl said. "Lightning like that always does damage."

Thunder roared again, and electricity flashed and sizzled outside the house.

"I'm not sure there's any point in going back to bed." Sarah now stirred the warming milk.

"We'll all be dead on our feet tomorrow," Mary Catherine

moaned. "No one could sleep through that storm. The family must be awake too."

"Keep your voices down," Mrs. Fletcher warned. "I don't want the family getting ideas about pushing annunciator buttons." She set out mugs for the milk.

The Bannings wandered into the dining room for breakfast slightly later than usual the next morning, but otherwise the pace of the day was as brisk as any Saturday. After breakfast, Sarah cleaned the parlor meticulously and polished the grand piano to a sheen that even Mr. Penard could not fault. The footman, Willard, carried in extra chairs.

Sarah nearly spoke to him, but his eyes gestured over her shoulders just in time. Flora Banning was right behind them.

"I want all the seating positioned to face the piano," Flora said. "My daughter will be playing for Miss Travers."

"Yes, ma'am," the footman said.

"We will move the settee, of course," Flora said, pointing.

We. Sarah glanced at the footman. What Mrs. Banning meant was that Willard would move the heavy settee.

"Sarah," Flora said, "make sure to raise the lid of the piano and then stand back to see if you missed any spots."

"Yes, ma'am."

"Willard, see what you can do with the seating and I'll be back in a few minutes to determine if it's adequate. We need to seat seventeen."

"Yes, ma'am."

Flora swept out of the room.

"Seventeen," Willard muttered. "I didn't know there were that many people in Chicago who liked opera."

"Don't be ignorant." Sarah gave the piano a final swipe. "The critics say Miss Travers has exceptional talent. I read it in the paper myself. It's an honor for the Bannings to have her in their home."

"It's still opera." Willard leaned into one end of the settee and shoved.

Sarah wondered what Brad Townsend thought about opera. If he invited Serena Cuthbert to a performance at the Auditorium Theater, she knew just the gown she would wear.

At three-thirty in the afternoon, Miss Travers arrived. Ten minutes later Lucy appeared, and the duo practiced behind closed parlor doors. Sarah laid the elaborate table with the gold-rimmed china and monogrammed white linen napkins. The table was extended to its full length to accommodate the diners.

At four-forty, the doorbell chimed with the first guests. Sarah was putting the finishing touches on the dinner table, a miniature vase with a single yellow rose next to the water goblet at each place setting.

Mr. Penard opened the front door, and Elsie took up her post. Flora Banning floated across the foyer to greet her guests. Sarah could not help but glance toward the front door to see who had arrived. First came the Herricks from two blocks south on Prairie Avenue, and right behind them were the Starkweathers from Calumet Avenue. Elsie took the light shawls the women carried, collected their hats, and politely inquired if they required her attentions. Conversation rapidly moved to the storms that had wakened the Banning staff and been the primary topic of conversation whenever any of the staff had been outside during the day.

"We're fortunate not to have more damage in our neighborhood," Mrs. Herrick commented. "The streetcars, telegraph, telephone lines—everything was put out of order in some parts of town."

"The barns of the Chicago Railway were struck by lightning," Mr. Herrick added. "A good chunk of the roof plunged down. It fell right through three stories. They lost four cars."

Mr. Starkweather scratched his temple. "Nine fire alarms in one hour. The property loss is overwhelming."

"Leo said he went past Chicago Brick today," Flora said. "The machinery is buried in debris."

"At least the storm has passed now," Mrs. Starkweather said with relief, "and fortunately for us Miss Travers was not delayed."

Flora's smile grew wide. "Miss Travers is right behind those doors! Penard, will you see our guests in and let Mr. Banning know we'll be ready to begin soon?"

Penard opened the pocket doors under the arch that led to the parlor and stepped to one side discreetly to usher the Herricks and Starkweathers in. Lucy rose from the piano to welcome the guests. With a clear view from the dining room and across the foyer, Sarah sneaked a peek at the visiting soprano, whose sapphire gown was the most spectacular silk Sarah had ever seen.

The doorbell rang again, and Penard dutifully crossed the foyer to answer it. Flora still stood in the foyer.

"Ah, you've come," Flora said. "I'm so pleased you could visit our home. Lucy, come meet the Wagners!"

Wagners!

Sarah sucked in a deep breath, abandoned the flowers, and stepped to the side of the room, where she would not be seen from the foyer but had an unobstructed view of the assembling guests. Samuel Banning appeared from his study.

"This is my husband, Samuel, and my daughter, Lucy," Flora said. "These are the Wagners, Frederic and Edith. They're new to Chicago. I just met Edith last week at a ladies' luncheon."

"It's nice to meet you," Lucy said. "I believe I've already met your daughter."

"Lillie sends her regrets," Edith Wagner explained. "She was disappointed not to be able to come, but she had a previous engagement for the evening." Edith chuckled. "In fact, we're all hoping it will lead to a formal engagement for the rest of her life."

When the bell rang again, Sarah hastened across the dining room and took refuge in the butler's pantry.

She put her hands behind her and leaned against the sink, weak in the knees. Sarah had become Serena Cuthbert and passed the test with people she suspected had never looked at her face. But the Wagners had. Serena had been in their home, sat at their table, told stories of a past that did not exist.

Perhaps they would not look at the face of a servant tonight. Why should they?

What if they did?

Even a glance across the room would be enough to make them look twice. She could not risk it.

Sarah took a deep breath and moved through to the kitchen.

"Is the table ready?" Mrs. Fletcher asked.

"Almost," Sarah answered. "There's still time. They won't even begin the concert for a little while."

"Why don't you just finish now and be done with it?" Mrs. Fletcher challenged as she tore lettuce into bits. "We have plenty of other things to do."

"I will," Sarah promised. Once the music started, none of the guests would dare leave the parlor during the performance. How to avoid clearing between courses was the more frightening question. The doorbell rang again, reminding Sarah of the gathering guests and the too-familiar faces among them.

"Mary Catherine, where are the beets?" Mrs. Fletcher demanded. She looked around, then flicked her gaze upward. "For that matter, where is Mary Catherine? Sarah, would you get the plates down for the staff dinner? We'll have to eat in shifts to make sure someone is available to attend to the guests at all times. Mary Catherine, the beets! Where is that girl?"

Sarah moved to the cupboard and took down the dishes. "I can go down to the cellar for beets."

"Mary Catherine has already gone. That's the problem. The girl doesn't have a hurry bone in her whole body."

Footsteps clicked in the hall, but they were not Mary Catherine's.

"Ah, there's Charlotte now," Mrs. Fletcher said, tilting her head toward the back door.

"I didn't know she was coming." Sarah glanced at the door just as Charlotte Shepard stepped through.

Mrs. Fletcher put the bowl of lettuce in the icebox. "I asked Charlotte to help in the kitchen tonight. Penard wants Mary Catherine to work in the dining room. It's too big a group for you to clear all by yourself."

Charlotte Shepard unpinned her hat and tossed it into the chair under the window. She pushed both sleeves up. "What can I do to help?"

"Check the potatoes on the stove, please, Charlotte."

Charlotte moved toward the stove.

Sarah pushed open the butler's pantry door just wide enough to peer through to the foyer. The Wagners still lingered next to the mahogany table with Lucy. The doorbell rang yet again, and Penard opened the front door. Simon stepped through.

Simon. Again?

Lucy made the introductions. Simon extended his hand, and Frederic Wagner shook it. Enthusiastic tidbits of conversation wafted through the fog of Sarah's mind.

Lillie.

Volunteer.

Grateful.

Eager.

Suddenly Sarah felt far more than a little shaky. Sarah Cummings and Serena Cuthbert were on a collision course.

Breathless, Sarah withdrew to the kitchen and reached for the plates for the staff meals. Mary Catherine appeared with the beets at last, with Karl in her wake.

"Karl Stenberg," Mrs. Fletcher said, waving a vegetable knife, "if you've been distracting my maid, I'll have your head."

Sarah was sure Mary Catherine blushed. The kitchen maid quickly busied herself with the beets. Sarah carried the plates to the wide-planked kitchen table and began to set them around, fearing that her own complexion had blanched, rather than blushed. She felt the tremble in her hand, but could not control it before the first plate clattered against the table.

"Sarah, are you all right?" Karl asked.

How should she answer that?

"I don't feel quite myself," Sarah flicked her eyes toward Mrs. Fletcher.

"You have a long evening ahead of you," Karl observed.

"I know." Sarah set down the next plate with a little less rattle. An idea flashed. "Mrs. Fletcher, I wonder if Charlotte might serve tonight. I could help you in the kitchen instead."

"You've been fine all day," Mrs. Fletcher said.

Sarah nodded. "I just started to feel shaky a few minutes ago."

"Are you sure you can't make it through the evening?"

"I would hate to drop something in the dining room in the middle of dinner."

That made the cook stop in mid-motion, a wooden stirring spoon in her hand poised above the soup pot. "Penard would have a conniption fit. None of us would hear the end of it for weeks."

"Please," Sarah said simply. "Charlotte knows how Mr. Penard likes things done."

"I don't mind serving," Charlotte interjected. "It would be like the old days. But I didn't come dressed for it." She gestured to her simple gray striped dress.

"You can wear one of my uniforms," Sarah said quickly.

"It will have to be something loose to hide the child," Charlotte said. "Mrs. Banning might not be as understanding as Lucy is."

"We'll find something."

Mrs. Fletcher grunted. "It's up to Penard."

"But you'll speak to him?"

"I'll speak to him."

23

illie leaned one hand against the carriage window as the horse slowed. She consulted the slip of paper in her hand to verify the address.

Yes, this was it.

She had not come all that far from Prairie Avenue—only a handful of blocks to the west—but the atmosphere of the neighborhood had changed. The mansions faded away in favor of homes that appeared more manageable even from the outside. Lillie had never known anyone who lived in a neighborhood like this one. She had seen the Banning house from the outside, and her parents had recounted details of the interior after their visit three days ago. Lillie had assumed their daughter lived in similar circumstances. This home, though, was just a square brick house with two stories and a porch stretched across the front behind a white wooden railing. Lillie rather liked it.

Her driver opened the carriage door, and Lillie stepped out.

"Thank you, Ronald," she said. "I'll look for you right here when lunch is over."

"Yes, ma'am."

Lillie straightened her hat and shoulders and followed the walkway to the stairs at the front of the house. Five stairs, then four more paces, and Lillie stood at the front door. She had barely rung the bell when the door opened and she was looking into the clear eyes of the maid who had been surrounded by children when they last met. Lillie rummaged through her brain for the name. Charlotte.

"Please come in." Charlotte stepped aside and gestured. "Mrs. Edwards is in the dining room."

As Charlotte entered the dining room, Lucy folded the last of the burgundy napkins into a perfect triangle and laid it on a plate. "Lillie! I'm so glad you could come."

"Thank you for inviting me. I've been looking so forward to this lunch."

Lucy crossed the room and took Lillie's hand. "I understand congratulations are in order on your engagement."

Lillie could not help but smile. "Mr. Gunnison asked me on Saturday evening."

"And you said yes!"

"I did! He had already asked my father for my hand."

"Have you known each other long?"

"We began seeing each other in April, and we are both quite sure of our decision."

"How delightful. When will the wedding be?"

"Christmas, we hope."

Over the next few minutes, Charlotte ushered in several other young women. Lucy invited everyone to take a seat at the dining room table. Charlotte served soup, tender roast beef under gravy, and a salad chock full of summer vegetables. The meal was filling and colorful, but uncomplicated, which Lillie found refreshing. While they ate, Lucy encouraged her guests to share their interest in St. Andrew's Orphanage.

As Charlotte served slices of warm blackberry pie, Lucy herself began to talk.

"I'd like to tell you about some of the children at St. Andrews. Let me begin with Sarah. She was a happy child, an only child. Her parents doted on her, but life can change in an instant. Sarah came home from school one day to discover her parents' carriage had overturned in an intersection. She went to school in the morning a content, well-loved daughter, and she came home an orphan." Lucy clapped her hands once sharply. "Just that quickly, she found herself at St. Andrew's. For years she struggled to make sense of what had happened to her.

"Alonzo and Alfred are brothers. They have three older brothers. When their father died of pneumonia, their mother found she could not care for the little ones and still scrape out a living. Alonzo and Alfred came to us four years ago. We all hoped it was temporary, but gradually they heard less and less from their mother. No doubt her own heart is breaking because she cannot reclaim her sons.

"Some of you have met Ben, my son. You might wonder how a woman my age can have a ten year old! Benny came to St. Andrew's as a newborn left on the steps. He and I were smitten with each other when I first began volunteering at St. Andrew's. When my husband met Benny, it seemed clear the boy was meant to be our son, and we adopted him two years ago. Ben is one of the lucky ones to find a real home, but far more children need homes than we have families able to take them in.

"These are real children who need to be loved, who have hopes and dreams. It's not easy for Jane to talk to people, so she writes things down. Jane keeps a journal of her hopes and dreams. I haven't read it, because it's personal, but I know she pours her heart into that brown leather book with a red stripe down the front cover."

Brown leather with a red stripe. A girlish scrawl.

Lillie could still feel the weight of that book in her hands. She saw again the outrageous accounts written between the covers. Jane was the name of the girl who had escorted her to Lucy Edwards's office. Now her face, with her dull dark eyes, hung in Lillie's mind.

But what was Serena Cuthbert doing with that girl's journal?

Simon handed his hat to Charlotte. "I telephoned to tell Lucy I would be late, but I had hoped to be here sooner than this."

Charlotte hung the derby on the hat rack next to the front door. "The ladies have been having a good discussion. Shall I bring you something to eat?"

"If it's not too much trouble."

Charlotte ushered Simon into the dining room.

"I'm sorry to be so late," he said as he took his seat. "Today has been one crisis after another."

"Ladies, I'd like you to meet Mr. Simon Tewell, director of St. Andrew's Orphanage," Lucy said. She made introductions around the table.

"It's generous of all of you to give us some of your precious time." Simon glanced around the table. If even one of these young women turned out to be half as committed to St. Andrew's as Lucy Edwards, the lunch would have been a valuable investment of his time.

"Are these crises that delayed you at the orphanage?" Lucy asked.

"Indirectly. The Haymarket Produce Bank failed today. They signed the papers this morning assigning their assets. The news is flying up and down the streets." Simon looked around the table, not sure how many of the privileged young women would immediately understand the implications of this particular bank failure.

"Don't quite a few of the truck farmers use that bank?" Lucy asked.

Simon nodded. "As soon as it was announced, a horde of farmers banged on the doors trying to get their money. The police cleared them away."

"It's disaster for the people who can least afford it." Lucy's shoulders sagged.

"But it's also a sign of the difficult economy in general. Some of those farmers donated to orphanages the produce they couldn't sell. Now they may lose their farms and have nothing to bring into the city at all. Everyone will feel it."

"Well, we can't save the Haymarket Bank," Lucy said, "but let's get down to business to figure out what we can do for the children of St. Andrew's."

The lunch dishes were cleared. Sarah tossed a towel on the counter next to the sink, where Mary Catherine faced the mound of dirty dishes. Sarah did not even look at the kitchen maid's face, resolute about not getting drawn into helping with washing up. That was not her job anymore. The afternoon lull was beginning, the hours of the day when the domestic staff might get to sit down for a few minutes and work on some handwork before preparations for dinner got underway and the family returned home with their demands.

But Sarah had other plans. She pulled her apron over her head and slung it across the back of a chair, deciding that the dark calico dress she wore underneath was not a complete embarrassment for going out on the street. Mrs. Fletcher was settling into the chair under the window, with her feet on a footstool. She had long ago given up pretending to do handwork during quiet hours. Sarah avoided meeting the cook's eyes, lest Mrs. Fletcher suddenly decide some obscure corner had to be scrubbed immediately. She was through the door and down the servants' hall before anyone could speak her name.

Outside, Sarah headed over to the Lexington Hotel. She had begun to go nearly every day now. If Brad or Lillie left a message for her, she needed to know immediately. Arranging a meeting could require finagling and would be impossible without advance warning.

The doorman was used to seeing her. He tipped his hat and held the door open, and Sarah sashayed through.

Kenny was clearly expecting her. "It's been a dry spell," he said, "but here you go." He held out an envelope.

Kenny did not even try to fluster her anymore. It was a seamless operation now. If there were no notes, she was in and out of the lobby in a matter of seconds. Sometimes she caught his eye from just inside the door. If he shook his head, she pivoted and went on her way. Most days she was back at Prairie Avenue before Mrs. Fletcher dozed off.

Sarah snatched the letter out of Kenny's grasp and turned it over to see the return address on the flap.

Brad. Finally.

Sarah stepped across the lobby, beyond the range where Kenny might express curiosity, and worked the flap open.

Thank you for your patience . . . pressing business matters . . . reception on Wednesday night.

Sarah stopped to read more carefully. It was yet another political affair, but he was inviting her out. Wednesday evening. Perfect! She would not have to negotiate the time off or make any explanations for her absence.

Wednesday. The textile show with Simon. He had taken pains to arrange his schedule to match her night off. Sarah sank into a chair. While she had not formally accepted Simon's invitation, she was interested in the textile exhibit and had been inclined to go. When would she have the chance to do something like that again? And she had come to think it might be rather nice to spend an evening with Simon Tewell.

Sarah tapped Brad's note with her forefinger. The show was just fabric. If she declined Brad's invitation, he might lose interest. Sarah pressed a hand against her forehead.

She had to see Brad. At the bottom of his note he had scrawled a telephone number. Sarah slid her steps back to the main desk.

"I need to use the telephone, Kenny," she said.

"Hotel guests only." He barely looked up from a stack of registration forms.

"You know I can't use the one at the house."

He shook his head. "I could lose my job."

"For letting me use the telephone at a hotel desk?"

A guest rang the bell at the other end of the desk and Kenny responded.

Sarah did not think twice. She picked up the telephone and gave the operator the number of Brad's office, where she left a message saying she was delighted to accept his invitation.

Eyeing Kenny, who was still occupied, she gave the operator a second number, hoping Simon would not be the one to answer the telephone. Surely he had someone to do that for him. Jane, perhaps, or one of the other girls who rotated duty in the office.

Sarah had counted four rings when the telephone was snatched out of her hands.

"I said no." Kenny glowered and hung up the telephone.

Sarah let her breath out slowly.

"I've taken one other person into my confidence with notes for Serena Cuthbert, because I'm not here every minute. But if my supervisor found out I was acting as your messenger service, I'd be out on the street."

"Are you threatening to stop?" she asked quietly.

"No means no. Three strikes and you're out."

Sarah moistened her lips while she thought. "All right. I'm sorry."

Out on the sidewalk she blew out her breath. At least she had gotten through to Brad's office. Simon would figure out for himself that she was not going to the textile show.

Simon scraped the last of the blackberry pie off the plate as Charlotte poured him a cup of coffee. All of the young women at the table had contributed to the discussion and all seemed interested to be involved at some level. But Lillie Wagner's eyes glowed the warmest, and the pitch of her voice rose with the most sincerity.

"My friend and I have been sewing," she was saying now. "We're starting with ten dresses, but I hope it will be much more than that. I haven't told Serena yet, but I've ordered a sewing machine. That will make the work go so much faster."

"I hope you will visit our sewing class one Friday," Simon said. "A young woman named Sarah Cummings runs it. She used to be at St. Andrew's herself, and now she is working. She sews clothing as well."

"Lucy told us about a girl named Sarah," Lillie said.

"It's the same girl," Lucy interjected. "She has developed into an accomplished seamstress, as well as having other talents."

"I'm sure she would love to have you visit the class." Simon was not sure at all that Sarah would welcome a guest, but it seemed to be the thing to say.

"I would love to!"

"Drop by any Friday afternoon. They begin about three o'clock."

24

*T*uesday crept by. Sarah mopped and polished and dusted and served dinner as she did every day, but all the while her mind was on Wednesday evening. Brad had never seen the crimson jacquard dress that flattered her so well. She would wear that, with the silver rose pinned at the neckline.

Sarah had promised Lillie they could sew together on Wednesday afternoon, and she was glad to have something to do to pass the time on her day off, while she waited for the hour when Brad would pick her up at the Lexington.

Lillie had been hard at work and had now started a fifth dress. Sarah inspected the handiwork closely and could find little fault with it.

"You must have spent hours on these dresses," Sarah said. "Where did you get this blue ribbon? It's a perfect match."

"I took it off an old dress," Lillie said. "I'm going to take the whole dress apart. There's so much yardage in the skirt that we'll probably be able to make two dresses out of it for the girls. It's perfectly good, just out of style."

"That's a wonderful idea," Sarah responded. Lillie would never suspect that the suit her friend was wearing had been taken apart and reassembled in just such a manner.

"Maybe there are sisters who would like matching dresses! Or best friends."

"I'll make inquiries," Sarah said agreeably.

"I can't wait for my sewing machine to arrive." Lillie settled into a chair with a pink and green floral project in her lap. "We'll be able to get so much more done."

"I suppose it would be faster."

"Surely your dressmaker uses one," Lillie said.

Sarah shook her head. "No, I'm certain she prefers to sew by hand. With a machine you can make a mistake before you realize it and ruin the client's fabric." Sarah had caused a run in precious fabric once, more than two years ago. That was a mistake she would never make again.

"If you ask me, a machine sounds grand. All the stitches are guaranteed to be even in length and equal in tension," Lillie said.

Sarah laughed. "You sound like an advertisement."

"I don't care." Lillie tossed her head. "The important thing is getting the work done for the sake of the children. Oh, Serena, I wish you could have been at Lucy Edwards's luncheon. She's doing so much, and she wants to do so much more! You just have to meet her."

"Were there many people?" Sarah asked cautiously.

"Just Lucy, me, and six other young women. And Mr. Tewell, of course. But I suppose you met him when you communicated that we were sewing dresses."

"Yes, of course." Sarah turned her face away and reached for a spool of thread. Now Lillie had met Lucy *and* Simon.

"He mentioned the same sewing class Lucy told me about when I first met her," Lillie continued. "He invited me to visit. It meets on Friday afternoons. I'd like to go. Why don't you come with me?"

Sarah shifted. "Wouldn't it be better to spend the time actually sewing? We'd just be in the way."

"I believe the invitation is sincere," Lillie said. "I want to go."

"I know you want to be personally involved," Sarah said, her heart racing, "but going to a class someone else is teaching may be a bit much. You should find your own niche."

"You always say that. But it can't hurt to observe what someone else is doing. I might get an idea what my niche is." Lillie groaned. "Oh no! I just remembered Mother arranged for a portrait painter to come on Friday. It's to be our first sitting. She'll have a fit if I suggest rescheduling."

"You should sit for the portrait," Sarah urged. "It's important to your mother."

"I suppose I must this week. But it doesn't always have to be Friday. Surely we can find another mutually convenient time during the week for the next sitting. I'm determined to visit that class. I do wish you would reconsider and come with me, Serena."

"Have you got any yellow thread?" Sarah asked. "I'm going to finish this hem, then I have to go. Brad is taking me out."

"Brad! Serena, why didn't you say something sooner? Where are you going tonight?"

"Unfortunately, it's another political affair." Sarah fiddled with a needle. "He promises that after the election things will be better."

"At least you get to see him," Lillie said. "What are you going to wear?"

Sarah breathed relief and let Serena answer the question.

⁓⟳⁓

Simon fingered the advertisement for the textile show for the twentieth time. He had never heard from Sarah and had no reason to think her silence meant anything but turning him down. Now it was too late to send a note with a fresh invitation.

He wished he had not let himself hope. When she had not immediately turned down his invitation to the textile show, Simon allowed himself to imagine she might agree to accompany him—out in public, without the cover of two dozen children as an excuse. In truth she had never given him any reason to hope for anything. Yet he had. He just had to wait for her to see in herself what he saw in her—what God saw in her.

Sarah sat alone in a chair on the perimeter of the room. In the hour since they arrived, Brad had spent perhaps twelve minutes at her side. Every time he turned around, someone was whisking him off to meet another visiting Republican dignitary. The first couple of times, he introduced Serena Cuthbert and kept her on his arm. After that he simply begged her indulgence and promised to return as quickly as possible, leaving her to smile at a roomful of strangers.

She took odd comfort in the fact that most of the people did not know anyone either. An inventory of the room from a safe corner convinced Sarah no one present had ever crossed paths with Sarah Cummings. She relaxed into Serena. The crimson jacquard gown had a scooped neckline, and, as she often did, Sarah had lowered it another inch when she fitted it to her own form. A dusty rose silk faille shawl draped off the ends of her shoulders. Sarah recognized a few people from previous outings with Brad and made sure Serena was cordial and greeted them by name. Emma Pearce was there with her husband, just as chatty as she had been every other time she saw Serena. She was harmless, Sarah thought, just too talkative and prone to flit from one conversation to another without ever finishing anything.

With a glass of punch in her hand, Sarah watched Brad from across the large room. She could not help wondering if he had political aspirations himself. He remembered everyone's name, always had a ready smile, and held an articulate opinion on any subject tossed before him. He charmed the women, who would surely influence their husbands to vote for him even though they could not do so themselves. She could so easily imagine herself at his side, confident she understood more about politics now than she had two months ago. She certainly understood that a beautiful, supporting wife was a requirement. Serena Cuthbert could fill the role.

Sarah wandered out through the French doors leading to a terrace and looked up at the night sky. This was the same sky she had gazed at in quiet midnight moments from the fourth floor of St. Andrew's Orphanage, the same sky she saw from the courtyard in back of the Banning house, but it was an entirely different view. Under this sky, now, was a city of promise calling her from the future. Serena Cuthbert was ready to answer.

Sarah leaned on a brick ledge and listened to passing carriages, fragments of conversation, the string quartet tuning and getting ready to play.

"Here you are, Serena!"

Sarah turned to find Brad standing between the open French doors, light from inside streaming around his handsome height.

"I just thought I'd take a bit of air," she said.

He walked toward her. "I had hoped this evening would be more fun for you."

"It's fine. I'm having a lovely time. I chatted with Emma Pearce and a few others. But mostly I'm just happy to get to see you." Sarah's pulse quickened.

He settled next to her at the ledge, and they turned toward one another. His breath grazed her face in the shadow of an overhang. Sarah dropped her glance, then lifted her eyes to meet his gaze. This could be the moment he kissed her for the first time.

She hoped so.

Brad took her hand and lifted it to his lips—not the kiss she anticipated.

"I must speak with a few more people," he said. "I'm sure you would enjoy some refreshment with my friend Mr. Curtis. He's just arrived—late—and he's here alone. You can relax and enjoy the string quartet while I finish my business."

Her lip quivered as she stifled the impulse to complain. Sarah would complain. Serena would do whatever it took. Too many other women would line up for the attentions of Bradley Townsend if

Serena were anything less than gracious. They walked back inside together and Brad led the way to a man slightly older than Brad who was sitting alone.

"Miss Cuthbert, I'm pleased to introduce you to Mr. Francis Curtis."

Mr. Curtis stood. "I've heard so much about you, but I have not had the pleasure of meeting you. I was beginning to think Miss Cuthbert was a figment of Brad's imagination."

Sarah laughed while her stomach took a twist. This man had sat at the lunch table with Leo.

That was weeks ago, she told herself. He would not remember her. After all, Thom Powell had been at the same lunch and danced with Serena Cuthbert with no suspicions.

<hr>

"It's almost time!" Edith Wagner announced on Friday at lunch. "Our first mother and daughter portrait sitting."

Lillie smiled. "Are you sure you've found the right artist?" She was not sure why this portrait was so important to her mother, but it seemed harmless enough to sit for it.

"He comes highly recommended. He has references from some of the finest families."

"Then I'm sure he'll do a splendid job. I'll change right after lunch." Her mother had been explicit about the pale green gown Lillie was to wear for the portrait.

Mrs. Burnett, the housekeeper, entered the dining room with a small silver tray. "A message arrived, madam."

Edith picked up the envelope and opened it. She read the note and threw her hands up. "He has fallen ill!"

"Who?"

"The artist, of course. He has been unwell all week and sends his regrets. We will have to reschedule."

"I'm so sorry, Mother. I know how much you were looking

forward to beginning." Lillie squelched a smile. Friday afternoon yawned open for something she was far more interested in.

—∿—

Sarah unfurled the green crepe on the table. Jane's eyes widened and her lips hinted at a smile. They were alone in the classroom.

"Are you sure I can catch up?" Jane asked. "Everyone else is nearly finished."

"Some of the girls are working faster than others," Sarah said. "You learned the stitches when we began and you did a beautiful job. I'm sure you can make a skirt every girl will admire."

"I've never had anything like this before." Jane stroked the fabric. "So smooth, so cool. Are you sure it's practical?"

"Won't it be enough that it's pretty?" Sarah asked.

"Around here everything is supposed to be practical and sturdy."

Jane was right. The crepe was not practical. She had said so herself the day Simon first showed her the donated fabrics. But giving it to Jane was worth the delight in the girl's eyes.

"You deserve it," Sarah said.

She heard footsteps slow in the hall, and the swish of a skirt, but she turned to the cupboard. "Let's find some thread for you to use. I think I saw a spool that is a very close match."

As she pulled the basket of threads from the cupboard and handed it to Jane, she heard more swishing. She looked up this time.

Lillie.

She was supposed to be sitting for a portrait. Sarah was supposed to have another week to distract Lillie from visiting the class.

The two women stared at each other. Sarah's heart battered against her chest, and words failed.

"Sarah, I don't see any green thread," Jane said. "Is there another basket?"

"I . . . sorry," Lillie said, "I am. . . ."

Sarah burned under her friend's inspection. She wore a simple broadcloth skirt and blouse, nothing to suggest Serena Cuthbert, and the confusion in Lillie's eyes was unmistakable. Sarah licked lips suddenly gone dry.

"I remember you," Jane said. "You're Miss Wagner."

"Yes, that's right," Lillie answered. "You're Jane."

Sarah busied herself rearranging fabric in the cupboard.

"Are you here for our class?" Jane asked.

"I thought I might observe. I wanted to meet your teacher."

"She's right here," Jane said. "Miss Sarah Cummings."

"I'm glad to meet you, Miss Cummings," Lillie said.

Sarah heard the edge in Lillie's voice scrape the sheen off friendship. She swallowed and turned to face Lillie. "Welcome, Miss Wagner." She nudged Jane's elbow. "Jane, would you please let the other girls know we might be starting a few minutes late while Miss Wagner and I talk?"

"What about cutting out my skirt?"

"We'll still do it," Sarah said. "Just give me a few minutes, please."

Jane looked from Sarah to Lillie with a puzzled expression, but she straggled out of the room.

"Sarah Cummings?" Lillie's jaw set firm. "You look remarkably like my good friend Serena Cuthbert."

Sarah opened her mouth, but nothing came out.

"Have you taken on a second identity to teach this class?" Lillie demanded. "Are the orphans not good enough for Serena Cuthbert?"

"That's not exactly the way it happened." Sarah gripped the back of a chair.

Realization dawned on Lillie. "You really are Sarah Cummings. You're the girl Lucy Edwards talked about at lunch on Tuesday."

Sarah said nothing.

"Do you work here?" Lillie asked.

Sarah shook her head. "I just come in to teach this class."

"I don't understand."

Sarah moistened her lips, considering her options. Her chest ached for breath. "I'm the parlor maid for the Bannings. I only come here on Friday afternoons."

"The parlor maid! Then who is Serena Cuthbert?" Lillie asked.

"I am," Sarah answered swiftly.

"But you can't be both."

"Why not? Serena is as real to me as she is to you."

"Apparently she's not nearly as real as I believed."

"Lillie, please, I can explain. Try to understand."

"What I understand is that I came here expecting to meet a talented young sewing teacher, and I discover my best friend is someone I don't know the first thing about."

"The girls will be here any minute," Sarah said. "Let's talk later."

"I don't see that we have anything to discuss." Lillie swished her skirts out of the room as the girls' voices wafted and giggled in the hall.

25

The class was a blur.

Serving dinner Friday evening was a haze.

The night was interminable. Sarah went through the motions of putting on a nightdress and lying in bed, but she never closed her eyes. In the morning after breakfast, drained and red-eyed, she dusted the parlor, polished the foyer table, and laid the table for lunch.

All Sarah wanted was to be unconscious. How could she possibly undo yesterday's events? The real question was, how long would Lillie wait before telling Brad? And then what? Sarah was running out of time.

Mrs. Fletcher stuck her head into the dining room just as Sarah finished the table. "I need you to go on an errand."

Sarah groaned. She could not possibly manage an errand.

"Mrs. Banning has asked for some pound cakes with almonds and rose water. Richard likes it, and she wants to have it one more time before he leaves for Princeton next week."

Sarah nodded. "From the bakery on Michigan Avenue."

"She never has a kind word to say when I try to make it myself."

"The bakery adds rose petals," Sarah said. "I heard the baker say so himself."

"It doesn't matter. I'm happy to have one less thing to cook. Go fetch it and we'll serve it with lunch."

"Yes, of course."

"You look a fright, Sarah. Don't bring that face to serving the table."

Mrs. Fletcher disappeared into the butler's pantry while Sarah rolled her eyes.

Sarah felt as if her blood had turned to sludge. The last thing that interested her was trudging over to Michigan Avenue to fetch pound cake. The grandfather clock in the foyer gonged ten times, and as its final tones faded, Sarah's mind quickened.

She did not have to go straight to the bakery.

Sarah set the last dessert fork in place, then hustled through the kitchen and up the back stairs. In her room, she stripped off her apron and added a striking yellow jacket over her black dress. With the right hat cocked at a precise angle, the ensemble was more than passable. If only her eyes were not so bloodshot. Sarah pinched some color into her cheeks and stepped as lightly as she could down the stairs. It would be better if no one saw her leave and watched the direction she chose.

Instead of heading west to Michigan Avenue, Sarah scurried south along Prairie Avenue. Lillie might not have spoken to anyone yet. Perhaps she would agree to see Sarah. Perhaps she would hear Sarah out.

Outside the Wagner house, Sarah paused to catch her breath and tug her jacket back into place. A lock of hair had sprung loose, and now she tucked it into a pin under her hat. When she felt she could control her breathing, she approached the door and pulled the bell.

"Good morning, Miss Cuthbert," the housekeeper said. "Is Miss Wagner expecting you?"

Miss Cuthbert. At least the Wagners' household help had not yet heard the truth.

"No, I don't believe she is." Sarah invoked as bright a tone as possible. "This is rather a spur-of-the-moment call."

"I will let her know you're here."

Mrs. Burnett escorted Sarah into the Wagner parlor, where she sat with her hands clenched in her lap, forcing herself to breathe at regular intervals without gulping.

Lillie descended the stairs in no hurry. The traitor could wait. When Mrs. Burnett announced that Miss Serena Cuthbert was paying a call, Lillie had been tempted to deny knowing the visitor. Serena Cuthbert did not exist, after all. But after sleeping hardly a wink the night before, Lillie thought it might do her some good to speak her mind to Sarah Cummings. She paused in the doorway to the parlor and crossed her arms.

Sarah stood up and pressed her hands together. "Hello, Lillie."

Lillie pressed her hands together in front of her. "Hello, *Sarah*."

"I was hoping we could talk." Sarah took a step toward Lillie.

"About what? More stories about Europe? New Hampshire? Lake Forest?" Lillie moved into the room, but she did not sit down. "My guess is you have never lived anywhere but Chicago."

"You guess correctly," Sarah said softly. "Is it so terrible for me to dream of going to those places?"

"Everything you've ever said to me was a lie." Lillie was just as furious at herself. How could she have been so naïve to believe every word that came out of this woman's mouth?

"Not everything."

"You did teach me how to cut out a dress," Lillie conceded. "Now I understand all the fashions I've admired in your wardrobe are your own work."

"My mother taught me early," Sarah said.

Lillie spoke softly now. "I'm sorry you lost your parents."

"Thank you."

"But you were wrong to lie to me all this time. I thought I had a friend. And I really need a friend. I was going to ask you to stand up with me at my wedding."

"And I would have said yes."

"You mean Serena would have said yes." The bite was back in Lillie's tone. She could hear it herself.

"I *am* Serena," Sarah said. "Don't you see that?"

"Serena is someone you created."

"She's someone I've become."

"But she doesn't exist."

"Doesn't she? Haven't you stitched dresses with her? Shared meals? When Paul kissed you the first time, didn't you tell Serena before anyone else?"

"You know what I mean," Lillie insisted. "There is no Serena Cuthbert. There can't possibly be a birth certificate or school records. She certainly has never been to France."

"That's all true," Sarah said, "but it doesn't mean she doesn't exist."

"You're confusing me."

"I don't mean to." Sarah crossed the room and put a hand on Lillie's arm. "Please don't tell Brad."

"How can you possibly think you can persist in this farce? You can't hope to marry a man without telling him the truth."

"But what is the truth? When I am Serena, I'm *real*. That's what Brad knows. It's what he wants."

"You're taking advantage of him."

"If he comes to care for me in a genuine way, how is that taking advantage of him? Serena can make him happy. *I* can make him happy."

"You don't even know who you are."

"I know what I want," Sarah said. "Yes, I lived in St. Andrew's. Yes, I am a parlor maid for the Bannings. Yes, I make my own clothes. Does that mean I can never have anything more, *be* anything else? You would never have spoken to me that first day in the hat shop if you knew I was in service."

Lillie squirmed out of Sarah's grasp and took a few steps across the room. Sarah was right. She had leaped at friendship with someone she assumed shared her background and her status. The way Sarah was dressed that day, the hat she was considering, the bag she carried.

"Are you going to break off our friendship now because I'm a maid?" Sarah asked.

Lillie shook her head. "No, not because you are a maid, but because you are a liar!"

"You don't understand!"

"The facts are perfectly clear."

"I'm not talking about facts," Sarah said. "I'm talking about dreams. Even parlor maids have dreams, and dreams are as real as facts."

Lillie stared vacantly at the landscape painting over the fireplace while she thought. "All right," she finally said, "I won't tell anyone. But we can't see each other, because I will not take part in actively perpetuating this deceit. It's sure to catch up with you. If Brad comes to care for you—and you for him—he deserves to know the truth."

Simon moved from shop to shop. This was not one of his favorite things to do, but experience had shown that if the director made the appeal personally, more shop owners responded. He simply wanted to place collection jars in the shops between now and Christmas and encourage generosity for St. Andrew's. A few pennies every week in each shop up and down Michigan Avenue added up. He progressed from dry goods stores and grocers to dress shops and hat shops. Today he was merely making a list. He would return in a week or so to place the jars.

A bell jangled when he entered the bakery. Any of the children would have squealed in disbelief at what the store offered—cakes, pies, cookies, breads of every variety.

"Hello, Simon," the baker said. "I think we made too much bread this morning. I may have the boy bring you a dozen loaves at the end of the day."

"Thank you, Roy." Simon knew Roy had baked too much bread quite intentionally. "Are you willing to take a collection jar again this year?"

"Why do you ask a foolish question, my friend?"

The bell jangled again.

"Ah, the lovely maid from the Bannings," Roy said. "What can I do for you today?"

Simon pivoted. "Good morning, Sarah."

She barely looked at him. "Morning, Simon. Roy, Mrs. Banning wants two of your rose water pound cakes. Have you got any today?"

"Certainly. I'll just wrap them in the back." The baker disappeared behind a curtain.

Simon and Sarah were left with each other. Simon thrust a hand into his patch pocket and twiddled his fingers. Sarah's eyes did not seem to settle on anything, Simon noticed. She stood perfectly still, not showing even a hint of interest in the three-tiered red velvet cake in the case in front of her.

"What a pleasure to run into you," Simon said. He moistened his lips.

"Likewise."

She could not mean that. She had not even looked at him.

"I was sorry you were unable to attend the textile show," Simon ventured, never having mastered the art of fishing for information in a subtle way.

"Oh. Right. The textile show. Yes, I'm sure I would have enjoyed that. Unfortunately, the schedule just did not work out."

"Did Miss Wagner find your class yesterday?" Simon asked. "She inquired in the office, but I'm afraid no one was available to escort her down the hall."

"She found me," Sarah said, "but it turned out she was not able to stay after all."

"Another time, then. She seems quite eager."

She turned her head slightly away from him, her complexion blanched with the effort of withholding tears. Simon had seen enough of the older girls on the brink of tears to recognize the expression. He had seen Sarah just yesterday, when he opened the classroom door for her, and she had seemed fine. Simon glanced toward the curtain.

"Sarah," he said, "if something's wrong, I hope you know you can always talk to me."

She did not speak. Simon saw the muscles of her throat struggle to swallow.

"Sarah, I want to help you."

"I'm not one of your orphans anymore."

Her words slapped him. "No, of course not. But I can see you're distressed."

"No, I'm not."

Even in her denial, her protest cracked.

"Whatever it is, Sarah."

She sucked in her breath and turned toward him.

Roy came through the curtain. "Here you go." He thumped a package down on the counter. "It's on the account."

"Thank you, Roy." Sarah picked up the package and left the shop without glancing at Simon.

"She dresses pretty smart for a maid," Roy said.

Simon watched the bright yellow jacket vanish into the flow of Saturday shoppers.

⌖

Sarah set a brisk pace back to Prairie Avenue. She had been gone far longer than the errand required and was counting on nobody being sure what time she had left the house. With relief, she found the kitchen unoccupied, although meal preparation was clearly in process for lunch. She left the pound cakes on the counter and scampered up the servants' stairs to retrieve her apron. As she tied it behind her back, she took several deep breaths.

She had not known what to expect from Lillie. A promise not to tell Brad was no small thing. At least it brought a reprieve while Sarah sorted out what to do next.

Under other circumstances she would have taken a few minutes to drop by the Lexington, and she hoped she still might sneak over in the afternoon. Brad had not sent a note since they'd seen each other on Wednesday. Sarah reminded herself that this was only the third day. The evening had not been particularly exciting, she had to admit. She spent more of it with Mr. Curtis than she did with Brad, and in the end Brad merely kissed her hand, claimed it was impossible for him to get away—again—and sent her home in his carriage.

Still, he smiled when he looked at her, and Sarah was sure it pleased him that she smiled back. He meant to pay attention to her, she was certain. It was just that his affairs were so complicated just now.

"After the election," she said aloud.

26

"You've been moping around for weeks," Karl said. "Do you need to see a doctor?"

"No, I don't need a doctor." Sarah shoved the mop into the pail, rung it out slightly, and slapped it against the floor in the second floor hall. "What are you doing up here, anyway? Don't you have somewhere to drive?"

Karl flexed his muscles. "Mrs. Banning asked for some boxes from the attic. Baby things for Miss Lucy, I think."

"I suppose it's beneath Penard's dignity to go to the attic himself," Sarah muttered.

"Don't be so glum."

"Mind your own business."

Karl grinned and continued down the hall.

Sarah shoved the mop again. Tomorrow would be three weeks, and she had not seen Bradley Townsend even once. Twice Brad had sent notes suggesting they meet for tea or a late supper, but both times, before Sarah could even try to finagle the time away from the house, notes had arrived to cancel. Sarah had seen enough of the headlines to know that Arkansas and Vermont had voted early and both states had gone to McKinley. William Jennings Bryan clearly was losing in the East, which surely pleased Brad. Surely his political commitments would ease up.

There was still the matter of the board of trade, of course. It had remained closed for weeks already. Now no one expected it to open again until after the election, but that did not mean business-men were not negotiating deals. Sarah supposed Brad was wheeling and dealing to preserve his financial prospects. In fact, she hoped he was, for the sake of her own financial prospects.

Lillie had not been back to St. Andrew's. At the Banning family dinner the previous Thursday night, Lucy had wondered aloud why Lillie Wagner had lost interest so abruptly. Sarah had simply cleared the salad plates.

Sarah had to admit to herself that she did not know Lillie well enough to be sure she would not let something slip. What if Edith Wagner asked why Serena was not coming around anymore? What would Lillie do with the dresses she had finished?

Sarah plunged the mop in the water again, releasing the dirt and watching it darken the liquid.

She was not going to mop floors forever.

She smacked the floor again.

She was not going to dust parlors. She was not going to lay tables. She was not going to make her own clothes from used fabric.

She had to find a way to see Brad—to bump into him casually somewhere—and remind him of Serena's charms.

Footsteps behind her made her turn around.

"When you're finished here," Mr. Penard said, "go to Mrs. Banning's room. She left three dresses on the bed. She would like you to repair the hem on the blue one. The others are for you."

Sarah clenched her jaw. "Yes, sir."

⁓

Sarah waited until Mrs. Fletcher put her feet up and Mary Catherine was up to her elbows in lunch dishes.

"I'm going to take a walk," she said casually.

"You take a walk every day," Mary Catherine observed.

"I like the fresh air."

Sarah went upstairs and changed her dress. She never chanced going to the Lexington in her uniform anymore. She was Serena Cuthbert, after all.

Kenny waved the gray envelope from across the lobby. Sarah maintained her composure as she clicked her heels against the marble floor at a dignified pace.

"You've been getting a lot of notes lately," Kenny said, "yet you don't look happy."

"I'm happy. Why wouldn't I be happy?"

Kenny held the envelope out. "You've been miserable for weeks."

Sarah flashed her brightest Serena smile as she took the letter. "Thank you, Kenny, for the message. I hope we'll see each other again soon."

"There's something else," he said, bending to a cubby below the desk. He slid a small blue velvet box across the desk.

Sarah stifled a smile. She would not give Kenny the satisfaction. "Thank you again," she said, picking up the promising box.

She carried the envelope and box to a chair near the window and opened them carefully—first the box. It contained a pair of small sapphire earrings. They were not ostentatious, Sarah was relieved to see, but tasteful and beautifully simple. A moan escaped as Sarah thought that Brad Townsend had the most exquisite taste. She turned to the note. *Dinner downtown . . . Saturday, September 26 . . . please do reply . . . affectionately yours.*

Sarah mentally composed her reply as she sauntered back to Prairie Avenue. She would write it on Lexington Hotel stationery and mail it tomorrow. Then she began to plan her dress. She needed something that would be perfect for showing off the earrings.

Sarah helped Mary Catherine with the dinner dishes. She even volunteered to scrub the pots. They climbed the back stairs together when the job was done.

"I have a favor to ask," Sarah said.

"I wondered why you helped with the dishes."

"I like to think we can help each other," Sarah responded. She opened the door to her room. "Let's talk in here."

"Do you want to trade your day off again?" Mary Catherine asked as she plopped on Sarah's bed.

Sarah nodded. "I need to have the night off a week from Saturday. I'll work Wednesday and you can go out, plus I'll work all day Saturday until the staff supper."

"I don't know," Mary Catherine said. "What if Mr. Penard won't allow it?"

"We've done it before," Sarah reminded her. "Remember when your sister had a baby and you wanted to go see her?"

"Yes, but that was a special case."

"How about when your friend from school invited you out?"

"She came all the way from Milwaukee in the middle of the week," Mary Catherine said. "I couldn't tell her I had to stay in and wash dishes."

"Mrs. Fletcher only cares if she has someone to help with dinner, and I will. I promise."

"It's Mr. Penard I'm worried about."

"He's been letting you serve dinner more often," Sarah pointed out. "You know how to do it."

"I don't want to get in trouble."

"You won't, as long as the work gets done. I'll even work two Wednesdays. I just need that Saturday night off."

Mary Catherine twisted her lips to one side. "I suppose it would be all right."

When Sarah was alone a minute later, she snatched the two new dresses off the trunk where she had laid them. One of them was an ordinary day dress, unremarkable striped chambray. The other was a silk organza gown with potential, the most delicate shade of peach Sarah had ever seen. She took the dress to her bed, where she could examine the seams in better light. Taking them apart without marring the fabric would be a fragile procedure.

—⟡—

Simon waited for the Friday afternoon knock. He looked at the clock three times within two minutes, thinking surely it must be time for Sarah. The precisely stacked papers on his desk were the fruit of his nerves. He had in front of him only the page where he had listed the reasons for and against accepting extra children at St. Andrew's. He would have to make a final decision soon. The practical reasons were all in the column against taking the children. The compassionate reasons were all in the column for welcoming them.

When the knock finally came, it startled him.

"Come in." The door opened and Sarah's dark head leaned in. Simon stood up. "Hello, Sarah."

"I don't want to disturb your work," she said. "I just need the classroom door unlocked."

"I wonder if we might have a word first."

"Of course." Sarah stepped into the room.

"A friend of mine is in a brass band," Simon said. "They're giving a concert next week—on Wednesday. I wondered if you might like to hear them play."

"Wednesday? I'm afraid not, Simon. I promised Mary Catherine I would work for her that day."

"I see. Well, another time then."

"Perhaps."

That was a polite non-commitment, Simon realized, first for the textile show and now for the band concert. He moved on. "I've also been wondering about Miss Wagner. She seemed so intent on becoming involved, and now we haven't heard from her in a while."

"I'm sure she's busy." Sarah adjusted her hat. "And didn't I hear she recently became engaged?"

"Oh? I hadn't heard that." Simon rubbed his temple with two fingers. "Still, it seems odd. I should telephone or send a note."

"Sometimes people think they want to do something, but it doesn't turn out to be practical."

"Are you sure she didn't say anything when she came to your class? Did you detect any slight hesitancy?"

"She left before the class even started," Sarah said. "We only spoke for a moment. Give her some time. If she's really interested, she'll be back."

"I suppose so." Simon stroked his chin.

"Simon, I was thinking of taking you up on your offer to use the sewing machine in the classroom. I'll need to practice on something before I try to teach the girls to use it."

"Of course."

"Does anyone know how to use it?"

"I believe it came with an instruction sheet. Let's look in the drawer."

~⌒~

By Saturday of the next week, Sarah derived her energy from anticipation. She had worked almost two weeks without a day off, and every night was spent working on the dress well past midnight. But it would all be worth it when Brad's carriage arrived at the Lexington Hotel to pick up Miss Serena Cuthbert in only a few more hours.

She was in the kitchen slicing bread for the staff's supper when Penard came in from his butler's pantry.

"Mary Catherine has informed me that she will be serving dinner tonight," he said.

Sarah's stomach heaved, but she remained calm. Mary Catherine was not supposed to say anything! Just do it.

"I asked her if she might," Sarah said. "I need the evening off for personal reasons." She drew the knife through the bread again.

"I'm afraid that is not possible." Mr. Penard stiffened.

Sarah's hand trembled and she put the knife down. "It's all been arranged. Mary Catherine will clear the family dinner dishes. The table is laid, and the food is under way. Mrs. Fletcher will have all the help she needs."

"It's a matter of principle," Mr. Penard said, and crossed both arms behind his back. "The staff assignments are my responsibility. I do not appreciate the maids repeatedly making their own arrangements."

"Mr. Penard, everything is accounted for! I've already worked through my day off so as not to cause anyone any inconvenience."

"It is not a matter of convenience. It is a matter of respect for the way this household is managed. You will not go out this evening."

"But Mr. Penard—"

"Do not be insolent, Sarah. You have my decision."

He pivoted and left the room.

Sarah breathed hard. If she defied him, he would dismiss her. She was too close to being out for good to risk having to find a new position even for a few months. And in a new position she would never manage any time off to see Brad. In another five weeks the election would be over. Brad would become more serious. And soon after that, he would propose. Serena would make sure he did. Then Sarah would walk out the female servants' entrance for the last time.

Sarah lowered herself into a kitchen chair, her chest heaving and her vision narrowing. She did not even look up at the sound of Karl's boots crossing the black and white kitchen tiles.

"Don't tell me you don't look glum now," Karl said.

Sarah looked up. "Karl, if I asked you to do something, would you do it, no questions asked?"

He did not answer immediately, but finally began to nod his head. "If you need something, I'll do it."

"I need you to deliver a note. That's all. But I don't want you to ask any questions about the name or address, because I can't answer them."

"Fair enough."

The note she handed Karl twenty minutes later, written on stationery from the Lexington Hotel, expressed deep regret at having to break the date at the last minute, and great anticipation at seeing Brad again very soon. By the time she finished writing it, Sarah had convinced herself that breaking a date with Brad—as he had done repeatedly with her—would only add to Serena's allure. Brad would know he could not take Serena for granted, and he would pay more attention.

27

"Where are you going tonight?"

Mary Catherine's curiosity more than two weeks later pleased Sarah, but she was not about to satisfy it. She made sure the sash knotted at her waist was secure.

"Ever since we came back from the lake," Mary Catherine said, "you don't just dress nice to go out on your day off. You look like you're going to a society party every time you leave the house."

Sarah adjusted the tops of her sleeves and examined her appearance in the mirror. "Maybe I am."

"You're a parlor maid. Who do you know who gives that kind of party?"

I am not a parlor maid.

"I have friends. Maybe someday I'll introduce you." *Never.*

"You got me in trouble, you know," Mary Catherine said. "You promised it wouldn't matter if we traded that Saturday night."

"It wouldn't have if you had not opened your big mouth and told Penard ahead of time."

"I didn't have a choice! The way he asked the question—I couldn't lie straight to his face. I promise I didn't do anything to make him suspect."

"Never mind," Sarah said. "We'll be more careful next time."

"I'm not sure I want to keep trading with you."

"I'll make it worth your while."

Mary Catherine threw up her hands. "Have a good time, wherever you're going."

"I will."

Sarah opened her top dresser drawer and took out the newspaper clipping. Leo had ripped something out of the bottom of the page Monday morning at breakfast and left the paper open. Sarah picked up the fragment when she cleared the table and scanned it without thinking. When she recognized some of the names mentioned, she paid closer attention. The names were not close neighbors of the Bannings, but they were well known in Chicago.

They were just the sort of people Brad Townsend would know, she had told herself as she tore the half-article out of the paper and tucked it in her skirt pocket. The Bannings themselves were not listed, nor had they given any indication they would attend the party the society page highlighted. Sarah's plan had taken form in an instant and Mrs. Fletcher's dinner menu for Wednesday night confirmed it. Flora, Samuel, and Leo would be dining at home, and there was no chance she would run into them.

Brad had not even acknowledged her note of regret. Words of his disappointment that he could not see her had never come. Was there any disappointment? As annoyed as Sarah had been at his making dates and breaking them, she preferred that to silence.

The party tonight could change the balance of their relationship. Serena would arrive at the party. She would meet people, chat with people, smile at people. She would glance over her shoulder at Brad and make him curious and wonder who she was with. He would cross the room to be with her. He would offer to escort her back to the Lexington.

Evenings were cool now, and Sarah was glad. She could wear a long cloak to protect her evening dress on public transportation. Her brown cloak was ordinary and was not a hand-me-down from Flora Banning or Violet Newcomb, but last winter Sarah had sewn in a new lining of sky blue silk. A simple practiced movement would flash elegant color at strategic moments.

Sarah made her way downstairs and into the back hall without acknowledging anyone in the kitchen. Where she was going was none of their business. She paused only long enough to put on the sapphire earrings before she found an elevated train and rode toward downtown Chicago. Two blocks from the hotel serving as the party's venue, Sarah got off the train and flagged a hansom cab. The driver gave her an odd look and glanced toward her destination, which they could both see easily from where they stood. His expression suggested she ought to just walk. Sarah ignored him. Serena Cuthbert did not arrive at parties by train or on foot.

⤙⤚

The hotel was modest—not nearly as lavish as the Palmer House—but the electric lights exuded welcome and anticipation. A doorman stepped to the curb to open the carriage door. Serena handed a coin to the driver and waited as a second doorman held open the door to the marble lobby. An attendant quickly took her cloak and directed her to a room where ladies could freshen up. Sarah took advantage of the amenities to be sure Serena Cuthbert would make a stunning impression. By the time she glided through the wide doors of the ballroom, Serena Cuthbert had arrived.

Sarah held her chin high as she surveyed the room. The silver gown competed well with anything she saw in the room. At the far end was a small stage and a collection of four chairs and music stands, but at the moment the only sounds to fill the room were the buzz of conversation and the rustle of full skirts. Tables were draped with gray jacquard cloths and adorned with pink roses. While the evening did not boast a formal meal, servers milled around the room with trays of appetizers and beverages. A young woman in ubiquitous black dress and white apron meekly offered refreshment to Sarah, who selected a shrimp canapé and held it delicately on a small plate.

She did not see Brad Townsend, but that did not mean he would not appear before the evening was over. Serena Cuthbert, though, would not wait for a man like a wallflower. Holding her canapé, Sarah drifted casually around the room, always seeming to be headed somewhere, toward someone, but without any real destination. She smiled and nodded her way in a wide circuit, occasionally pausing to converse with someone she had met at one of Brad's political events. She did not see many of that crowd, however, which discouraged her. If few of his friends were at this party, would Brad himself come? Nevertheless, she chatted with his friends about the good news that Florida's early voting had gone for William McKinley and the threat of William Jennings Bryan as a serious presidential candidate was fading. Bryan had already conceded most of the Eastern seaboard and turned his campaign efforts to the West.

As she sauntered across the far end of the room, Sarah finally ate the canapé and accepted a beverage from a passing waiter. She began to wonder what the musical entertainment would be. A string quartet, certainly, but what group would perform on the stage?

"Sarah!"

Sarah gasped at the voice calling her name and spun around. "Jane! What are you doing here?"

"Singing, of course, with the choir. Well, we're not really a choir, just some orphans singing a few songs. But Mr. Tewell likes to call us a choir."

"You're singing here?"

"Well, yes. Didn't I just say so? I love your dress, Sarah!"

"Thank you." Sarah glanced beyond Jane and saw a handful of children milling around the side of the stage. Through the doorway behind them, she saw even more children in a hallway.

And she recognized them all. Every single one. Why was a group of children from St. Andrew's Orphanage preparing to sing at a society party?

"Sarah, do you think I'll ever be able to make a dress as pretty as yours?" Jane asked.

Sarah stifled the urge to simply tell the girl to be quiet. Jane had managed to say "Sarah" three times already—loudly.

Jane prattled on. "I suppose I'll have to practice on a few more skirts and blouses, and maybe I should learn to use the machine. But someday I'll make an evening dress."

"I'm sure you can if you put your mind to it." Sarah craned to look over her shoulder.

Mr. Curtis, Brad's friend, was headed directly toward her.

"It's lovely to see you, Miss Cuthbert," he said.

"Good evening, Mr. Curtis," Sarah answered.

"Did Mr. Townsend know you were going to be here?"

"No, I don't believe so." Sarah was counting on Jane's polite silence. Though the girl had become more at ease with Sarah, she was still shy by nature. At the moment her eyes were wide and fixed on Mr. Curtis's formal wear with silk lapels.

"I'm sure had he known," Mr. Curtis said, "he would have made more of an effort to attend this charity event."

Charity event? It did not sound as if Brad were coming, but at least now Sarah could be fairly sure he would learn Serena had been there. The evening was not an entire waste. But the presence of the children from St. Andrew's and the description "charity event" made Sarah nervous.

After another moment of small talk, Mr. Curtis moved on.

Jane looked puzzled. "Why did he call you Miss Cuthbert?"

Sarah took a deep breath. "Because to him I am Miss Cuthbert."

"Does he think you're Sarah Cuthbert instead of Sarah Cummings?"

"Let's talk about this over here." Sarah put an arm on Jane's shoulder and nudged her toward the wall. "Miss Cuthbert's name is Serena."

Jane's eyes flashed. "You're pretending to be this Miss Cuthbert, aren't you?"

"Not exactly. I am Serena Cuthbert."

"But you're Sarah Cummings."

"Jane, you write your dreams down in your journal, right?"

Jane nodded. "I used to. Before."

"Well, I'm old enough that I don't have to just write them down. I can make them happen."

"That's why you told me it's okay to imagine."

Now Sarah nodded. "You understand, right?"

"I'm not sure." Jane creased her forehead. "Aren't you lying?"

"Are you lying when you write in your journal?" Sarah countered.

"Well . . . no . . . I guess not. I'm imagining. Just like you said."

"So am I. How can a dream come true without imagining?"

Alonzo thumped toward them. "Come on, Jane. We have to get ready to sing. Then the people will give their money."

"I have to go now," Jane said, and Sarah was alone again.

She let out her breath. She had exchanged political fund-raisers for an orphanage fund-raiser. The scrap of newspaper that had steered her here had not mentioned that detail. If only she had seen the headline.

She had to get out of there. Sarah set her drink down on the nearest table and maintained a stately composure as she took a more direct route across the room.

She was almost to the door when Emma Pearce grabbed her arm. "There you are, Serena! I heard you were here."

"Hello, Emma!" Sarah offered Serena's dazzling smile.

"I think it was a darling idea to have the orphans come tonight, don't you? It's lovely to think that someone is teaching them music."

"I was not aware they had a choir," Sarah said truthfully. In the background a string quartet began to tune.

"Of course, I hope they're also learning some more practical skills," Emma continued. "I doubt we'll find a Franz Liszt or Johann Strauss among them. But they'll be able to comfort themselves with a ditty now and then."

"Comfort themselves?" Sarah echoed.

"They have such difficult lives and so little to look forward to." Emma stated this sentiment as if it were proven fact.

"If they aspire, they might achieve their goals," Sarah said, a smile still plastered on her face.

Emma suddenly waved a hand. "Oh, there's the orphanage director now! Mr. Tewell!"

To Sarah's horror, Simon responded to his name and approached them. "Good evening, Mrs. Pearce."

"Miss Cuthbert, I'd like you to meet Mr. Simon Tewell. Mr. Tewell, this is Miss Serena Cuthbert."

Simon extended a hand. "It's delightful to meet you, Miss Cuthbert."

His words were even and polite. But he held her hand a fraction of a second too long. Its warmth lingered when she broke the clasp and squirmed under his gaze.

"It's a pleasure to meet you, Mr. Tewell," Sarah said.

"I was just telling Serena it's a darling idea to have the children here," Emma said.

"They seem excited to sing," Simon said pleasantly. "I hope you and Miss Cuthbert both will enjoy the music."

"Serena, those earrings are absolutely stunning!" Emma said.

"Thank you." Sarah surrendered to the blush as she felt Simon's eyes on her.

"They are most becoming." Simon tilted his head and gave a small smile.

"I'll leave you two to get to know one another," Emma said. "I seem to have misplaced my husband."

When Emma was gone, Sarah swallowed hard. "Thank you, Simon."

"What are you doing?" he asked, his voice low, his eyes pained.

Sarah could not stand to look at his face. "I was just leaving," she answered. "I think it's best under the circumstances, don't you agree?"

"You're here, whatever the circumstances. Why don't you stay and hear what the children can do. It would mean something to them."

Sarah eyed the door. "You're most gracious, Simon, but I'm certain it's best if I go."

She snatched her cloak from the attendant and ran for the nearest elevated train station. Only once it was in motion did Sarah allow herself to exhale.

28

*S*arah stood frozen outside Simon's office door.

All morning she had tussled with not coming.

She could say she was sick, but Simon would know she was not. Eventually she would have to face him.

Leaving things the way they were with Jane caused a physical pain in Sarah's stomach.

Ending the class abruptly—never going back—seemed cowardly, and the last thing Sarah would allow herself to be was a coward.

So she exhaled, smoothed her skirt, and knocked as she did every Friday afternoon.

Simon, sitting in the chair behind his desk, looked up and she met his eyes. The questions he did not ask hung between them, a thick but transparent wall. Sarah waited to see if he would speak—undecided whether she wished he would. She twisted both hands around the strap to her handbag.

"I came a little early today." Sarah broke the silence. "I thought I might try using the machine."

Simon stood up and walked around his desk. "Very well. I'll open the room." He fumbled in a pocket for a ring of keys.

"Also, I want to explain about the other night." She might as well get it over with.

Simon stopped his steps and sat on the corner of his desk, his feet planted solidly on the floor and his arms crossed.

"Serena Cuthbert—she just happened one day." Sarah was talking too fast, but she could not stop. "I met someone new, and she asked my name, and that's what came out."

"I don't understand." Simon measured his questions. "Why would the name of someone who does not exist be the first thing to come to your mind?"

"It just did. Then she wanted to be friends." Sarah's breath caught. "No one has wanted to be my friend in a long time."

Simon uncrossed his arms and held his palms up. "I rather hoped you had noticed that I wanted to be your friend."

Sarah had no response and settled for focusing her eyes on a globe between two thick books on the credenza under the window. Of course she knew.

"What would make you persist with this fiction?" Simon's voice had softened. "Clearly you thought that party was something other than what it was. You couldn't get out of there fast enough once you realized the truth."

"I . . . miscalculated, that's all."

"Why do you deny yourself, Sarah?"

Sarah swallowed. He had it all wrong. "I don't think of it as denying myself. I think of it as finding myself."

"In a life you made up?"

"In a life I hope someday to have."

"I see."

She was not convinced he did. "What do you see, Simon? Do you see a girl who is deluded, or one who is determined? A woman who has lost her mind, or one who is using her mind to find a better life?"

He spoke quietly. "I see a woman who wants to be loved. A woman who was well loved as a girl and has been afraid ever since that no one will ever love her again. So she gives up on love, even God's love, and chases the next best thing."

"You don't understand." Sarah broke her fixation on the globe and looked at Simon through misty eyes.

"Don't I?" He moved toward her, took both her hands in his, and pulled her to him.

The gesture sent a shiver up her arms. When he leaned in, her breath caught.

"I feel as if I have waited years for you," Simon murmured. "I'm not going to let Sarah Cummings disappear into Serena Cuthbert without letting you know my true feelings."

His hands moved to her face, and Sarah trembled. She had not been touched with love in so many years she had nearly forgotten the mystery.

When his lips touched hers, she briefly thought she ought to be offended, but she wasn't. This was not like the kiss Kenny had attempted when she was sixteen and he was an under-coachman on Prairie Avenue. Nor was it like the one a footman had once offered in the back hall. The softness of it, the gentleness. This was a kiss of love that layered trustworthiness and security and faith.

But it was not Brad's kiss, not the one she had been dreaming of. Sarah pulled away and put two fingers to her lips.

"I suppose this is where I am supposed to beg your forgiveness," Simon murmured, "but I would be insincere in doing so."

Sarah tried to catch her breath, but had no words.

"Will you have dinner with me on Wednesday evening?" He held his face close to hers. "That is still your day off, is it not?"

Sarah nodded.

"Yes, it's your day off, or yes, you'll go to dinner?"

Sarah nodded again.

"I'll wait for you outside the servants' entrance at six."

⁓⁓

They walked awkwardly to the classroom, where Simon unlocked the door, then left Sarah alone. It was still early. Sarah sat at the sewing machine and pulled out the instruction sheet. She studied the diagram for how to thread it. It seemed to her that threading the contraption was the most difficult task. If she could do that properly, working the treadle with her feet would just be a matter of discovering an efficient rhythm.

When she sensed a presence in the doorframe, Sarah looked up expecting one of the girls had arrived early.

"Hello," Lillie said.

The instruction sheet fell to the floor as Sarah lurched to her feet. "Hello."

"I'm not sure what to call you," Lillie said.

"I've missed you," Sarah blurted out, because it was true.

"I've missed you, too," Lillie said. "I mean, I've missed my friend Serena. I don't really know you."

"Yes, you do." Sarah took a tentative step toward Lillie. The table consumed the space between them.

"I'm here for the class." Lillie ran a gloved hand along the table's edge. "I realize it's awkward for both of us, but I've decided I'm not giving up on it because . . . because—"

"Because I lied to you." Sarah moved around the end of the table, closer to Lillie.

"Well, yes. I suppose that's it. But I do want to help with the children, and clearly you are a talented seamstress and I can learn a great deal from you."

"You're welcome to stay." Sarah was standing beside Lillie now. "It would be nice to spend some time together."

"Do you seriously still expect we could be friends?" Lillie paced around the table until she was again staring at Sarah across its width.

"I'm not expecting you would want to have anything to do with a parlor maid," Sarah said flatly. She moved back to the machine and picked up the instruction leaflet again.

"You said you've missed me."

"I have. You were my friend."

"Friendship is based on truth," Lillie said. "You said it yourself. I am not hesitant because you are a maid, but because you deceived me."

"You haven't walked in my shoes." Sarah tossed the instructions at the machine and spun toward Lillie. "You've never wanted for anything. You don't understand."

"Being in want is no excuse for deception."

"I did not set out to hurt you."

"Nevertheless you did hurt me. I trusted you."

"You still can," Sarah said.

"You grew up in an orphanage, and I grew up in a big house in Cincinnati," Lillie said. "But if you think that makes any difference in who I really am, then *you* don't understand *me*."

They regarded each other in silence.

"Brad deserves to know the truth," Lillie finally said.

"Truth comes in many colors," Sarah answered. What color was Brad's truth, she wondered. Even as she spoke, though, Simon's kiss lingered on her lips.

A gaggle of girls tumbled through the doorway.

"Did we get any new fabrics?" Melissa asked.

Mary Margaret went straight for the cabinet. "Let's just look."

"Girls," Sarah said, "let's get out your projects and see where everyone stands. We'll sort things out from there." She looked at Lillie, then clapped her hands to command attention. "I'd like you to meet Miss Lillie Wagner. She's come to help us. Miss Wagner does some very nice stitching herself."

The girls murmured a polite welcome.

Jane was missing. A few more girls straggled in, and in another ten minutes everyone was hard at work. Jumping right in, Lillie undertook to help Melissa measure a hem. Sarah had to concede that Jane was not coming.

It was because she knew, Sarah thought. And despite her own journal, Jane's color of truth was the same as Lillie's.

Kenny.

Jane.

Simon.

Lillie.

Too many people knew. If Lillie was so committed to the truth, how much longer would it be before she crossed paths with Brad and revealed the secret?

Sarah's stomach burned, and she lost the flavor of Simon's kiss.

—⁓—

On Saturday morning, Sarah laid the table for breakfast as usual. She glanced at the clock, calculating whether she had time to inspect the newspaper before Leo would come downstairs expecting to find it in pristine condition. Cautiously, she opened the pages, scanning for election news.

What caught her eye was an advertisement rather than an article. Reward! The Democratic National Convention offered a five hundred dollar reward for evidence and conviction of anyone bribing or attempting to bribe a voter, or coercing votes.

If the Democrats were offering the reward, obviously the Republicans were the target. Was this the sort of political maneuvering Brad thought Serena could not understand? Of course, Brad would not personally approach anyone with a crisp five-dollar bill. Sarah had seen how smooth Brad was in action. He would not sully himself with direct contact with the working class.

On the other hand, he would not think twice about providing the funds for whatever it took for his candidate to win the election. But bribing voters? Sarah hated to believe Brad was involved.

Five dollars a head does not seem too much to ensure we win the election, he had said to Mr. Sattler at the ball.

Five hundred dollars—the reward was easily four times what Sarah earned in a year.

Sarah scanned the articles around the advertisement but found nothing incriminating or suggestive of foul play. No mention of specific names. No quotations from anyone who had been approached and offered money to vote for William McKinley. But what little doubt Sarah tried to muster about Brad's involvement dissipated.

She was so absorbed in the paper that she did not hear Leo coming through the lobby. By the time she realized he was in the room, he was lowering himself into his chair. Rapidly, Sarah folded the paper and placed it beside his plate.

"I'm so sorry, Mr. Leo. I should not have been reading your paper."

"Do we have eggs today?" he asked, unperturbed. "What were you reading about?"

Sarah moved into action at the sideboard and spooned scrambled eggs onto a plate, then added some mixed fruit and a roll. "Would you like coffee, sir?"

"Yes, please," he answered. "You haven't answered my question."

"Sir?"

"What were you reading about that was so absorbing?"

"Nothing of consequence, sir."

"You can tell me, Sarah. I won't let on to Penard."

She lifted and lowered one shoulder. "Is it true the Republicans are buying votes and the Democrats are offering a reward to anyone who can prove it?" She set the plate before him and turned back to the sideboard for the coffeepot.

"I suspect it's true, yes," Leo said, "though I doubt it is on a scale large enough to influence the election results. It's a scare tactic, more than anything. Big business has a lot at stake in this election. Mark Hanna has organized a money machine for the Republicans."

Sarah poured coffee. "If you don't mind my saying so, Mr. Leo, you don't seem very political."

Leo laughed. "You mean, for a resident of Prairie Avenue?"

Sarah blushed.

"You've served enough dinner guests here," Leo said, "to hear for yourself what the conversation is like. My father represents his share of big business clients. I have no doubt that people like Mr. Pullman are working closely with Mr. Hanna. But I'm an engineer and a scientist. I'm interested in manufacturing technology on a research level. As much as Pullman and the others dislike it, the labor force is changing. The way things are manufactured in Chicago is changing, and economic policies will have to adapt."

"Yes, sir." Sarah wondered whether she was supposed to decipher from Leo's explanation which presidential candidate he favored. She could not bring herself to voice what was really on her mind. Bradley Townsend was almost certainly among those trying to buy votes.

29

$\mathcal{S}$arah flopped onto her bed, hands over her head.

No matter how many ways she turned things over in her head, they never came out right. Lillie refused to understand. Jane was angry. Brad was unpredictable. And Simon was befuddling.

Simon. Sarah had chosen a suit to wear to dinner, a beige lightweight wool with forest-green trim. His kiss had persuaded her to go to dinner with him, but her head argued that she should not encourage him. Serena's future lay with Brad. Despite Lillie's stand on the matter, Sarah had not given up hope. One day Lillie would accept Serena again.

Already four days had passed since Simon kissed her, four days since Lillie visited the class—and weeks of not being certain what Brad was thinking. How much more of this anguish could she withstand? Tomorrow night Simon would arrive to take her to dinner, and that would likely thicken the muddle.

Footsteps clunked in the hall, coming to a stop outside her room. Sarah sat up with the first rap on her door.

"Yes?" she said.

Mary Catherine turned the knob and leaned in through the doorframe. "You have a visitor."

"A visitor? Who would be coming to see me?"

"It's that Kenny fellow, the one who used to be coachman for the Pullmans."

Sarah was on her feet. "He was only an under-coachman. What's he doing here?"

"He says he has to talk to you on an urgent matter. He's in the courtyard. The poor man can hardly breathe."

Sarah pushed past Mary Catherine and scrambled down the stairs and out the door off the kitchen that led to the courtyard. Kenny leaned against a ledge, his shoulders heaving.

"Kenny!" Sarah cried. "What's going on?"

"He's there. At the Lexington."

Sarah needed no explanation.

"Are you sure? You've never met him."

"I know his carriage and his driver. He came to the desk to ask after you personally."

Sarah's eyes widened. "What did you tell him?"

"I said I had not seen Miss Cuthbert all morning. Then he said he would wait for a while to see if the lady might arrive. He's having a cup of tea in the lobby. So I hightailed it over here. Can you get away?"

"I'll have to finagle the afternoon off." Sarah's mind churned with rapid possibilities. "But Kenny, why would you do this for me? I mean . . . you know . . ."

"I know you're not really Serena Cuthbert, and I could lose my job for leaving my post. Is that what you mean?"

She nodded.

"I've been following the saga for months," he said, grinning. "I don't want to miss the drama now that it's getting good!"

"Oh, stop it, Kenny."

"No, really. I hope you find the happy ending you're looking for."

"Thank you, Kenny." Sarah nearly leaned forward to kiss Kenny's cheek.

"What do you want me to tell him?"

"Keep stalling," she answered. "Tell him you've just received word that Miss Cuthbert is due within a half an hour."

"Done!" Kenny was out of the yard before Sarah could get back in the house.

Mary Catherine lurked in the servants' hall. "What is it?"

"I need a few hours off," Sarah said.

"Oh, no. Not this again."

"It's just lunch," Sarah said. "Mrs. Banning is the only one home. I'll be back in plenty of time for dinner and I'll do the washing up for you."

Mrs. Fletcher barked from the stove. "Mary Catherine, the vegetables."

Mary Catherine glanced into the kitchen. "I have a feeling I'm going to be sorry, but all right. You're meeting a man, aren't you! It's so romantic."

"Thank you, Mary Catherine!"

Sarah clambered up the stairs, threw open one of the trunks, and pulled out a fashionable blue paisley day dress. She unbuttoned the dark gray calico she had put on in the morning and stepped out of it. The blue dress slid over her head, her shoulders, her hips, and she buttoned it quickly. In the morning funk, she had taken no care with her hair. Now she had to brush it thoroughly and pin it up under a hat.

In twelve minutes, Sarah was ready to leave the house, wearing both the silver rose pin and the sapphire earrings. She took the stairs more gracefully this time, careful not to put her clothing in disarray while she pulled a wool shawl around her shoulders.

Mary Catherine was at the bottom of the stairs holding two heads of lettuce. "Are you really not going to tell me where you're going?"

"That's right." Sarah was out the door.

Simon paced around his desk. The orphanage board was pressing for his recommendation. He could think of no good solution to the dilemma, but he knew he could not accept forty-eight more children at St. Andrew's. That was more than a ten percent increase at a time when cash donations were dropping off severely. Despite the recent party, fund-raising efforts were falling short of what he had hoped for. He could not ask the cooks to thin the soup or minimize the portions any further for growing children. He had no bed space. He had no money to hire more teachers for the school or more staff for the afternoon hours. The overcrowding would escalate the safety problems already weighing on him.

In his mind, Simon turned phrases and arranged sentences of his written decision. He did not know where else they could go, but the extra children could not come to St. Andrew's.

One thing intruded on his concentration: Sarah. It was barely lunchtime on Tuesday, and fragments of a dinner yet to come on Wednesday bounced around his mind. Simon was convinced Sarah had felt something when he kissed her. Tomorrow he would seek confirmation.

He reached for a fresh sheet of paper and dipped his pen.

─⌒─

"I'd prefer to go somewhere else," she said when Brad suggested that he and Serena might have an impromptu lunch in the restaurant at the Lexington. "For variety."

"Yes, I suppose you eat a lot of meals here." Brad took his pocket watch out of his vest pocket and examined it. "I guess I have time to go somewhere else, if it's close."

"There's a place I love only a few blocks over," she said brightly.

In truth, Sarah had never been in the restaurant, but she had heard the Bannings recommend it. If the Bannings would dine there, surely it would satisfy Brad.

He offered his arm. "The carriage is just outside."

Inside the restaurant, landscapes of the European countryside adorned the limestone walls, spaced tastefully apart so the viewer could focus on one image at a time. Elegant calligraphy identified each of the featured locations. Sarah immediately noted the precision with which the tables were set, the plates and goblets situated in precise relation to each other and strict measurement apart. The tablecloths dropped exactly the same length on each side of the table, and the napkins, tented slightly in the center of the plates, were creased identically. Sarah doubted Brad would appreciate the care it took to make a table look this elegant.

Brad ordered. Sarah barely heard what he said. She was still recovering from the shock of his midday appearance at the Lexington. Whatever the price was when she returned home, a stolen lunch with Brad would be worth it. The waiter bowed slightly and backed away from the table, assuring Brad that he had made an admirable selection.

"I'm so glad you waited for me," she said. "If I had known you were coming by, of course I would not have gone out this morning."

"I did not know myself," Brad said. "A meeting nearby concluded sooner than I expected, and I found myself in your neighborhood. I thought I could at least try to see you."

Sarah's heart swelled. "I'm flattered."

"You've probably wondered about my intermittent attentions," Brad said.

"I know you are busy." Sarah spread her napkin in her lap. "Your political involvements and business affairs must be quite demanding just now."

"The fact is I'm never sure when I'll have some free time. It makes it difficult to plan social engagements."

"I'm quite busy myself," she said. "I've barely kept up with writing to my parents, and making afternoon calls can be so consuming."

"I have been pondering our dilemma," he said, "and wondering how we might see each other more regularly."

"Oh?" This was the turning point Sarah had been waiting for. She put one elbow on the table and leaned toward him. "And have you discovered a solution?"

"I think so." Brad answered. "We need more flexibility, don't you think? Formal invitations and notes back and forth—we lose precious time with the social conventions."

Sarah narrowed her eyes. What was he saying?

"And then of course, we lose more valuable time with the carriage. I don't like to just send my driver for you, but it's cumbersome to come myself, and then there's the time we spend driving to our destination. It seems to me there ought to be a simpler way."

This was not the romantic proposal Sarah had envisioned, but her heart quickened anyway. Yes, if they were married and living together, they could see each other so much more easily.

"We need to be out of the public eye," Brad said, his voice low.

"I beg your pardon?" Sarah said.

"If we had a place where we could meet," he said, "without all the time-consuming entrapments, we could spend so much more time together. I can arrange such a place. We can shut out the whole world and focus only on each other."

The waiter arrived with the soup. Sarah sat back in her chair as he served. If Brad would say something suggestive to Serena Cuthbert, what would he say to Sarah Cummings?

With the arrival of food and the hovering attention of the waiter, Brad shifted the conversation to the progress of the political campaign and the opportunity he had to meet with Mark Hanna. He did not mention again his suggestion that they should meet out of the public eye. When they finished the meal, he dropped her back at the Lexington, politely seeing her into the lobby and kissing her hand before proceeding to his next business meeting with no mention of when he would see her again.

—⚬—

Sarah stoically held herself together to help prepare and serve the Bannings' dinner on Tuesday evening, but on Wednesday afternoon, when her time was finally her own, she lay on her bed red-eyed and stunned for several hours. When Mary Catherine knocked, Sarah told her in no uncertain terms to mind her own business. At five o'clock, though, she splashed cold water on her face, brushed out her hair, twisted it on top of her head, and donned the beige wool suit. Hurting Simon's feelings would not change what happened with Brad. By six o'clock she was downstairs in the servants' hall. When Simon arrived, she took his arm and let him lead her to the streetcar.

The restaurant he had selected was an Irish pub. Simon assured her it had the best corned beef outside of Dublin. One waitress served the small cluster of tables, and Sarah suspected the girl had not had a clean apron in three days. The walls were unadorned rough brick.

They bantered about the Colts and Sarah's growing interest in base ball.

They talked about the girls in the sewing class—carefully avoiding Jane.

By the time their food arrived, Sarah felt a hundred miles away from the previous afternoon.

Sarah learned that Simon's parents farmed rented land in Pennsylvania but had scraped and sacrificed for their son to earn a college degree. Out of gratitude, he sent them a few dollars whenever he could, which was not often. His two older sisters were married with children. He played the banjo. He loved his church, though most weeks he could not attend because he felt he should be with the children at St. Andrew's. He made sure Sunday mornings brought hymns and sermons sensible for children to hear. He was a good storyteller, making her smile with his descriptions of the farm and his accounts of conversations with some of the smallest children.

Simon Tewell had a life.

She'd been so busy inventing Serena Cuthbert's life, Sarah had never imagined what was plain to see now.

She knew nothing of Brad's life, beyond politics and the board of trade.

Simon said nothing of Serena Cuthbert, asked nothing of Sarah. He set aside the formalities of his position as the orphanage director.

After dinner, they ambled back toward Prairie Avenue.

"Do you ever think about going back?" Sarah asked.

"Back?"

"To Pennsylvania. Not to the farm, but Philadelphia, perhaps. You could be closer to your family."

"I think of it occasionally," he admitted. "I've had offers. But something holds me in Chicago."

"The children would be lost without you."

He nodded. "Among other things. What about you? If you had the chance to leave Chicago, would you?"

"I've never even thought of it seriously." She glanced at him. "In my circumstances, how could I?"

"What if I were to take you?" Simon asked softly.

Sarah turned her eyes forward again, warmth oozing through her chest. *I might just go,* she thought, but she said nothing.

"I'm getting ahead of things, aren't I? I don't mean to embarrass you. Let's catch a streetcar on Indiana Avenue," Simon suggested. "I can tell your feet are hurting."

She had to admit he was right. But how had he known? Even she had not noticed her limp until that moment.

At the servants' entrance to the Banning house, Sarah wondered if he would kiss her again.

She hoped he would. When she saw him glancing down the side of the house in both directions, as if to be sure they were alone, she felt her shoulders relax.

"I don't want this evening to end," he said, "without making it unequivocally clear how I feel about you. You don't have to say anything."

When he leaned in to kiss her, she leaned into him.

30

The card shook in Sarah's trembling hand.

I've taken the liberty of making some provisional arrangements on the matter we discussed. I beg of you to meet me on the afternoon of Election Day at 3:30, at which time I have every expectation to be celebrating the success of Mr. McKinley. We can explore the question between us further when we are alone together.

At the bottom, below the flourish of Brad's signature, was the address of an apartment building. Just from the address, Sarah knew it was a luxurious building.

This was Brad's first communication since the impromptu lunch two weeks ago. It was already three in the afternoon of Tuesday, November 3. The city buzzed with election speculation. Every conversation Sarah had overheard all day touched on it. By this time, though, the question had become simply how wide McKinley's margin would be. No one seriously projected any outcome other than his victory. Brad would be exuberant.

"What does he want?"

At the sound of Kenny's voice, Sarah thrust the card into her lap. Uncharacteristically, Kenny had stepped away from the hotel desk and crossed the lobby to approach her.

"He asks that I meet him." Sarah slid the card into her bag.

"Now?"

"Yes."

"Why didn't he come for you?"

"He has pressing engagements because of the election, but he's eager to see me."

"A gentleman would call for you," Kenny said.

Fury rose through Sarah's chest and neck. "Don't you have a bell to answer or something?"

"Don't say I didn't warn you." Kenny pressed his lips together and sauntered back to the main desk.

Sarah studied the clock on one wall of the lobby. The Bannings were hosting an election party later that evening, which meant Mrs. Fletcher would be barking orders in the kitchen earlier than usual. Sarah did not really have time to meet Brad without risking the wrath of Penard.

If she did not go, she could never be sure what he meant.

She stood up and pulled the warm cape around her shoulders. The address was just off a train line. It might not take long after all.

The building was a short two blocks from the elevated train stop. Sarah approached it slowly, soaking in the sweep of the front steps and the wrought iron fence marking the boundaries of the property in a tidy but definitive manner. She ascended the steps gracefully and pushed the handle of the polished oak door. Inside, her steps halted briefly, as if she were uncertain where to go—or whether to go. The lobby of the building was modest and functional. It was not meant to encourage anyone to linger, Sarah decided, which was probably an attractive feature for Brad. The elevator was mere steps from the door, with its ornate copperplated bronze grillwork. She entered the cage and asked the operator for the third floor.

Sarah stepped out of the elevator into a wide hall with nine-foot ceilings, crown moldings, and plush carpets. Paneled walls suggested sophisticated isolation, and she had to look twice to see that periodically the pattern of the panels included doors finished to the same mahogany shade. Apartment 3E was at the rear of the structure, she deduced, and turned right to proceed down the hall.

Outside 3E, Sarah knocked nervously, glancing in both directions down the hall as she did so. The door opened almost instantly, and Brad took her hand and pulled her into the apartment. A gold and alabaster chandelier hung from the vivid sky motif on the ceiling in the main room, and a collection of red-toned handwoven tapestries were laid at random angles around the room. Furniture was sparse, amounting to one love seat and a few side tables.

"What do you think, Serena?" Brad gestured widely. "We'll get furniture, obviously, but I love the roominess."

"It's beautiful," Sarah said, because it was. A limestone fire-place dominated one wall, and a hall led to what she presumed were the kitchen and bedrooms. Unquestionably the space had the potential to be an inviting home for intimate dinner parties. She hardly heard a whimper of street noise. Inside, the apartment was insulated, protected.

Yet she felt exposed, insecure. Just how intimate would the dinner parties be?

"Let's sit while we soak it in." Brad took her hand and pulled her to the gray and crimson love seat.

"I'm afraid I can't stay long." Sarah trembled as she sat down. "I have another engagement in only a few minutes."

"That's all right," he said. "I was eager for you to see the place. This can be where we truly relax with each other." He still held one of her hands in his.

Sarah's nerves rattled.

"You must be very pleased about the election," she said. "It's all anyone is talking about today."

"It will be a relief to have it behind us. We probably did not have to engage in certain persuasive tactics with the voters, yet it is nice to be sure of the results. But I don't want to talk about politics, Serena." He twisted in the love seat to face her and put a hand at the back of her head, then lightly traced his fingers down the side of her neck, pausing at the collar of her tweed suit.

Sarah shivered.

"The election is over," Brad said. "Now it's time to focus on you and me."

She put a hand on his wrist and stilled his roaming hand. "Is there a 'you and me'?"

"Of course there is. We're here, aren't we?"

"These are not quite . . . the circumstances . . . I imagined . . ."

"We can create our own circumstances, Serena. We'll make our own world here in this apartment."

"And someday?" she asked.

He shrugged. "Today is all that matters."

He leaned in and kissed her fully, his hands gripping her shoulders and his lips in no hurry. Breathless, Sarah squelched the welling confusion. Brad's kiss had come—and she wanted only for him to stop.

She pulled back at last. "I really must go."

"Promise me you'll come back." Brad reached into a suit pocket and pulled out a key. "I have to go out of town for a few days. Come back while I'm gone and decide what furnishings you would like. Meet me here again next Monday and you shall have your every wish."

Sarah stared at the key in his open palm. Slowly her fingers rose to claim it.

⁓

Sarah jumped off the streetcar at Michigan Avenue still trembling, whether from Brad's kiss or his daring, she was not sure. She was already late enough to warrant a tongue-lashing, so she reasoned she had nothing to lose by slowing her steps enough to get a grip on herself before arriving home at the Banning mansion.

She walked past the hat shop where it had all begun. If that crimson beaded hat had not been in the window, if she had ducked into the store thirty minutes earlier or the next afternoon, there would have been no Lillie, and without Lillie, no Brad, and without Brad, no apartment 3E.

"Sarah!"

She steeled herself not to turn in response. She knew the voice—Simon's—and she could not face him right now, not with Brad's kiss on her lips. Not with the key to 3E in her bag.

"Sarah Cummings!"

She picked up her pace, still refusing to turn her head, and heard the footsteps behind her quicken as well. At Eighteenth Street she turned toward Prairie Avenue, intending now to go home as quickly as she could.

"Miss Cuthbert!" the voice said now, but it was still Simon's, so she still did not turn.

Sarah's throat thickened. Under no circumstances could she talk to Simon now!

"Serena!"

Salty liquid oozed in her eyes, but at last the sound of steps behind her ceased. When she reached the Glessner house and turned the corner, she dared to glance over her shoulder.

He was a block away, shoulders stooped, retracing with defeat his steps in the other direction. Her chest heaved.

What had she done?

31

"It's nice to have all the fuss of the election behind us," Flora Banning said at dinner on Thursday evening. "Now we can get on with our lives."

Sarah calmly removed Flora's meat plate. Everyone had finished nibbling at the crown pork roast with apple-walnut stuffing. Mrs. Fletcher had prepared two roasts for the weekly family dinner. Glancing around the table, Sarah moved from Flora's place to her sister, Violet Newcomb. Will and Lucy were there—thankfully without the children—and Oliver and Pamela sat in their usual spots. Leo had brought Christina Hansen to dinner again. This was the fourth time now, Sarah calculated. He must be serious about her.

She used to wonder what it would be like to meet Brad's family. But she never would. A sigh escaped as she collected the next plate.

"Now we just have to wait for Mr. McKinley to take office," Samuel Banning said.

"That's hardly going to solve everything," Violet said. "The Democrats have a strong presence in Congress. They are sure to make their voice heard on economic questions."

"Everything will be sorted out," Oliver said. "Money will start flowing again without getting mixed up in the silver business."

"I wonder if the ranchers and miners of Colorado would share your sentiment." Violet Newcomb leaned back in her chair, but kept a firm gaze on Oliver.

"The backbone of the economy is manufacturing and industry," Oliver countered. "Wouldn't you agree, Leo?"

"Manufacturing and machinery are changing rapidly," Leo said. "It's difficult to predict the implications for the labor force."

"As long as men like Pullman and Armour can fund their businesses, workers will be employed and the economy will recover."

Lucy spoke up. "I hesitate to speak unkindly of a neighbor, but Mr. Pullman is not the most popular of employers. Surely you haven't forgotten the mess caused two years ago when the railroad workers went on strike against Mr. Pullman."

"He is not immune to the recession. He was just trying to keep his business open and profitable," Oliver said.

"By cutting the pay of his workers and sending them into squalor while he lives in that never-ending monstrosity across the street?"

"Lucille Eleanor!"

Sarah's heart skipped a beat at the tone in Mrs. Banning's voice. She could hardly believe what she was hearing. With two plates still to collect, she reached delicately between Lucy and Will.

"I'm sorry, Mother." Lucy tempered her voice. "I mean you no disrespect. It seems to me, though, that the bottom line of big business is not the answer to every need. A measure of humanity would go a long way. Every person deserves to be treated with dignity. Is that too much to ask?"

"I do wish Richard would write more often," Flora said. "Is it so much trouble to send his mother a letter?"

As Sarah carried the plates to the sink in the butler's pantry and Mr. Penard entered with the vegetables tray, table conversation drifted to family matters.

Sarah swallowed, Lucy's question suspended in her mind. Was dignity too much to ask from Brad?

Sarah opened the big red door of St. Andrew's the next afternoon and paced down the hall to the offices. She was not looking forward to facing Simon.

Jane stepped into the hall from Lucy's office. "He's not here."

"Oh. Hello, Jane. Actually, I'm glad to catch you." The thought of talking to Jane put a lump in Sarah's stomach, but the relief of not seeing Simon bolstered her. She would face one difficult conversation at a time.

"I'm sure Miss Lucy will open the room for you." Jane started to turn away.

"I'd like to talk to you first." Sarah reached for the girl's shoulder.

"I have papers to put away. I'll tell Miss Lucy you're here."

Jane disappeared before Sarah could protest further. Skirts rustled and feet scuffled within the office, and in a moment, Lucy appeared with a key in her hand. A few minutes later, Sarah stood in the classroom alone. After putting down her tapestry bag and removing her hat, Sarah shifted to the cupboard and began extracting projects the girls had been working on.

The green crepe lay on the third shelf, now in the form of a skirt basted together with one side seam carefully stitched and the other awaiting attention. Pressing her lips together and setting her jaw, Sarah pulled the project out of the cupboard and marched back down the hall to the offices. Lucy sat at her desk, and Jane was sorting papers on a long table.

Lucy looked up. "Did you forget something?"

"I'd like to speak to Jane about her project." Sarah held out the green fabric.

"I'm busy," Jane mumbled.

"It's all right, Jane." Lucy caught Sarah's eye. "The work will wait a few minutes. Why don't you use Mr. Tewell's office?"

With a grunt, Jane released her clench on the papers in her hand

and laid them on the table. She followed Sarah into Simon's office. Jane closed the door and crossed her arms.

Sarah moistened her lips and swallowed. This is where Simon had first kissed her—where the confusion began. His scent hung in the air, his presence nearly palpable. She saw the indentations his form had left in the leather desk chair from years of use. A coffee cup still held brown liquid, and he had laid a pen on the desk without putting it away in its holder, as if he would be right back.

"That's my skirt." Jane pointed at the green crepe.

"It's not a skirt yet." Sarah roused to the moment. "It's only half-stitched—useless at this stage. But it can still be a skirt if you come back to class."

"I don't need it anyway." Jane pivoted away from Sarah, arms still crossed.

"But you want it, don't you?" Sarah was betting on the answer to that question.

"I don't get everything I want," Jane said. "I'm going to throw away my journal. Burn it!"

"Don't do anything you'll be sorry for," Sarah cautioned.

Jane spun around and glared at Sarah. "You're not even sorry! After everything you've done, everything that's happened, you're not even sorry!"

Sarah took in a deep breath. "I'm sorry I hurt you. I didn't intend to, and it doesn't mean you have to give up your dreams."

Jane's glare persisted.

Sarah smoothed the green crepe. "Your life might not turn out like the journal, but it can be a good life."

"I don't believe you."

"Why not?"

"Because you don't believe that for yourself." Jane rounded the desk and plopped into Simon's chair. "If you believed what you say, then you wouldn't be ashamed of your own name."

Sarah nodded. Jane's words stung. "You're a wise young woman,

Jane." She held out the green crepe. "Forget about me. What do you want from your life? Come back to class and consider the future."

Jane reached out and snatched the fabric. "I'll think about it, but I might have learned everything I can from you."

Sarah took three deep breaths under Jane's slapping glare. Sarah may have scrambled her own life, and she might never make things right with Simon, but she did not want to be responsible for muddling Jane's future.

—⁓—

"Am I interrupting?" Lillie stuck her head in Simon's office and looked from Jane to Sarah, their eyes fixed on each other across the width of the room.

Sarah turned. "Come in, Miss Wagner."

Lillie stepped tentatively into the office. Something was wrong. "When I didn't see you in the room, I wondered if everything was all right. Mrs. Edwards said you were in here."

Jane folded the green crepe over one arm. "I'll go now."

Lillie watched the girl slip out of the room, her shoulders drooping unevenly and her step sluggish.

"Is she all right?" Lillie asked.

Sarah moved toward the window. "I tried to talk to her."

"About the journal? It was hers, wasn't it?"

Sarah's response faltered. "About . . . dreams."

Lillie moved farther into the room. "Yes, I suppose the two of you would have a lot to talk about." She let a bag slide off her shoulder in a deliberate choice to let that thread of conversation go. She brightened her tone. "I've been working on the dresses. I'd like you to look at them and tell me whether they're good enough to give to Lucy or Mr. Tewell now."

Sarah turned away from the window and pulled a dress out of the bag. She held it by the shoulders, letting the hem drop. A bit of lace here and there brightened the dark blue broadcloth. Sarah turned the dress inside out and ran a thumb and forefinger over the seams, feeling for knots and gaps. The inspection revealed neat, evenly spaced stitches. She turned the dress right side out again. Lillie's own heartbeat thudded in her head as she awaited the evaluation.

"It's beautiful, Lillie," Sarah said. "You've done exquisite work. I can't even see the hem stitching from the outside."

"The credit goes to you," Lillie said, letting out her breath. "Without you I'd still be cross-stitching table linens instead of making something practical."

"Table linens are practical. You'll need them when you and Paul have your own home."

"You know what I mean." Lillie's voice wavered. Whatever she thought of Sarah Cummings, Lillie owed her a debt. "Thank you."

"You're welcome, Lillie." Sarah riffled through the other dresses in the bag, seven in total. "I have the ones I worked on as well. I'll get them all together and talk to Mr. Tewell soon about who needs them."

Lillie hesitated, then said, "There is one more thing, Sarah." It sounded so odd to use that name. She still was not used to it.

"Yes?" Sarah folded a beige calico dress and picked up a gray-and-green-striped garment.

"I promised I wouldn't say anything to Brad, and I haven't." What Lillie was about to say could shatter the woman before her, whatever her name.

"Thank you," Sarah said. "I appreciate it more than you know."

"However, I did not promise not to tell you if I heard something." Lillie hated to think of the pain her words might cause.

Sarah looked at Lillie expectantly as she laid one dress on top of another and took a third from the bag.

"It may just be a rumor." Lillie began to pace around the office. "I have no business repeating it."

"Lillie, just spit it out," Sarah said. "Surely we're past the point of pretenses with each other."

"Yes, we are." Lillie stopped pacing, leaned on the credenza with her hands behind her, and looked squarely at Sarah. "In spite of what has happened between us, I can't stand the idea of your being hurt."

"Thank you, Lillie." Sarah's motions had slowed. "What do you need to tell me?"

"The rumor is that Bradley Townsend has been courting a woman in Lockport. Occasionally she comes into the city, but more often he goes out there. He goes on the train. It's someone he has known for a long time, so he stays overnight with her family when he visits."

Lillie watched the color seep out of Sarah's face and into her neck. Her impulse was to move toward Sarah, but she resisted.

"I don't know for sure," Lillie said. "I have no proof, not even a name, but I think he may be there right now."

"He did say he had to go out of town," Sarah mumbled. Lillie could barely hear her.

"I don't know what's between you and Brad right now," Lillie said quietly, "but I thought you should know. From what I have heard, it is a serious relationship that their parents approve of."

Sarah licked her lips. "Thank you for telling me."

"I don't want you . . . just . . . don't do something foolish."

Sarah picked up the stack of dresses with an overly deliberate gesture. "I should get back to the classroom. The girls will be coming soon."

"I want to see how the sewing machine works today." Melissa burst through the classroom door. Several other girls arrived in Melissa's wake.

Sarah put a smile on her face. "I figured it out last week." She was glad to have something specific to focus on after hearing Lillie's news.

It should not have surprised her. What Lillie reported certainly explained events in recent weeks.

"Can I learn, too?" Mary Margaret asked.

"You can all learn." Sarah moved toward the machine. "I'll show you how to thread it. If you don't get that right, it will just be a big mess."

Sarah glanced toward the door, hoping for a flash of green crepe. She sat in the chair at the sewing machine while four of the older girls gathered around her. "You have to be careful," she said. "You can put a needle through your finger faster than you can blink." Two more girls straggled in.

She demonstrated how to thread the machine, then pulled the thread out and let Melissa try. Each of the four girls took a turn trying out the treadle while younger girls found their projects and arranged threads and scissors on the work table.

Sarah had just about given up when Jane stood in the doorway at last, the green crepe draped over one arm.

Sarah slung the tapestry bag over her shoulder. It was fuller now with Lillie's dresses. She had briefly considered just setting them in a cabinet but decided to take them home and combine them with the ones she had worked on herself. She could present the entire batch as a peace offering to Simon.

Sarah knew she should go straight home, but her steps hesitated at the streetcar stop as it rumbled toward the intersection. If she boarded now, she could catch a smooth transfer to the elevated train. The streetcar heaved to the curb with its bulk and noise, and Sarah got on.

A few minutes later she again stood outside the building, this time with a key in her hand. She felt its shape impressed on her skin inside her fist. And then the allure of the building was too strong, the tug to go up in the elevator irresistible.

The key turned easily in the lock, and she entered apartment 3E. The sparse furnishings were as she had left them three days earlier, but in her mind's eye, colorful chairs and tablecloths sprang up around them, throw pillows bounced around the room, lamps lit the shadowy corners, floor-length velvet drapes framed the symmetrical windows.

She had wanted everything she imagined now. The maid's uniform would be a thing of the past as she chose the fabrics and furnishings of her own home.

But she had wanted Brad's name as well. And he was not offering it. She wanted a ring, and he would not give one. Sarah backed up against a bare wall to quash the shudder that ran from head to toe. As the first tears rolled down her cheeks, she slid to the floor. Surely she had not sunk so low that she would consider what he proposed.

For the proposal—the arrangement—was clear.

Expelling her breath, Sarah recomposed herself and stood up, the key to 3E still in her clammy hand. She thought about simply laying it on one of the tables. She would stop going to the Lexington, just tell Kenny to throw away any more notes for Serena Cuthbert.

"No," she said aloud to the empty room. "If he is going to shame me, I will tell him to his face."

32

For most of the church service, Sarah wondered why she had let Karl drag her to Second Presbyterian again. It seemed that whenever the Bannings were gone on a weekend, going to church was at the top of his list. But her mind was so scattered, she could hardly make sense of anything. She had shattered a jar of jam on the kitchen floor the day before. When she remembered the way Brad leaned toward her on the gray and crimson love seat, her fingers forgot their grip. Later she had walked off and left a pail of dirty mop water in the middle of the foyer when she felt herself again sliding down the wall of apartment 3E. When Mr. Penard barked a reprimand that the temporary absence of the Bannings was no excuse for slovenly work, Sarah barely heard him because Lillie's words about Brad's betrayal rang in her ears. She left the vegetable oil tin open on the dining room table and dropped four peeled potatoes in the trash bin before she came to her senses.

So far Sunday morning had not been any better. Mrs. Fletcher had said, "Get out of my kitchen before you destroy it," and Sarah had meekly allowed Karl to take her by the hand and lead her out of the house.

Now, sitting in the balcony, she saw a piece of paper on the floor, and she bent to pick it up. The paper had nothing in particular to do with the service. It was a card someone had left in the wooden pew, perhaps a bookmark, with the words set in a narrow strip down the center. Who knew how many weeks it had lain there before Sarah picked it up? Words leaped up at her eyes.

"For what does it profit a man if he gains the whole world, and loses his own soul? Or what will a man give in exchange for his soul? Matthew 16:26."

She had come perilously close, she knew, to plummeting into those very questions. Tomorrow that descent would end.

As the minister approached the pulpit to give his sermon, Sarah wondered where Simon was. Was he in the church he loved? Or was he at that moment in the dining hall with all the children old enough to sit still for a brief service? Was he singing a hymn? Was his head bowed in prayer? Was he worshiping because he was sure of God's love in a way that Sarah was not?

Tomorrow she would make things right. Sarah bowed her own head as grief and remorse gripped her breath. If Simon was right, love could make the difference.

On Monday morning, Mr. Penard admonished Sarah to pay attention to what she was doing. He would not tolerate another day of distractions and accidents.

Flora Banning sat alone at the dining table, leisurely flipping through the latest edition of *The Ladies Home Journal* long after Leo and Samuel had left for their offices. She seldom came to breakfast as early as they did, preferring instead to have a tray in her room or enjoy the solitude of the dining room at mid-morning with the attention of one of the maids.

Sarah refilled Mrs. Banning's coffee cup just as the front door opened. Lucy bustled through the foyer and into the dining room, her baby in her arms.

Flora offered her cheek for her daughter's kiss. "What are you doing here, Lucy?"

"I thought I would drop in to see how your weekend away

went." Lucy settled into the chair around the corner from her mother. "Besides, your granddaughter was begging to see her grandmama."

Flora smiled. "Of course she was." She reached over with one hand and moved the blanket back from Stella's face. Then she put out both arms. "Take off your cloak, Lucy. Sarah will pour you some coffee. Have you had breakfast?"

Lucy deposited the baby in her mother's arms. "I am hungry," she confessed. "Ben didn't seem to want to go to school today, and the baby spit up at a moment that was unpropitious. I had to change my dress. Between the two of them, I never had so much as a piece of toast."

"You really must get some live-in help," Flora said, cooing at the baby. "Sarah, fix Lucy a plate."

Most of the breakfast offerings had been cleared away or grown cold. Sarah did what she could with a croissant and fruit, remembering that Lucy preferred a simple breakfast anyway.

"We manage quite well with Charlotte most of the time," Lucy said. "I have to be at the orphanage this afternoon. Charlotte will pick up Benny from school and then come fetch Stella so I can go to a meeting."

"It's not one of your regular days for the orphanage," Flora remarked.

"No, but Simon wants to have a meeting with some of the advisors and asked me to be there. And Miss Wagner would like to come by and learn how the office runs."

"Is she thinking of volunteering there?"

"She seems keen to understand everything she can about St. Andrew's." Lucy scooped some fruit onto a fork.

"She ought to be planning her wedding."

"I'm sure she is, Mother. But it's still seven weeks away."

Seven weeks. Sarah set the coffeepot down harder than she meant to. Lillie must have fixed the date. How strange it felt not to be privy to the information. Sarah would have liked to stand up at Lillie's wedding.

———— ❧ ————

"They're unhappy, of course," Simon told Lucy, "as I expected they would be." Simon plunged one hand into the pocket of his jacket, where he could run his thumb over the pads of his fingers, over and over again, without being observed. He had made the difficult decision about the new children.

"Disappointed, I'm sure." Lucy leaned forward, her elbows on Simon's desk opposite him. "Are they pressuring you to reconsider?"

"Not yet. I spelled out my reasons explicitly. I don't think they dispute them."

"What do you think will happen to the children when the facility closes down next month?"

Simon dropped his head and closed his eyes for a few seconds. "I honestly don't know. A settlement house, perhaps. I believe they are talking to Jane Addams. Or a train to farms downstate."

"How many children still need places?"

"About forty." Simon felt one knee start to jiggle.

Lucy shook her head. "There are no easy answers. I wish I could take them all home with me."

Simon stilled his anxiety long enough to regard Lucy Edwards. "You are the biggest-hearted person I know."

"Thank you. That doesn't solve the problem." Lucy pressed her lips together. "We just have to do what we can, one small step at a time. Sarah's sewing class seems to be a success. We need more programs like that. Volunteers could teach more real life skills."

Simon nodded. "I think in the spring I'll ask her to start a new class of beginners, once these girls are well on their way."

He doubted Sarah would agree, though. Every week he feared she would call an end to the class she already had—especially after she would not speak to him in the street. He had made his feelings clear, and she had turned a deaf ear. He would have to make his peace, one way or another. The offer of employment in Philadelphia was still available. If the board could find someone to take over St. Andrew's, it would be best to move away.

At the sound of a knock, Simon and Lucy turned their heads in tandem toward the door.

"The gentlemen from the board are here," Jane said. "I've seated them at the table in the spare office."

"Thank you, Jane," Simon said. "You've been a great help. Why don't you go back to class now?"

⌇

"You have to promise to cover for me," Sarah said to Mary Catherine.

"Mrs. Fletcher knows exactly how long it takes to go put in an order at the butcher's." Mary Catherine closed the icebox firmly.

"She'll sit down with her feet up in a few minutes," Sarah said. "She won't even be sure when I've left. Make her a cup of tea. She might even drop off for a while."

"You always ask me to do things like this, but you never even tell me where you're going." Mary Catherine tossed a wooden spoon in the sink. "You have all those pretty dresses, and you never leave the house without one."

"If you do this for me one last time," Sarah said, "I'll give you one of the dresses. Then things will go back to normal. I'll help you with anything you ask."

Mary Catherine perked up. "Can I have the beige suit?"

"It's yours." Mary Catherine had not set her sights very high, Sarah thought. "Just make sure no one comes looking for me."

Sarah now leaned against the train's window as it rumbled above the city blocks. She would give away all her dresses. What was the point of keeping them now? It would take a miracle to get what she wanted from Brad—and she was no longer sure she wanted it.

At the apartment, she put the key in the door. Brad was already there and stood up as she entered.

"I've missed you," he said.

"How was your trip out of town?" Sarah clenched the strap of her bag.

"Unimportant," he answered. He kissed her cheek. "Mundane business."

Oh really?

"Have you thought about how you would like to furnish the apartment?" he asked. Holding one of her hands, he led her into the room.

"I've had a few ideas," she answered truthfully. With her free hand, Sarah pressed the key against the nearest table. Something splintered inside her as she let go.

He smiled slyly. "I had a few things delivered this morning."

"Oh?" Sarah saw nothing different in the main room.

Still holding her hand, Brad led her down the hall to one of the bedrooms. Her eyes widened and her heart thudded when she saw the double bed with a rich red and gold covering.

"Brad, I don't think—"

"If you don't like it, we'll send it back." Brad still held her hand and pulled her into the room. "If you don't like the bedding, we'll change it." He laid the back of one hand against her cheek.

"Brad," she said, her voice hushed, "if only you had shown me this place because you wanted me to be your wife."

"Marriage is an outdated convention," he said. He tugged on her hand again, and now they stood at the edge of the bed, where he leaned in and placed his lips softly on hers.

Sarah put her hands on his chest and pushed gently. "No, Brad. Not this way."

"What way, then?"

"As your wife," she insisted.

His tone steeled. "Surely you know that is not going to happen." He stepped away.

"Why shouldn't it?" He owed her that much.

He chuckled. "Did you seriously think I would not find out the truth?"

Sarah could barely breathe. "What do you mean, Brad?"

"You remember my friend, Mr. Francis Curtis, I'm sure."

"Yes."

"It turns out he's a friend of a young man named Leo Banning, from the university."

Sarah blanched.

"He thought Serena Cuthbert was most enchanting—but also vaguely familiar. One night he saw her at an affair for the orphans. Something fell into place."

Sarah refused to tremble.

Brad continued. "A few simple inquiries put all the pieces in place, Miss Cummings."

She let her shoulders sag and exhaled slowly. "So that's why—all this." She swept her hand around the room. "That's why you won't speak of marriage."

He reached for her and captured a hand again. "It's one reason."

"Does the other reason live in Lockport?" she asked. Heat flashed through her face.

"You are an exquisite creature," he said, "even when you're incensed. I don't care what you call yourself. You can be Serena Cuthbert and enjoy everything I'm offering you here."

"Don't you care for me at all?" Sarah barely found the breath to speak.

"I care for you a great deal," he answered. "Have I not demonstrated that to you here?"

"And Lockport?"

"A political necessity."

"I wanted to marry you," she said.

He shook his head. "Perhaps. But you don't love me. You love all this. You can still have it, and marriage is not a requirement."

She backed away from him. "Actually, Mr. Townsend, it is. You're right. I was nearly willing to sacrifice love for what you could offer me. I was a fool."

―――ᴄᴩ―――

On the train home, Sarah swallowed hard and let her stop pass. Mary Catherine was going to be frantic, and Mrs. Fletcher would soon wake from the doze she would deny taking. But as long as Sarah had been gone this long already, she might as well make things right with Simon while courage still pulsed through her veins. She got off the train only a few blocks from St. Andrew's—and Simon.

She had to tell him how sorry she was. She had to make him believe it. Sarah lifted her eyes toward the familiar brick building.

Something was burning.

A dalmatian ran past Sarah in the street and shooed off a stray dog. That meant the fire wagons would be right behind. The dalmatian was doing its job in clearing the way.

Sarah started to trot toward the smoke as a team of horses careened past her in the street, pulling a steam pump. The hook and ladder team was on its heels.

St. Andrew's Orphanage was on fire.

33

A string of trucks stampeded down the street, ferrying items needed for the assault—the hoses, ladders, chemicals, the water tower, another steam pump. One team of horses after another pounded the road, yanking behind them wagons and wheels painted bright red and carrying the best of Chicago's firefighting equipment. Stunned pedestrians jumped out of the way.

By the time Sarah penetrated the crowd across the street from St. Andrew's to get a clear view, the hose carriage had unfurled fifty-foot lengths and the steam pump was fastened on a hydrant. The hoses stiffened with the rush of water through them. Ladders had come off the truck, and dalmatians circulated to keep interference at bay. The water tower on the back of one truck was raised and aimed at flames belching from the upper floors as children clattered down the fire escape on one side of the building. Horrified, Sarah saw children still at the windows on the other side. She shoved people out of the way and slithered between the fire trucks, ignoring the dogs that protected the working horses.

A uniformed arm went down like a gate. "Miss, you can't go through there," a man's voice boomed.

"I have to," she pleaded. "I know people inside." She looked past the uniform, her attention fixed on the building.

"No, miss, you're not going inside." The fireman was firm. He pointed down the street. "You can wait over there."

"No, you don't understand! I have to know—"

"No. You have to get out of the way. We know what we're doing. You cannot interfere."

The fireman herded Sarah, along with a few others who had ventured close, away from the trucks.

"I want to help!" Sarah shrieked.

"Then comfort the children coming out," the fireman directed. "Over there!"

Coughing and spluttering, children tumbled off the staircase and followed instructions to move down the street, away from the scene. Dozens of them, then scores. Orphanage staff speckled the amassing huddle.

"Mrs. Davis!" Sarah screamed above the din.

Some of the younger children were screaming themselves. Older children clutched toddlers and babies. Siblings latched on to each other. The stream of people flowed steadily from the orphanage down the street until there were hundreds.

Sarah touched a few shoulders and faces as she passed by, murmuring words of assurance she could not be sure were true. Vacant, shocked faces mingled with terrified grimaces. Those she recognized, Sarah called by name as she wiped grime from their eyes with the corner of her cape.

"Mrs. Davis!"

At last the housekeeper turned.

"Are you all right?" Sarah reached the familiar figure now covered in soot.

Mrs. Davis nodded. "I was downstairs. The fire started upstairs. It's mostly smoke."

"What happened?"

"No one knows yet," Mrs. Davis answered. She looked around. "Where is Mr. Tewell?"

Sarah scanned the amassing crowd as well. "I haven't seen him."

"And the others?"

"What others?"

"The people in the office," Mrs. Davis said. "He had some visitors, but they'll have to look after themselves. I've got to help the children." She wiped the back of her hand through a streak of soot across her forehead, and both of them surveyed the growing crowd of children. "How will we ever account for everyone?"

"Sarah!"

Sarah turned toward the scream and Lillie stumbled into her arms.

"I'm so glad to see you!" Lillie's chest heaved in its quest for air. "Where's Lucy? Did she make it out?"

"Miss Lucy was still there?" Sarah asked. "What about—"

"Charlotte was there too," Lillie said. "She came with Benny and Henry to pick up the baby. Lucy was in a meeting. I had just arrived to wait for her."

"So Stella was not with Lucy?" Sarah asked.

Lillie shook her head. "No. One of the older girls was watching her. It was only supposed to be a few minutes."

"And Simon?"

"In the meeting with Lucy," Lillie said. "They were almost finished."

"We must find them." The urgency in her voice surprised even Sarah.

"They have to be here," Lillie insisted. "They have to. We'll find them."

Smoke and ash painted a monochromatic picture. Sarah struggled to distinguish one form from another, but she began to move quickly through the huddle with Lillie right behind her. More of the St. Andrew's staff emerged and began to take charge. Sarah heard them asking basic questions as they probed for injuries and instructed the children to arrange themselves according to their dormitories so they could discern who might still be missing. Sarah squatted to question a few children herself.

Sarah stood and shook her head. "There should be more children," she said to Lillie.

"How can you tell?"

"Four hundred children live at St. Andrew's. This crowd doesn't look big enough to me."

"They're still coming."

The winds that carried smoke also bore the wails of children still caught inside the building.

"They have the ladders up," Lillie said. "They'll get them out. We have to believe that. Look, there's Jane!"

Sarah instinctively opened her arms and the girl plunged into them.

"It's my fault!" Jane howled, hiding her face against Sarah's chest. "It's my fault."

"What are you talking about?" Sarah took the girl by the shoulders and searched for her reluctant brown eyes.

"I burned my journal!" Jane covered her face with her hands and sobbed.

Sarah's knees went weak. "We can't be sure what happened," she said. "The important thing is you're safe and all these other children are safe."

And Simon? Was he safe? And Lucy and Charlotte and the children?

"They should have let me burn to death," Jane bawled. "I did this!"

Sarah looked at Lillie. "Keep looking for Lucy and the others," she said. With an arm around Jane's shoulders, she steered the girl to the edge of the crowd.

"Jane," she said firmly, "you must get a grip on yourself."

"You don't understand! I wanted to burn my journal. It was all lies, and I wanted it to go away. So I stole matches out of Mr. Tewell's office, from the fireplace mantel. I remember that they were Diamond matches. I took a tin wastebasket to the back stairwell on the fourth floor, and I put the journal in it and dropped in a match. This is all my fault!"

Sarah shook Jane by the shoulders. "Jane, listen to me—"

Jane twisted from her grip. "Don't tell me it's going to be all right! It's not! Nothing ever will be again! Mr. Tewell came running up the stairs yelling for everyone to get out."

Simon. "Did you see where he went?" Sarah asked.

"He went into the boys' dormitory room. I couldn't see after that. It got smoky really fast. Everybody was screaming."

"There's Lucy!" Lillie's cry cut through the pandemonium, and Sarah peered in the direction where Lillie pointed.

To her relief, Lucy carried the baby in one arm, and Benny clutched her skirt. Lucy's other arm gripped Charlotte's shuddering shoulders. Sarah broke from Jane and ran toward Lucy.

"Henry!" Charlotte shrieked, twisting to look back at the burning structure.

"Where is Henry?" Sarah asked Lucy, meeting weary eyes.

"He let go," Lucy said quietly. "He's too big for Charlotte to carry now that she's so far along, and he let go somewhere in the front hall. We couldn't find him in the smoke. The firemen insisted we had to get out before . . . before . . ."

Charlotte crumpled to the ground screaming her son's name. Sarah's heart threatened to stop.

She took off before anyone could stop her.

⁓•⁓

This time Sarah was more devious in her approach. Every step along the way, as she staggered against the tide, she examined faces of small boys, but she also took careful note of where the firemen had stationed themselves and what consumed their attention. She knew the kitchen entrances, the delivery entrances, the cellar. The front door was not the only way into St. Andrew's.

Sarah broke from the congestion at the front of the building, where firemen were helping children down ladders. She dodged the water tower truck that spewed a steam-powered gush at the upper floors. She avoided the tangle of hoses with copper rivets and brass fittings. At the back of the building, Sarah kicked the latch on the old cellar doors. The storage space had been replaced by a walk-in pantry on the ground level when she was twelve. Sarah yanked open the doors and stepped down into the darkness.

Her mind knew the way. Not being able to see was almost a help, as memory revived and she counted steps and trailed fingers along splintered wooden shelves. No one knew she used to come down here. She had not cared about the darkness in her pursuit of solitude. Now the girlish habit served her well.

At the other end of the cellar, Sarah counted rising steps. Seven. Eight. Nine. The door gave easily enough, and she was in the kitchen.

Then she was in the dining room, knocking against tables she did not see in the smoky gloom. Coughing, she lifted the hem of her skirt to cover her mouth and nose and fought to keep her stinging eyes open. As the dining room gave way to the hall, she stumbled again.

Something soft.

Sarah fell to her knees and gasped.

Melissa lay sprawled in the doorway. Next to her was Alonzo. She shook them both. No response. Vacant eyes above mouths frozen open stared back at her. A hand laid lightly on each still chest confirmed her fear.

Sarah started to cry, which gave way to a wracking cough. She covered her face again and crawled toward the front hall, still feeling her way by memory.

"Henry!" she gasped at random intervals. "Henry!"

A whimper.

Sarah stilled herself to listen below the roar of rushing water and swinging axes and slapping flames.

There it was again. She moved toward the sound and scooped up Henry.

Now she was on her feet, feeling his weight and staggering from breathlessness. She could see the front door, though. Charlotte had been so close to getting her son out safely.

"What in tarnation are you doing here?" the voice thundered. "I thought I told you to get out of the way." The same fireman who had stood guard when Sarah first arrived now bundled her toward the fresh air.

"There are two others in there," she gasped. "Dead, I think."

"I can't send a man in there now." The fireman shook his head as a fresh burst of flame startled them both.

Sarah did not wait for further scolding, instead racing with Henry in her arms to where she had left the child's mother.

Charlotte was not there.

Sarah sank to the ground, gasping for air and gently slapping Henry's round face.

"Wake up, Henry. You have to wake up." She rubbed his chest vigorously.

Finally his blue eyes opened. "Where's my mama?"

Relief made Sarah fall back against a tree.

"Where's my mama?" Henry demanded again.

"She's fine. We'll find her."

Henry started to cry, and Sarah knew he was all right. She scanned the block and realized she had misjudged her location and fallen against the wrong tree. By now, though, Lucy and Charlotte had spotted her and were hurtling toward her. Charlotte collapsed with her son gathered against her chest and her belly heavy with the future.

Sarah's shoulders heaved.

"Are you all right?" Lucy asked.

"Melissa," Sarah muttered, "and Alonzo."

"I haven't seen them," Lucy said.

Sarah put her head against the tree and closed her eyes. She inhaled deeply, begging her lungs to function. "What about Simon?"

"I haven't seen him, either," Lucy said, "not since he ran up the stairs."

Simon. Sarah shuddered in fear she would never have the opportunity to make things right. Simon did not deserve to go to his end this way.

When the image of Melissa and Alonzo invaded her eyelids, Sarah forced her eyes open.

"I know it's chaotic," Lucy said, "but I am going to try to find a cab to take you all to my parents' house. Charlotte, you can wait for Archie there. Sarah, I want you to take my children. Will is out of town on business, but my mother can look after them." She put the baby in Sarah's arms and turned to her son. "Benny, you go with Sarah."

"I want to stay with you!" Benny wailed.

"No, Benny," Lucy said. "You go to Grandmama's."

"But Miss Lucy—" Charlotte protested.

"I have to stay," Lucy said. "I won't have any argument. We have to figure out who is missing and make some arrangement for everyone else. I don't know what we'll do with four hundred homeless children, but I'm going to stay and help the staff."

"Find Simon," Sarah said.

Lucy nodded. "Of course. Now stay right here. I'm going to get someone to drive you all home. I don't know how I'll find a cab in this mess, but I have to try."

"Lillie," Sarah said. "I mean, Miss Wagner."

"She's fine," Lucy said. "I just left her."

"No," Sarah said, "what I mean is her driver is probably nearby. He would have been waiting for her."

"Good thinking!" Lucy said. "Don't move!"

Sarah dared not close her eyes again. The scene before her could not be happening. She had read newspaper accounts of dozens of fires in the last several years, but still it seemed this could not be happening. Not now. Not to Simon.

A man in a tweed suit squatted next to her. "I'm a reporter from the *Chicago Tribune,*" he said. "I saw you come out of the building with that boy and followed you over here. Can I get a statement from you?"

Sarah looked at Charlotte, who had eyes only for her son.

"People will want to hear this story," the reporter urged. "Let's start with your name."

Sarah looked him in the eyes. "My name is Sarah Cummings. I grew up in St. Andrew's."

34

We can't go in the front door!" Charlotte gripped her son's hand as she huddled with Sarah at the bottom of the steps leading to the Banning front door. At the curb, Tillie's driver clicked his tongue and the horse pulling the carriage heeded the command to continue the journey to the Wagner home.

"I can't very well take Lucy's children through the kitchen," Sarah said. She coughed and moved Stella to the other hip. "Besides, these are not usual circumstances." The truth was she was not sure she could walk any farther than the front door.

Sarah led the way up the stairs with Ben and Stella, leaving Charlotte no option but to follow with Henry. The door was latched on the inside, as she expected it would be, so she pulled the bell. Stella squirmed in her arms. Every muscle inside Sarah screamed with exhaustion.

"Is my mother going to be all right?" Benny asked.

"Yes, of course," Sarah said. "She just wants to help the other children because she knows your grandmother will take care of you."

"I'm worried," he said.

But you're safe, alive, she wanted to say, shaking off the image of the two children lying still in the dining hall.

"Pull the bell again," Sarah suggested.

But the door opened before Benny's hand reached the bell.

Mr. Penard's eyes flickered slightly as he considered the scene before him.

Sarah pushed past him. "There's been a fire."

"Grandmama!" Benny ran to Flora, who had stepped from the parlor into the foyer, and wrapped his arms around her waist. When he separated, he left a streak of gray down the front of her yellow dress.

Flora took the baby from Sarah just before she squalled. Sarah sank on the bottom marble step, indicating Charlotte and Henry should sit beside her.

"What happened?" Flora demanded.

"A fire," Sarah answered. Her chest still heaved with the effort to breathe, and speaking provoked coughing. "At St. Andrew's."

"Where's Lucy?" Flora made no effort to mask her anxiety. "Penard, bring some water!"

"She's fine, ma'am," Sarah said quickly.

"You know Miss Lucy," Charlotte added. "She stayed to help."

"Sarah, I didn't realize you were going to St. Andrew's today," Flora said, smoothing her granddaughter's grimy dress.

"It's a long story, ma'am."

"I suppose it doesn't matter now," Flora said. "Was anybody hurt?"

Sarah nodded. "I'm not sure how many, ma'am."

"Penard, the children will need baths. Send some extra towels to my bathroom. I'll see to the baths myself."

"Yes, ma'am." The butler bowed slightly.

"And ask Mrs. Fletcher to put the kettle on. The girls need tea."

"Yes, ma'am."

"Mrs. Banning," Charlotte said quietly, "if I might use your telephone to reach my husband at work."

"Penard can call him for you. He works for Mr. Glessner, does he not?"

"Yes, ma'am."

"I'll take the children. The two of you go through to the kitchen," Flora instructed. "Penard will see you get some nourishment."

Flora Banning's answer to everything seemed to be to enlist Penard, which Sarah found vaguely amusing until the room began to spin and she slumped off the step.

⁓

Sarah woke, in darkness, in her own room with fragmented recollection of how she arrived there. Smelling salts. Mrs. Fletcher insisting she sip water. She did not remember climbing the narrow stairs to the third floor, but she had a hazy recollection of Elsie and Mary Catherine stripping off the day dress she had been wearing and seeing the ashes in its fibers launched into the room.

She was alone, wearing a white nightdress, and under her own blankets plus one more, a quilt from the guest room on the second floor. Mrs. Banning must have ordered its use. No one else would dare. Though it was the middle of November, the window was open. Fresh air streamed through steadily. Sarah experimented with a deep breath and found it less troublesome than a few hours earlier.

Suddenly she wanted to know what time it was. The sky was black, but darkness came early at this time of year. How long had she been asleep? The thought of getting out of bed to pull the chain on the electric light bulb overhead was too much, but she could manage to light the kerosene lamp at the side of the bed. Sarah pulled herself half upright, fumbled on the table for matches, and struck the second one she tried.

They were Diamond matches.

Sarah lit the wick, then fell back in bed wondering if anywhere in the Banning household she might find a brand of matches that did not remind her of Bradley Townsend and his anticipated fortune. She lay there watching the light grow to brightness, banishing images of apartment 3E. Simon was the man who mattered now, the only one who ever had.

Was Jane right? Was it possible the girl had started the fire? Sarah moaned with the conviction that her own actions somehow had driven Jane to destroy the journal.

"*Mr. Tewell came running up the stairs yelling for everyone to get out,*" Jane had said.

Something did not add up. Simon had run past Jane and her tin-can fire and into the boys' wing.

"Jane did not start the fire," Sarah said aloud. "Something else happened, something worse."

The door opened and Mary Catherine came in. "I heard you talking," she said.

Sarah moved her gaze to the kitchen maid, who must have been holding vigil outside her door. "What time is it?"

"About ten o'clock."

"It's still Monday?" The only day that rivaled this one in Sarah's life was the day she came home from school to find her world destroyed. Only twelve hours ago she had fixed a breakfast plate for Lucy. "Benny and Stella?" she asked suddenly.

"Asleep in Richard's room. Mrs. Banning has taken them in hand herself," Mary Catherine said. "She's quite good with children when she wants to be."

"Charlotte and Henry?"

"Archie left work and came right over. He took them home hours ago."

"Miss Lucy?"

Mary Catherine shook her head. "She hasn't come home yet."

"Mrs. Banning must be frantic."

"She says she'll wait up all night if she has to. I'm supposed to stay up all night with you. Mrs. Banning says you are to stay in bed as long as you like in the morning."

Sarah shook her head slightly. "Go to bed, Mary Catherine.

You've done so much for me today already. Put out the light, please. I'm going to sleep."

But she would not sleep, not right away. Where was Simon?

※

In the morning, Sarah slept through the hour when Leo and Samuel Banning would have their breakfast, but she was dressed and downstairs when Flora and Benny came in for their morning meal.

"Miss Newcomb is here as well," Mrs. Fletcher told her as she set a bowl heaped with oatmeal in front of Sarah.

"Still no word from Miss Lucy?"

"Not yet. Mrs. Banning dozed in the parlor all night waiting for her. She never even changed her clothes. It's strange to see her looking a mess."

Mary Catherine came in from the dining room. "Sarah, Mrs. Banning is asking for you."

Sarah pushed back from the table, her own breakfast untouched. "I'd better see what she wants, then."

Flora Banning had the morning newspaper spread out before her.

"Sarah," Mrs. Banning said, "it would seem you did not tell us the whole story yesterday."

"Ma'am?" Sarah looked from Flora Banning to Violet Newcomb.

"You're in the newspaper! Leo left the page open for me."

Sarah stared at the headline: "Fire Ravages Orphanage." She scanned the details reported.

The first fire truck left the station within twenty seconds of the alarm, followed by four more fire apparatus vehicles.

Four hundred children were believed to reside at St. Andrew's.

It is unknown how many staff were present in the structure at the time.

At the time of going to press, there were two known deaths, and a small number of children and staff were unaccounted for, among them orphanage director Simon Tewell.

Sarah sucked in her breath.

Flora thumped the paper. "There! Read that. They quoted you. It says here that you went into the building and pulled out Henry Shepard. Neither you nor Charlotte said a word about that yesterday."

"We were just . . . grateful he was safe . . . and worried . . . about . . ."

"Of course that is what is important," Violet Newcomb said. She held a bottle while Stella's cheeks flapped with the motion of consuming the formula.

Ben's fork clattered to his plate. "Where is my mother?" he wanted to know.

"I'm sure she'll be here as soon as she can," Mrs. Banning said. She pointed at his plate. "She would want you to eat your breakfast."

"I don't have to go to school today, do I?" he asked.

"No, not today, dear."

"Good. They might have a fire there, and I don't ever want to be in another fire for the rest of my life."

"May I?" Sarah picked up the newspaper to read more carefully. "It doesn't say what caused the fire."

"They might never know," Violet said. "I'm sure right now the authorities are concentrating on accounting for everyone."

The front door opened.

"Mama!" Benny was out of his chair before anyone could stop him.

Lucy knelt between the pocket doors to the dining room and gathered him in her arms.

Flora and Violet were on their feet, rushing toward Lucy. Sarah quietly laid the newspaper down and moved to her familiar post at the sideboard, but Lucy met her eyes.

"Aunt Violet," Lucy said, "I wonder if you would take the children to the parlor for me. I'll fill you in later."

"I want to stay with you, Mama," Benny insisted.

"I'll only be a few minutes," Lucy assured him. Violet gripped Ben's shoulder and steered him across the foyer.

"Lucy, you're a mess," Flora observed. "Did you sleep at all?"

"Only an hour or so," Lucy said. "I'm so dirty, I hate to sit on your William Morris furniture."

"Sit!" Flora ordered, pointing at a dining room chair. "I'm tired of this pattern anyway."

Lucy lowered herself into the chair, and Sarah automatically carried the coffeepot to the table and poured Lucy a cup. Lucy took a long grateful draft.

"Sarah, how are you this morning?"

"I'm well, ma'am."

"No cough? No burning in your lungs?"

Sarah shook her head.

"You'll tell somebody if you don't feel well?"

"Yes, ma'am." How she felt was inconsequential to Sarah at the moment.

"I'm sure you want to know the news," Lucy said.

Tell me they found Simon. Tell me he is all right. "Yes, ma'am."

"By midnight, we accounted for nearly all the children," Lucy said. Her voice caught as she looked at Sarah. "I realize now what you meant when you spoke of Melissa and Alonzo. Alfred is inconsolable about losing his brother. Mrs. Davis has taken him under her wing. We're looking for his mother, but we haven't heard from her in over a year."

"Did these children succumb?" Flora's face paled.

"Smoke inhalation," Lucy said. "Something about the construction of the building. The fire was on the fourth floor, but the smoke spread rapidly through the ventilation system. A few of the children were taken to nearby hospitals with damage to their lungs, but most of them remembered the instruction to cover nose and mouth while they got out of the building. We're hoping the ones still missing will turn up in the hospitals as well. The firemen are sure no one is inside."

"Where are most of the children now?" Flora asked.

"Schools. Churches. It was heartwarming to see how quickly organizations opened their doors to us. Mats and blankets came from everywhere."

Lucy had not yet mentioned Simon, and Sarah could not intrude with her question.

"The paper said the damage is still being assessed," Flora said.

Lucy nodded. "The preliminary report suggests the real damage is limited to the fourth floor. It seems the fire started when one of the staff turned on a gas lamp affixed to the hall. There was an explosion. I don't know all the details."

A gas lamp? Not Jane burning her journal.

Lucy continued. "It's really a matter of how much damage there is from smoke and water. We won't know for a few days." She held up her coffee cup for Sarah to refill. "Simon always dreamed of electrifying, but it's so expensive to bring electricity to a building of that size when we need so many other things."

"Electrical fires happen, too," Flora pointed out. "Crossed wires. You hear about it all the time."

Lucy drummed three fingers on the table. "We have a lot of decisions to make, but first we have to find Simon."

"Mr. Tewell is still missing?" Flora sounded alarmed.

The coffeepot shook in Sarah's hand.

"We all heard the explosion even though we were downstairs, and he took off immediately," Lucy said. "Enough of the children have said they saw him that we know he was upstairs moving around, getting children out. The firefighters assure us he is not inside the building, but ambulances were everywhere, so he might have been taken away. We're still looking for him."

Simon.

Jane.

"Miss Lucy," Sarah said. "If I may?"

"Yes, Sarah?"

"Do you know where Jane is?"

"Why, yes. She's at one of the churches—though she seems to be in shock and won't speak to anyone."

Sarah swallowed. "She believes she started the fire. She told me she struck a match to burn . . . a personal item."

Lucy shook her head. "No. The fire department is sure it was a gas line fire. It started in the boys' wing. Jane shouldn't have been anywhere near there."

"No, ma'am. She wasn't. She said she was in the stairwell on the other side of the building."

"I'll have a word with her," Lucy said. "I was able to telephone Will. He's on his way home on the late train today. I'd better spend a few minutes with Ben, but I'll have to go back, at least until we find Simon."

Sarah backed away to the kitchen. She needed to sit down.

⁓

Despite suggestions from both Mrs. Banning and the other staff that it might be wise to rest, Sarah stayed awake and on her feet all day. Occasionally, a fit of coughing consumed her, and Mrs. Fletcher kept the tea pot filled and steaming.

All Sarah wanted was to know if Simon was all right. She forced herself to eat lunch. Though Mr. Penard excused her from duties, she wandered the downstairs rooms to dust and wax. Resting seemed an impossibility.

Lucy returned to the house in the middle of the afternoon and rang for Sarah immediately. Sarah scuttled across the dining room and the foyer to present herself in the parlor.

"They found Simon!" Lucy's face beamed. "I was certain you would want to know."

Sarah exhaled. "Thank you, ma'am. I'm very glad."

"I thought you might be."

Sarah considered Lucy's green eyes and wondered what she knew. What had Simon said?

"Is he all right?" Sarah hoped her effort to restrain her eagerness for news was more convincing than it felt.

Lucy's face turned somber. "He turned up in one of the hospitals. He has suffered burns. I don't have any information on how extensive they are. No one is allowed to see him. The hospital only confirmed he had been admitted for care."

"But surely—"

"Don't worry. I'm not giving up. A lot of people are worried about Simon Tewell. I will wring information out of those doctors personally. I will make sure you know. Simon would want you to."

"Thank you, ma'am." Sarah blushed.

Lucy rubbed one eye with three fingers. Sarah saw the exhaustion in the gesture.

"Can you find my children for me?" Lucy asked.

"Yes, ma'am," Sarah answered. "And I'll bring you something to eat."

"Thank you, Sarah. We'll get through this."

Sarah started to leave the room, then turned back. "Miss Lucy, it's a small offering, but I have a few dresses ready for girls. A friend and I have been sewing. It's only ten dresses, but it's a start."

Lucy nodded. "Every contribution matters, big or small."

35

Two days of waiting felt like holding her breath at the bottom of Lake Michigan. Sarah was not sure which direction was the way up.

Lucy telephoned a few times and spoke to her mother. Will had come home, and Charlotte had recovered her wits, so Lucy did not bring the children to Prairie Avenue again until the weekly family dinner on Thursday evening. Sarah volunteered to greet the guests in the foyer and take their cloaks and hats. Mr. Penard looked at her as if he found the request odd, but he acquiesced. Oliver and Pamela arrived first, then Leo and Christina, then Violet Newcomb. After each entry, Sarah carried coats to the master bedroom and hurried back to the foyer. While she made an effort to attend to small requests of the group gathering in the parlor, primarily she was glancing out windows on the front of the house, watching for Lucy and Will. Karl had been dispatched to fetch them in a Banning carriage, as he was every Thursday evening, since Flora Banning found Will and Lucy's penchant for using public transportation in poor taste. Finally the carriage rolled to a stop in front of the house.

Ben held his mother's hand unashamedly, with the same desperation Sarah had seen in his clutch of Lucy's skirt on the day of the fire. Sarah could not blame him. Benny had already lost one mother. No child should lose two. He would likely sit through the formal dinner tonight without causing undue distraction even if he did not understand most of the conversation. Stella, on the other hand, was not quite old enough to sit up in a high chair. Inevitably, Flora would scowl, then snatch the child from one of her parents and settle her in her own lap. By dessert, Violet would have the baby. Sarah saw the same series of handoffs happen whenever the children came to dinner.

Sarah opened the front door in perfect timing, and the Edwards family stepped through seamlessly. She collected their wraps and said quietly, "Miss Lucy, I wonder if I might have a word."

"Of course," Lucy said. "Will, take the children in. I'll be right there."

Together Lucy and Sarah walked to the master bedroom, where Sarah laid the coats down with care.

"You're wondering about Simon, aren't you?" Lucy asked.

Sarah nodded, her throat a knot.

"I finally saw him for the first time this afternoon."

Sarah released a moan. "How is he?"

"He has burns on both hands and one side of his face. They're still evaluating the damage to his lungs from the smoke."

Involuntarily, Sarah closed her eyes and steadied herself on the bedpost.

"It's difficult for him to talk," Lucy continued, "because of the burn on the side of his face. But he seemed well."

"I'm so glad."

"He asked about you."

Sarah's eyes opened. "He did?"

Lucy nodded. "He saw you out a front window. He said you were arguing with a fireman next to one of the trucks."

"I was," Sarah admitted, "before I found any of you."

"He was afraid you would do something foolish, he said."

"For instance, run into a burning building?" Sarah expelled pent up breath.

Lucy smiled. "Yes, like run into a burning building to look for a lost little boy. I told him all about it."

"What did he say?"

"He said he knew you had love in you all the time."

"I want to see him."

"I'll arrange it," Lucy said. "I have a feeling that seeing you would be the best medicine Simon could have."

An unfamiliar shyness washed over Sarah.

"Let's plan for Saturday afternoon," Lucy said. "I'll let you know what arrangements I am able to make."

Lucy was there in the hospital lobby, just where she had said she would be, at three o'clock on Saturday afternoon. Sarah had not sneaked out of the house this time during the afternoon lull. Lucy had made sure her mother consented to the absence.

"Thank you for arranging this visit." Sarah sucked her lips in.

"I'm glad to help," Lucy said simply.

Sarah believed her. Lucy would not be Lucy if she were not helping someone, but Sarah had not expected to be in this particular receiving position. They walked together to a staircase, up a flight of stairs, then down a long hall.

"You can't stay long," Lucy said as she paused outside a door. "The doctor has given the nurses strict orders to monitor visitors, and they are quite vigilant."

Lucy pointed to a nearby nurses' desk. A white-capped woman there met Sarah's eyes and let her know without question that she was being watched.

Sarah had rehearsed for days what she would say to Simon if only she could see him. Now the words jumbled together and she was afraid they would not sort themselves out again. "Did you tell him I was coming?"

Lucy smiled and nodded. "He's eager to see you." She pushed open the door. "I'll wait here."

⌐✵⌐

Sarah slipped into the room, already gray in afternoon shadows. Pressure building in her chest reminded her she was holding her breath, and she let it out slowly.

"Hello, Sarah."

He spoke out of one side of his mouth and sounded as if he had a mouthful of pebbles, but Sarah had never been more grateful to hear her name. Her *real* name.

"Hello, Simon." She moved closer to the bed, examining him, looking for a safe way to touch him without hurting him. Finally she settled on putting her hand on his ankle under the white sheet, away from the dressings on his hands and face.

"You're a hero," he said.

She shook her head. "No."

"I'm sure Henry would say you are. Charlotte too."

She brushed away his compliments. "Simon, they won't let me stay long."

"It means a great deal to me that you came."

"I've been a fool. And I hope you can forgive me." Her practiced speech crumpled into pieces that could not be reassembled. Not a single phrase rose in her throat. There was no time for it anyway. The short version would have to do for now. "I was on my way to tell you that on Monday when I saw the smoke."

"I wondered why you were out there."

"I wish I'd seen you."

"You were beautiful, as always. Determined. I saw it in your face just the way I always do."

"When you look at me," Sarah said, "I sometimes wonder who you see."

"You should look at yourself sometime," Simon answered. "See what is really there, not what you think ought to be there. See what God sees and loves."

"You told me once I had been well loved and was afraid I never would be again."

Simon turned his head away. "In my own feeble way, I was trying to offer you my love. But even that could never replace what you need most."

"God's love."

He nodded.

"I came to see that for myself. I nearly traded it in for the opposite of everything I need, but I couldn't forget what you said."

He met her eyes again now.

Sarah glanced over her shoulder. "They won't let me stay much longer."

"Come back."

"I will." As soon as she could. As often as she could.

"Come back for the rest of your life." His eyes bore past the bandages on his face and fixed on hers. This was a proposal she could accept.

"I will." Every day.

"I'll be waiting for you for the rest of my life."

His ankle moved under her touch, and she moved her hand to squeeze his toes just as the nurse put her head through the door.

After one last intake of air, the words she most wanted to say finally formed. "I love you, Simon Tewell."

36

Sarah walked with Simon through the empty upstairs hall of St. Andrew's a few weeks later.

He nodded in satisfaction. "The work is almost finished. We'll be able to bring the children back sooner than we hoped."

Sarah ran her finger along one wall, hardly believing it showed no evidence of being buried in layers of soot. Volunteers had scoured smoke-damaged walls, and fresh paint made the walls look better than Sarah ever remembered they had.

"Structurally, the building is sound," Simon said. "Brick and stone have their benefits." He sniffed the air. "The smell of smoke might haunt us for a while. They tell me it will likely seep through the new paint eventually."

Sarah looked at Simon's red-scarred face and thought he had never looked more handsome. She had to quell her impulse to reach up and touch his cheek, lest she cause him pain. "Are you in pain today?"

He shook his head. "You worry too much."

"How about your hands?"

"I only wish I could have helped with all the clean-up." He turned his wounded hands palm up. "With time I'll be fine."

"Promise me you're following the doctor's instructions."

"I'll promise whatever you ask, Sarah Cummings."

They moved into the fourth floor corner girls' room. The furniture was all pushed to the middle of the room. Lillie and Lucy had their sleeves rolled up with rags in their hands and a bucket of water between them.

"It looks like you're almost finished in here," Simon said.

"We are," Lucy said. "We're just wiping up the last of the paint dribbles. That will be everything except the boys' dorm where the fire started. The walls still have to be plastered in there, and of course we need all new furniture."

"We'll get there," Simon said. "The boys will just have to double up in the other rooms until then."

"All the children I talk to are eager to come back." Lucy used a thumb to scrape at a stubborn dried paint drip.

"What about Jane?" Sarah asked.

"Jane is a special case." Lucy dipped her rag in the bucket. "She still blames herself. She cannot accept that she was not responsible. She focuses on what she might have done with that match if she had lost control."

"Jane needs a fresh start," Simon said. "We were able to arrange a foster care setting for her."

"You haven't put her in service, have you?" Sarah asked, panicked.

"No," Simon assured her. "She's with a couple who are both teachers. They don't have any other children and can give her the attention she needs. Even as muddled as she is right now, they can see how bright she is."

Sarah laid a palm over her heart. "I'm so glad."

Simon gestured around the room. "Lucy, you've done an amazing job mobilizing volunteers for the clean-up work."

Lucy waved a hand toward Lillie. "I could not have done it without Lillie. She has turned out to be quite the administrator."

Sarah looked at Lillie and smiled. "Thank you, Lillie. You've really thrown yourself into whatever St. Andrew's needs." And she had never mentioned Serena Cuthbert again.

Lillie blushed. "I didn't know I had it in me until the job had to be done."

"You've been spectacular," Lucy said. "Clean-up crews, painters, making sure everything touched by smoke was laundered, getting the gas lines fixed. And all while you've been planning your own wedding. Only two more weeks!"

Lillie laughed as she twisted her rag above the bucket. "I'm not looking very bride-like at the moment. My mother has taken over the wedding. I've found it's wisest to just stay out of the way."

"I remember," Lucy said. "I had to put my foot down with my mother on more than one point."

"I hope you'll be there." Lillie looked around the room. "All of you."

Sarah met Lillie's speckled eyes and swallowed.

"Sarah, I wonder if I might have a word with you alone," Lillie said.

Sarah glanced at Simon and Lucy. "Of course."

In the hall, Lillie took both of Sarah's hands. "I'd like you to stand up for me at my wedding. Would you?"

Sarah's pulse surged. She had a friend. Serena was not between them anymore. She blew out her breath. "After I lied to you? Are you sure?"

"I've never really wanted anyone else," Lillie said, "and Paul agrees."

"Does he know . . .?"

"He knows everything. And he wants you there."

"And your parents?"

"I'll explain to them that the past doesn't matter. It's forgiven."

"But what about . . .?"

"Mr. Townsend?"

Sarah nodded. "He's a friend of your father, isn't he?"

"I insisted that he *not* be invited to my wedding." Lillie smiled slyly. "Besides, my mother heard the most scandalous thing the other day from Mrs. Pullman. It seems that Mr. Townsend's lady in Lockport has changed her mind. She received information that his attentions were not as ardent and exclusive as he had led her to believe for the last few months."

"Lillie, you didn't—"

Lillie waved a hand. "It was anonymous information. No names were mentioned. Will you stand up for me or not?"

Sarah's throat swelled and tears welled. "I would love to."

Lillie grabbed Sarah's wrist and dragged her back into the girls' dormitory room. "Sarah is going to be my attendant!"

"Delightful!" Lucy bent and swiped a baseboard with her rag. "I have a feeling Simon and Sarah will have an announcement of their own pretty soon."

Sarah blushed.

"Frankly," Lillie said, "I don't know what's taking them so long."

"We'll make it official," Simon said, "as soon as my hands heal enough to hold hers firmly."

Sarah turned her head to meet Simon's eyes. How could she have ever seen anything there other than what she needed most? She put her arm through the crook of his arm and gently kissed his scar.

Acknowledgments

With each book I have growing appreciation for the skill and attention of the Revell publishing staff. Whether editors, marketers, designers, or publicists, I have come to feel encouragement simply upon seeing their names pop up in my email. Over the course of this series they've become a set of people I confidently depend on to help give readers a better book. Thank you. You know who you are.

Once again Steve Reginald, my research partner on the ground in Chicago, has been a cheerleader, an eager pair of hands when my own seemed too full to hold everything, and a spare pair of eyes when mine were too blurry to delight in the small stuff any longer.

My family has gotten used to seeing the back of my head from my office door, and I'm grateful for their respect of the writing process.

And thank you to Rachelle Gardner, the agent who makes sure I'm not walking this publishing journey alone. Grace and peace.

Author's Note

The Great Fire of 1871 is the most famous devastation in Chicago history, but records of the late nineteenth century show that fire remained a constant threat in daily existence for many more years. A tipped candle, a spilled lantern, a lightning strike, a warming flame—all of these had the potential to burst into disaster. The electrical storm that woke Sarah and the rest of the domestic staff in this story set off a wave of destruction on August 22, 1896. Newspapers of the last decade of the century are full of headlines about lives lost to fires, including those in orphanages.

The setting for this story was also a time of shifting social policies. Philosophies for how to care for swells of children without parents transformed from the idea of simply housing and feeding them to genuinely envisioning their futures and well-being. Although St. Andrew's is a fictional orphanage, its story represents both the philosophic and economic challenges of the end of the Gilded Age.

The country was in an economic depression, and feelings ran deep and strong about how government ought to respond and who should benefit. We will never know what might have happened if

William Jennings Bryan's famous "Cross of Gold" speech had won him not only the Democratic Party nomination but also the national election, but I would like to think we learn something from national history.

Steeping myself in these social, economic, and political facts about the year 1896 makes me feel keenly the reality that we face many of the same challenges today. I hope this story of Sarah Cummings realizing her own worth in the eyes of God and digging deep inside herself will inspire readers to consider what contribution they can make—no matter how small—to bring healing and health to someone else's life.

Olivia Newport's novels twist through time to discover where faith and passions meet. Her husband and two twentysomething children provide welcome distraction from the people stomping through her head on their way into her books. She chases joy in stunning Colorado at the foot of the Rockies, where daylilies grow as tall as she is.

I'm imagining you. You walk past as I
water my front flower-beds and we
wave. You check the time as we both
stand in a long line at the grocery
store. You sit in front of me in church.
I'm at my table in the coffee shop and
you're at yours.

We may smile politely and move on with
our separate lives. Or one of us may
speak, a simple invitation to conversation,
and the words flow between us.

Here the adventure begins. When we
meet someone new, we never know
where it might lead.

— Olivia Newport

www.olivianewport.com

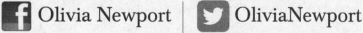 Olivia Newport | OliviaNewport

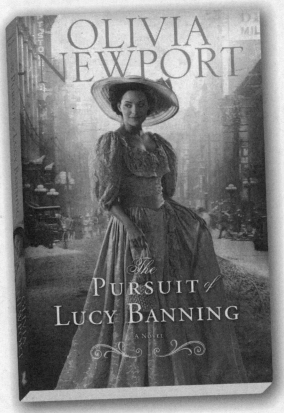

"A wonderful historical romance that has everything fans of this genre look forward to: romance, intrigue, and secrets, as well as characters that are rich in detail but not over the top."

—*RT Reviews*

This compelling story of courage, strength, and tender romance captures the tension between the glittering wealthy class and the hardworking servants who made their lives comfortable.

"Historical romance specialist Sundin (Wings
of Glory series) opens another WWII-era series with
a well-researched and absorbing tale."

—*Publishers Weekly*

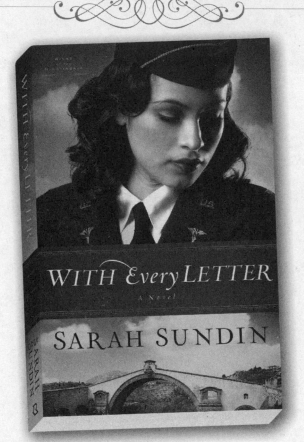

Combining a flair for romance with excellent research and
attention to detail, Sarah Sundin vividly brings to life the perilous
challenges of WWII aviation, nursing—and true love.

Revell
a division of Baker Publishing Group
www.RevellBooks.com